Betrayal

A Julian Mercer novel

G.K. Parks

Copyright © 2016 G.K. Parks

A Modus Operandi imprint

All rights reserved.

ISBN: 1942710046
ISBN-13: 978-1-942710-04-2

For my mom

ONE

"Julian Mercer for Logan Porter," Julian said, resting his hip against the front desk while he surveyed the area.

His eyes scanned the lobby of the high-rise. A dozen men in dark suits accessorized with earpieces and semi-automatic weapons were scattered throughout the room. The clacking of high heels echoed against the tile floors as women hurried past, carrying folders and documents. Despite the numerous business professionals bustling about, typical corporate offices didn't require that level of firepower. Mercer didn't turn, but he knew his second-in-command was taking in their surroundings too. Regardless of what they'd been told, it was obvious this elegant building was a front for something.

The receptionist glanced up, realizing the man before her was speaking. "Mr. Porter is busy. You'll have to reschedule your appointment." She tapped the screen a few times. "May I have your name, sir?"

"Mercer. Julian." The former Special Air Service commander drew himself to his full height, practically standing at attention. "Your boss is expecting us, and I do not believe he would appreciate our meeting being rescheduled."

The receptionist fixed Julian with an icy glare. "Excuse me?"

From behind, Bastian Clarke sighed dramatically. "You'll have to excuse Jules. He's been hit in the head far too many times for his own good. Occasionally, he believes he's a spy for MI6." Bastian handed the woman a business card. "We're the kidnapping and ransom specialists that Mr. Porter hired. Would you be so kind as to let him know we're here, love? I believe we're the reason he's asked you to cancel his appointments for this afternoon."

She smiled at Bastian. "One moment please, Mr. Clarke."

Moving to the end of the long desk, she picked up a handheld radio and held it to her mouth, speaking quietly. Seconds later, two men in dark suits flanked the former SAS members. Mercer shifted his gaze but remained motionless while the men swiftly disarmed him and Bastian.

"Your firearms will be returned after your meeting is concluded," one of the men said. "If you'll follow me, Mr. Porter is expecting you."

The guard turned, not waiting for a response, and headed down the corridor. Julian and Bastian exchanged a look and followed the man while the second guard brought up the rear. At the end of the hallway stood an oversized door with a palm scanner. The door opened, and the two K&R specialists entered alone.

"Mr. Mercer, I'm glad you could make it," Logan Porter said, standing and extending his hand. "You were on the shortlist for personal security experts, but I didn't expect you to arrive until tomorrow. Did you catch the red-eye from London?"

"We're not based in London," Bastian said, making small talk while Mercer studied the extravagant office. "Even though our team is comprised of former Special Air Service members, we no longer call the United Kingdom home. We spend far too much time away, handling sensitive issues," he narrowed his eyes, "but you already know this. You also know that time is of the essence, so shall we cut through the pleasantries and job interview and get to it?"

"A man of action is precisely what I need. Has the agency informed you what's happened?" Porter asked.

"We'd like to hear it from you," Mercer said, sizing up Logan. The corporate bigwig was half a foot shorter, balding, and soft underneath the expensive suit, practically the exact opposite of Julian Mercer, who was also in his early forties but comprised of nothing but hard planes and rough edges. "Start with when she was taken."

"She has a name," Logan snapped. "It's Sarina." He sighed, squeezing the bridge of his nose. "I apologize. It's just...I don't know what to do."

"That's why you called us," Bastian said. "Why don't you take a seat and tell us when Sarina was taken. We'll need to know where she was, who was with her, and who was aware of her itinerary."

"Sarina was at home. Alone. She had a meeting scheduled later that afternoon. At three o'clock, I think, but she didn't show up. It's my understanding that someone phoned Sarina's assistant to see why she missed the meeting. When I got home that night, she wasn't there." He tilted his neck from side to side as if working out a kink. "Our home security footage caught the kidnappers on tape. They left a note stating that I was not to involve the police. That was three days ago."

"Regardless, did you contact the authorities?" Mercer asked.

"No." Porter inhaled and swallowed. "I expected some type of follow-up communication. A letter. Phone call. E-mail. But there's been nothing but radio silence since the abduction. The day after Sarina was taken, I spoke with the men in charge of our corporate security. My position here provides certain extraordinary protections, including ransom insurance. They felt it was imperative to have negotiators on-site who were prepared to deal with any incoming demands, so the agency hired you."

"Are you sure someone abducted your wife?" Mercer asked, his voice harsh and accusatory.

"Do you think they killed her?" Porter asked, his voice rising an octave in surprise.

"It's possible but unlikely. By now, her body would have been discovered," Mercer said. "Without proof, it is unreasonable to jump to such conclusions. However, she might have staged this abduction to escape from you."

"How dare you," Porter shrieked. He stormed across the room, standing toe-to-toe with Julian. Despite the height difference, Porter didn't back down. He shoved Mercer, which had the same effect as pushing against a brick wall. "That's my wife. My Sarina. She loves me, and I love her. She would never do something like that." He shoved Mercer again. "Take it back."

"Did you push her around too?" Mercer asked, glowering.

"Jules," Bastian said, interrupting and taking Porter by the arm before the commander decided to push back, "that's enough. Mr. Porter is distraught.

You are not helping matters." Bastian led Porter to the nearest chair. "We'll gladly assist, but there are a few ground rules that need to be established. First, you do what we say, when we say it. No questions. No hesitation. Second, we'll need full access to your home, your personal records, and your security system. We won't be able to do anything else until we determine this is a kidnapping. Normally, a demand is issued. Without one, it'll be more difficult to make a recovery."

"A recovery?" Porter blinked. "You mean getting Sarina back."

"Yes." Bastian's gaze flicked briefly to Mercer.

"If this is not a kidnapping, you'd be better off contacting the authorities," Mercer declared, moving toward the office door. "We'll need access to your home now. You'll have our assessment by the morning."

Porter handed Bastian a set of keys and a folder from the top of his desk. Inside were the details on his home security system, including access codes and a list of personal employees. The information had been compiled earlier that morning, based upon the timestamp printed on the pages.

"A car will take you to my home. If you find something or encounter any problems, my cell phone number is listed," Porter said. "Please, you have to save Sarina."

"We'll do our best," Bastian promised. "The sooner we get started, mate, the better off she'll be."

Porter nodded and pressed a button, summoning building security to his office to escort the specialists back to the lobby. Taking back his gun, Mercer checked the clip in his Sig, tucked it into his hip holster, and gave the waiting town car an uneasy look. He found something about the situation unsettling, but Bastian simply slid into the back seat without a second thought. Worst case, Julian wasn't above shooting his way out, but with any luck, this job wouldn't require expelling lead.

TWO

"Bloody hell," Bastian said when the car stopped in front of a guard stand. The driver spoke to the sentry on duty, prompting the opening of the gate and allowing the vehicle to enter. "We picked the wrong profession."

"I wouldn't be too sure of that," Mercer retorted. His eyes scanned the grounds. The lawn was manicured. The shrubbery that lined the driveway was perfectly trimmed and even, and the infrared cameras that covered the exterior were placed strategically to minimize blind spots. The car stopped in front of a fountain, and the driver opened the rear door. Mercer stepped out, studying the man. "Do you always service the Porters?"

"No, sir. They pay a monthly fee for the car service. We rotate."

"Very good," Bastian said, coming around the car. "Are you our ride back this evening?"

"I'll be here whenever you're ready," the driver replied.

"We shouldn't be too long," Bastian said, opening the folder and approaching the front door. He took out a key, read through the security protocols, entered a code, and unlocked the door. "Jules, are you sure we didn't pick the wrong profession?"

Mercer stepped inside, closing the door and examining the interior. A crystal chandelier hung from the ceiling. The foyer branched out, leading in three directions. A staircase on the side led to the floors above. Everything was pristine, not a single crumb or speck of dust covered any of the gleaming surfaces.

"I'll begin on the upper level. Find the security footage and start your analysis. I'd like to be gone before Logan returns." Mercer headed for the staircase, "and let's keep it clean and quiet." He met Bastian's eyes. Until they had a chance to suss out precisely for whom they were working, he didn't trust Logan Porter or the mysterious corporation with armed guards installed in the lobby, so leaving prints, DNA, or discussing the potential abduction inside a home that was likely being monitored was to be avoided at all costs.

The top level of the three story mansion contained the master suite. Deciding that was the best place to begin, Mercer began in the bathroom, searching for signs of a struggle. The mirror wasn't broken, and the smallest crevices didn't contain any blood residue. If Sarina fought against her kidnappers, it hadn't been inside this room or the bastards were meticulous in the cleanup.

Next, Mercer searched the bedroom. Inside the first closet, he found clothing and accessories of the female persuasion. The second closet held Logan's clothes. Two dressers stood on either side of the room. Disassembling Sarina's, Mercer searched each of the drawers and checked the surfaces for a hint as to who might be responsible. Aside from lingerie and a few other items that would indicate Sarina had a kinky streak or Logan was failing to satisfactorily perform his husbandly duties, Mercer didn't find anything of use.

Repeating the process with Logan's belongings, he discovered a thumb drive. Pocketing the USB, he gave the room a final once-over, checking for blemishes on the pristine paint, a random shard of broken glass, or something that would indicate Sarina was forced to leave her home. On the nightstand was a framed wedding photo.

Sarina appeared to be at least a decade younger than Logan. She had dark blonde hair, an airbrushed tan, and the body one would get from hours spent with a personal trainer. Frankly, she was out of Logan Porter's league. Perhaps she was a gold digger or legally blind. Then again, maybe her attributes ended with her looks. A photo didn't exactly depict personality or level of intelligence.

Continuing the exploration, Julian went through the rest of the rooms of the house, finding very few personal effects and no indication that foul play was involved in Sarina Porter's disappearance. Perhaps Sarina staged the abduction and simply left. Surely, she had means available to her. She could have emptied out a bank account and ran off to live on a sunny beach with her personal trainer. At least, that was the best case scenario. On the other end of the spectrum, she was taken somewhere and killed. Unfortunately, there were plenty of possibilities that existed in between those two extremes.

"Bas," Mercer called, descending the staircase, "how much progress have we made?"

"Leaps and bounds," Bastian said sarcastically.

"Bugger." Mercer continued his perusal of the home. He entered the kitchen, searching the cabinets and refrigerator before studying the cooking implements that had a permanent position on the counter. A single knife was missing from the block. Opening the dishwasher, Mercer didn't find the missing utensil. It wasn't in the sink either. Frankly, the kitchen was as immaculate as the rest of the house. No one lived that neatly. He marched into the office where Bastian was transferring the security logs and footage onto his laptop. "That wanker had the place cleaned after Sarina went missing."

"That's not all he did." Bastian shook his head in disdain.

"Is it an abduction?"

"Too soon to say." Bastian drummed his fingers against the desk. "It's a bleeding mess." He hit play and pointed to the screen. "We have a glitch."

"Bollocks." Mercer sighed. "I'll check the grounds. Will you be ready in twenty minutes?"

"I'll meet you outside."

Julian exited through the rear door, hearing the security system beep, but since the alarm was deactivated, no fanfare or sirens were triggered. Circling the exterior, he examined the windows of the first floor, checked the surrounding foliage and adornments for footprints or other disturbances, and stumbled upon the cobblestone driveway. Everything looked perfect. Too perfect. There wasn't a single oil stain or tire mark on the driveway. Kneeling down, Mercer studied the tan and brown stones, finding only the vaguest sign of use in between the large slabs.

"They power scrub," the driver said from his position next to the vehicle. "Mr. Porter is one anal son of a bitch. He's phoned the car service several times in the last three months to complain about air conditioning fluid being left on the path. Eventually, he ordered the groundskeeper to power scrub the driveway twice a day to keep things neat and tidy."

"Is Mrs. Porter just as finicky?"

"Nah, she's cool. I don't see why she puts up with him," the driver glanced at the house, "but I could take a guess."

"When's the last time you saw Mrs. Porter?" Mercer asked, catching a glimpse of Bastian exiting the house and reengaging the security system.

"It's been two or three weeks. I've been on vacation. I just got back a few days ago, and today's the first time I've been assigned to the Porters. Why?" He narrowed his eyes. "Did something happen to her? You're investigators or consultants or something, right?"

"That's none of your concern," Mercer replied, slipping into the back seat. "What's your name?"

"Stan Appleman."

"Nice to meet you," Bastian responded, joining Julian in the car.

For the duration of the ride, Bastian made pleasant small talk with the driver, believing a friendly exchange would provide answers and insight. Once the waters were smoothed, Bastian jotted down the man's name and the car service. Then he and Mercer exited in front of a block of hotels.

From there, the two ex-SAS members entered the adjacent parking structure, located their rental, and drove to the flat they were using as one of their safe houses for the duration of this assignment. Despite the fact the insurance company was picking up the tab for accommodations, hotels were far from secure, and their last assignment had been compromised by valet parking and easily accessible suites.

"When are Donovan and Hans arriving?" Mercer

inquired.

"They're waiting until we're positive it's an abduction before they cut their holiday short."

"They're not going to be happy."

"You believe she was taken against her will?" Bastian asked.

"Frankly, it doesn't matter. The bird's gone. Either she faked the abduction or someone made her leave. Eventually, we'll determine which is accurate."

"So we're staying?"

"I don't know yet."

Bastian raised a questioning eyebrow. "Then why are we sending for Hans and Donovan?"

"In the event we need the additional support, there needn't be a delay. That office building is a cover. It won't matter what we determine. Logan Porter isn't prepared to just let us walk away."

"Jules, you're paranoid."

"That house has been scrubbed. Frankly, I'd be surprised if the Porters even live there. Everything is too pristine. It looks staged."

"The driver said Logan is a neat freak."

"How would the driver know about the inside of the house? He doesn't even drive for them regularly, or so he said. Not to mention, he was conveniently away on holiday and out of rotation until after Sarina's disappearance."

"That's called paranoia. Everyone's not out to get you." Bastian knew that was precisely how Mercer felt most of the time due to his wife being murdered. "Did you find anything that might be useful?"

"They're missing a kitchen knife."

"Quick, someone phone the bobbies, we have a missing knife," Bastian mocked. Then his face contorted into a smug grin. "I can't be positive she was taken, but I'll see your missing knife and raise you, mate." Bastian powered on his laptop and took a seat at the kitchen table. "Hand me that bag of crisps, and I'll show you what I found."

Mercer rummaged through his pocket, removing the USB and placing it on the table next to the bag of junk food. "Logan had that hidden in his drawer. It could be corporate secrets or something untoward."

"Where shall we start? The USB or the security footage?"

"You decide."

Bastian plugged in the USB and crunched away on a handful of crisps.

THREE

The USB drive Mercer discovered was encrypted, so while Bastian's decryption protocols ran in the background, the two men reviewed the security footage from the Porters' security system. The files Bastian copied covered the entire month of surveillance, including three and a half weeks of footage prior to Sarina's disappearance. Having access to that information would help establish daily routines and build a list of possible suspects and witnesses. Most professional kidnappers had an inside man or some type of insider knowledge about the family and daily routine. If anyone had been stalking Sarina or casing the estate, it would be on the surveillance tapes.

The Porters followed a similar routine. The car service arrived between 7:15 and 7:23 every morning. Logan exited the house at 7:30 with his briefcase in hand and slid into the back seat of the car. At 8:20, the groundskeeper would hose off the walkways. On Mondays, Wednesdays, and Fridays, Sarina would leave the house at 8:15 with her gym bag and yoga mat. She'd return three hours later. Sometimes, she used the car service. Other times, she drove a silver luxury vehicle. Aside from her yoga class, Sarina didn't stick with a strict schedule. A few times, she left around noon, and other times, it'd be three or four in the afternoon. Occasionally, she'd stay in the entire day.

"She's a marketing consultant. Some of her work is done online. As far as I can tell, she has an office and assistant, but she picks and chooses her clients," Bastian said. "It leaves her schedule fairly open."

"We'll need a dossier on her associates."

"It's in the works."

The men fell silent as they recorded the details of the couple's nightly routine. Most nights, Logan arrived home between six and seven. Occasionally, they'd go out, presumably to dinner or some type of event, but they were always home by midnight. The weekends were the only exception. There was no pattern to their travel or plans, either together or separate, but the frequency they went out together would indicate they enjoyed one another's company. Perhaps she hadn't fled from her pushy husband, after all.

"This is the day of the abduction." Bastian slowed the speed of the playback.

As usual, Logan left at his normal time, and Sarina departed for her Wednesday morning yoga class. She returned home before noon. The only person who appeared on the feed during her time away was the groundskeeper. From the footage taken at the guard post, the only vehicles that entered and exited were part of the car service and the Porters' employees. The groundskeeper and the sentry stationed at the guard post were the only staff members present. The cleaning staff worked on Mondays and Fridays, and no one else had access to the house.

At approximately two p.m. the day of Sarina's disappearance, the footage blinked out for a few seconds. Bastian rewound to two minutes prior to the glitch, slowed the speed to one fifth, and hit play. Nothing strange occurred on the monitor, but for three seconds, there was nothing but blackness. He switched to a different camera, but it blacked out at precisely the same time.

"What would account for that?" Mercer asked.

"A power surge, a computer glitch, the system resetting, or tampering." Bastian took another chip out of the bag and crunched thoughtfully. "I'll check the power grid to see if it was widespread, but that doesn't seem likely."

"Was the system bypassed remotely or placed on a loop?"

"I can't be sure."

"Well, figure it out," Mercer said.

While Mercer watched the rest of the footage from the day in question, Bastian keyed in a few things on a secondary laptop. Ten minutes after the glitch, two masked men were caught on screen. They waited for Sarina to descend the staircase and grabbed her from behind. They carried her off to the side, out of view of the cameras. A minute later, one of the men returned, leaving a piece of paper on the kitchen table. He looked straight at the camera, a smug arrogance resonating from his posture before he disappeared.

No one entered or left the estate until Logan's arrival at seven that evening. The next three days continued normally. Logan left on time. The car service arrived without hesitation. No additional security was hired or told to guard the premises. The cleaning lady came on Friday and scrubbed the house.

"We'll need to speak to her too."

"Yes, Jules, I'm well aware of how we work a kidnapping. We've been doing it for years." Bastian glanced at the screen and returned to his current task.

"This is different. They haven't issued a ransom demand yet. That's the primary objective of a kidnapping. What the hell are they waiting for?"

"Maybe they want to make sure they're in the clear before they risk compromising themselves again."

"Bullshit. They knew how to maneuver around the cameras or bypass them completely." Mercer pointed to a screen capture of the masked man. "He looks too damn smug to think he's compromised. They must be familiar with the layout. Hell, it could even be the bloody security guards."

"The city's power grid didn't experience any surges that day," Bastian announced. "I'll need to see the schematics for the house to determine the location of the power supply, if they have backup generators or other surge protections in place, and when the system normally resets. But realistically, someone altered the footage. It could easily be a cut and paste job."

"Bloody fantastic." Mercer snapped his focus back to the screen when something beeped.

"The decryption software is finished."

Bastian scanned the USB drive again, finding a single video file stored on the device. He opened it, unsure of what they were about to watch. The video was grainy and filmed in low resolution, but it was clear the woman on tape was Sarina Porter.

"Jules," Bastian began cautiously, afraid of what the commander might do, "it needs to be authenticated. We don't even know if Logan has seen this."

"Bollocks." Mercer stared at the screen. The USB contained a fifteen second video clip of Sarina bound and gagged. Mascara streaked her face, and her eyes conveyed panic and pain. "You honestly can't believe a man that meticulous wouldn't notice a misplaced USB drive in his sock drawer."

"It depends how many pairs of socks he has."

Mercer stalked the path next to the table like a caged lion. "Someone has her. They left that behind, or they had it delivered. It's bloody likely they already issued a demand, and that arsehole didn't tell us." He lifted the untraceable phone, dialed a few digits, and hit end call, slamming it down hard enough that it was a miracle the screen didn't crack. "When was it recorded?"

"I don't know."

"Figure it out."

Mercer stormed out of the room. Hostage negotiations were meant to be impersonal, cold and calculating. An emotional response would lead to mistakes or a shoddy deal. It was imperative the kidnappers believed they didn't possess all the power, so Mercer took a moment to let the rage boil to the surface. He saw red, and his pulse pounded in his ears. Someone would pay. He'd make sure of it.

The question on his mind was how Logan Porter could fail to disclose such a vital piece of information. Was their client one of the kidnappers or working with them? Maybe it was an attempt to defraud the insurance, have a ransom payout issued, and then abscond with the practically untraceable cash. The thought was repulsive, and Mercer forced it away. They needed more information.

When his hands began to tremble, he opened his eyes and took a few deep breaths, counting to ten. The counting never helped. It was rubbish that some psychologist had given to him when he was forced to endure counseling on Her Majesty's order. The counting was an irritant, like most things, but he did it anyway. It was a testament that he had himself back under control. On the rare occasions the anger and rage were overpowering, the counting would send him over the edge, oftentimes resulting in something being broken. A time or two, it had been his knuckles, but mostly, the damage was doled out to the closest object.

As soon as his emotions were in check, he returned to the kitchen, picked up the phone, and dialed Donovan Mayes. He and Hans Bauer made up the two missing parts of the four-man team. Despite the fact they were each a decade younger than Julian, they had left the Special Air Service as a show of their loyalty to their commander. They had no qualms working as kidnapping specialists, even if they were highly trained for tactical resolutions. Quite often, negotiations devolved into armed combat, and it was a relief to have two of the best shooters on the planet working on the same side.

"It's an abduction. Get here soon." Mercer disconnected without another word.

"I'll have the technical aspects fleshed out by the morning. I'd advise you not to speak to Logan before then. We need to determine what side he's on. And if he doesn't know about the USB drive, he'll want answers, and we don't have them. The last thing we need is someone else blundering about."

"You have twelve hours. In the meantime, I'll perform some recon." Mercer picked up the car keys and went to the door. "Ring me if you determine any additional points of interest."

FOUR

Mercer found himself parked across the street from the Trila International office building. He scrubbed a hand down his face and studied the Lucite and steel construction. Despite the glass and airy feel, the building wouldn't be easily penetrated. The executive parking structure was beneath the building in a subbasement. Two access points allowed entry on the northern and western sides. Each had a guard station, keycard access, and surveillance cameras. Not only was identification required for admission, but the cars were swept for explosives before being allowed entry. Anyone who believed this building only served as the corporate offices for a tech startup was an idiot.

Mercer had seen plenty of buildings like this, and more often than not, they held government secrets. Normal security guards didn't carry automatic weapons, nor were they prepared to deal with kidnappings. However, Logan Porter spoke to the company's security personnel about Sarina's abduction. It was Trila International's insurance firm that contacted Bastian about performing a negotiation and retrieval. That wasn't typical of corporations either.

Sure, Logan seemed distraught, but he also appeared to be hiding something. The USB drive in his sock drawer spoke volumes, and Mercer wondered the real reason Porter concealed the fact. Obviously, Sarina's abduction happened for a reason. The kidnappers wanted something, and Mercer considered it might have to do with whatever actually went on inside Trila International. An uneasy feeling grew in his gut, and Mercer shook it off as he watched a luxury sedan pull out from beneath the building.

"Bollocks," he muttered, catching a glimpse of two security guards approaching from the rear of the vehicle. Turning the key in the ignition, he gunned the engine, pulling into traffic. A car horn blared, and Julian rolled his eyes.

At least he uncovered one thing on his outing – Trila's security monitored the entire vicinity surrounding the building. If they kept such close tabs on the building, they probably kept eyes on their employees as well. Someone inside probably knew who had taken Sarina Porter.

He continued to drive, carefully monitoring the area for a tail. The best surveillance relied on multiple vehicles that would cut in and out of traffic, appearing behind and in front of the car, and trading off before the driver got suspicious. In the cover of night, Mercer couldn't be certain he wasn't being followed, but it seemed unlikely. However, he circled the city, finding a smaller residential area with a few stores, restaurants, and pubs. He parallel parked on a side street and waited inside the car for fifteen minutes, watching traffic patterns for any repeat offenders. Then he exited, walked to the nearest restaurant, requested a table near the window, and ordered dinner while he kept one eye focused on the exterior.

After eating, he returned to the car, examined it for signs of tampering, and headed to Logan Porter's estate. Pulling up to the guard stand, Mercer rolled down the window, handing the guard his business card. Without a word, the guard called inside, listened for a few seconds, and then waved Mercer through. Apparently someone was home.

"Mr. Mercer," Logan said, opening the front door before Julian could press the doorbell, "where's your associate?" Logan stepped onto the porch, tilting to the side to look into the car for Bastian. "Didn't you say you'd provide your report in the morning? Has something changed? Have you already made progress discovering who took my Sarina? Do you know where she is?"

"Do you?" Mercer retorted.

"I don't understand." Logan glanced back at the front door nervously.

Julian inhaled, composing himself into the unemotional, stoic negotiator. "After our preliminary examination, we have a few questions. Your answers will allow for a more complete report. Shall we?" Mercer gestured toward the door.

"Do you mind if we speak here? It's a lovely night." Logan started to sweat.

"As you wish." Mercer narrowed his eyes but shook off the question. "Why did you allow the house to be cleaned after Sarina was taken? Your cleaning lady likely destroyed evidence that would have led to identifying Sarina's abductors."

"There was nothing, except the note. I checked. The house was pristine as always. It wasn't until I listened to the message from Sarina's assistant that I realized anything was amiss. Then I found the note in the kitchen."

"Do you still have it?"

"I'm afraid I don't. I gave it to Trila's security staff to analyze."

"Fine. What about the glitch on your security footage? Do you have an excuse for that too?"

"What are you saying?" Logan asked. "Do you think I'm behind this? Why would I kidnap my own wife? That's just stupid."

Mercer studied the man, observing the nervous tics and habits. "Have they communicated with you? Proof of life is fundamental to ransom negotiations. Photos, videos, and telephone calls are commonplace. Has anything been delivered to your home or office? Perhaps someone you employ may have been contacted to hand deliver such evidence." It was the perfect opportunity for Logan to come clean about the USB, but he remained tight-lipped. "Is there any particular reason you don't want to let me inside? Is someone here?"

"A business associate." Logan's eyes communicated something Mercer couldn't quite discern. "If there's nothing else, I should get back to him."

"You failed to provide us with a list of people who have access to your home and Sarina's office, aside from your staff. We will need that tonight."

"Can I e-mail it to you?"

"Very well." Bastian had created an online dropbox for this exact purpose, so Mercer took out another business card that contained nothing but the url and handed it to Logan. "Perhaps we should meet for breakfast tomorrow morning to discuss our findings. Kidnappings are personal, and meeting at your office is far from it."

"Yeah, okay, whatever. I'll e-mail you." Logan stepped backward, glaring briefly at the car on the path. "Don't drive up here again. Oil stains are a pain in the ass to get out of the cobblestone."

Mercer nodded, getting into the car and slamming the door. "Obsessive compulsive wanker," he mumbled. Once he was back on the main road, he found the perfect spot to stake out the property. The supposed business associate sounded like a crock, and he suspected whoever was inside had something to do with Sarina's disappearance.

An hour later, headlights bounced off the cobblestone driveway, and Mercer sat up straight. He didn't have a plan. Normally, a demand was issued, and the abductor's identity was determined. This time, things were moving in reverse, and Julian didn't care for it. Frankly, he didn't care for Logan Porter or Trila International either, but having an affinity for the client wasn't a necessity. The black limousine turned onto the main road and passed Mercer's parked vehicle without slowing. The only thing Julian could do was memorize the license plate number. Following the limo would tip his hand and possibly endanger Sarina, and neither of those was acceptable.

Briefly, Mercer considered returning to Porter's estate, but after their earlier encounter, it would likely force Logan to clam up. And if Logan tightened his mouth any more, they'd have to get a crowbar to pry the man's lips apart. Why wouldn't Logan assist the K&R specialists to the best of his ability? Only two possibilities came to mind. The kidnappers threatened to kill Sarina, or Logan was in on it. Already, this abduction was functioning beyond the typical scope. Normally, that meant it wasn't about fulfilling demands but gaining access to someone or something. In those instances, the endgame was usually bloody. Situations like that rarely ended well.

"Goddamn," Mercer swore, heading back to the

safe house.

FIVE

"Jules," Bastian rubbed a hand over his face, "I've teased every digital crumb out of the thumb drive, but she's not saying much."

"Sarina?" Mercer asked. He had fallen asleep after his research resulted in nothing but uselessness. A quick glance at the grey-blue sky assured him it was early morning, and he hadn't missed his meeting with Logan.

"No, mate, the computer." Bas gnawed on a pen cap. "I hope you had better luck. What'd you find on the employees?"

Mercer shook his head. He'd spent the better part of the night performing background checks on Porter's employees. The two sentries who worked the guard post at the entrance to the estate, Will Franco and Thomas Redding, were nothing more than rent-a-cops supplied by the security company that installed the home security system and surveillance equipment. Neither man had a criminal record, and there hadn't been a sudden change in spending patterns or an influx of funds into either of their accounts. On paper, they appeared clean. Gabrielle Turner performed the thorough scrubbing of the estate. She was the Porters' primary cleaning lady, but like the guards, she was also provided by a service. The groundskeeper, Bill Fulton, was the only private hire. He also performed landscaping for many of the other homes in the upscale neighborhood. He was a regular fixture, and since his daily duty involved nothing more than hosing off the driveway, he had plenty of time to fulfill his other clients' needs. On the weekends, when the Porters were out, he'd perform yard work and lawn maintenance. His entire schedule was posted online on his business website.

"The security and maid service are provided by Trila," Mercer said. "The groundskeeper was a private hire, but he works the area. He's been a staple in the community his entire life, and he's done exceptionally well for himself. He earns six figures a year."

"To weed the garden?" Bastian asked. "Bollocks, now I know I picked the wrong profession." He drummed his fingers against the desk, antsy to make some real progress. "It could be a personal dislike or obsession with Sarina, but behavior like that never remains hidden. If that's the case, he would have acted before." Bastian clicked a few keys, running the same search Mercer had performed hours ago. "He looks clean."

"I know. Did you make any progress on determining who took Sarina?"

"Two men. I have approximate heights and weights." Bastian keyed in a few more things. "Given Trila's involvement in the Porters' personal affairs, I'm searching their employee database for possible matches. So far, it looks like eighty-five percent of the men who work at the company fit the description." He poured a cup of coffee and sat across from Julian. "Whoever shorted out the Porters' home security system is a bloody genius. There's no trace of the intrusion or the file being deleted or altered. It's possible the glitch is nothing more than a glitch, but timing is everything."

"So we're looking for someone with technical expertise?"

"Perhaps."

Mercer hated uncertainty. "Yes or no?"

"Yes."

"Fantastic, and Trila International is known for employing a host of tech-savvy wankers." Mercer stood, leaving the paperwork spread across the coffee table. "Unless there's something more useful you haven't shared, we'll discuss these things with Porter in person. It's time we give the nut a squeeze."

Bastian grumbled something and took his coffee cup into one of the bedrooms to change.

*　　*　　*

"What type of assessment did Trila's security team provide?" Bastian asked. They'd been sitting in a tiny café for the past thirty minutes. Logan Porter had only spoken a few polite words, instead focusing on the menu before him and the specials scrawled across the chalkboard in the corner. "Have any previous threats been made to Trila or you?"

"Huh?" Logan bit his lip and glanced around the room again. "Trila's the company where I work. It's not a person."

"You didn't seem this stupid yesterday," Mercer grumbled. "Did someone suggest you play dumb or was yesterday one of your lucid days?"

Bastian shot a look at the commander but didn't

say a word. He settled his unwavering gaze on Logan and waited.

"I don't know what types of threats the company receives. I'm not in charge, and I don't deal with that. I'm not in the mailroom or the PR department," Logan huffed. "Security said they'd contact the appropriate agency to handle Sarina's disappearance, so I need not worry." He shifted his gaze to Mercer. "But I am worried."

"You probably should be. Two men entered your home, abducted your wife, and knew exactly how to cover their tracks. They must be intimately aware of your routine, the layout of your home, and your security measures." Mercer let the implication hang heavily in the air, but Logan didn't make a peep.

"It's in your best interest to tell us everything," Bastian insisted.

"I am."

"No, you're not." Mercer pulled the USB drive from his pocket, but Logan didn't react. "Who was at your house last night?"

"I told you — a business associate."

"The limousine was registered to a foreign embassy. Do you care to explain?"

"Trila *International*, what part of that don't you understand?" Logan fixed Mercer with a hard glare. "I didn't hire you to spy on me. How is any of this relevant to getting my wife back?"

Before Mercer could say or do anything, Bastian intervened. "Did your wife have any enemies?"

"No. We're happily married. Everyone likes Sarina." Logan picked up the knife and buttered his biscuit for the third time, placing it untouched on the plate.

"Former flames?" Bastian asked. "Maybe a jealous ex or recent paramour?"

"No." Logan's face reddened, and he let out a disgusted snort.

"What about her job?" Mercer asked, hoping to cover everything in one fell swoop.

"I don't know much about her daily activities. Her assistant would be more helpful." Logan took a card from his pocket and passed it across the table. Then he made a show of looking at his watch. "I really must be going." He laid some cash on the table, but his hands trembled.

Mercer pinned Logan's hand against the table. "Tell us the truth."

"Please," he lowered his voice, "you have to find her. They'll kill her."

Before Bastian or Julian could say another word, Logan slipped his hand free and went out the door. The two men exchanged a look, and then Bastian turned the card over. Written on the back were the words: *They're listening.*

"Well, let's follow up with the assistant." Bastian swiped the uneaten biscuit off the table. "Perhaps she'll be able to shed some light on Mrs. Porter's abduction."

He took a bite while Mercer gave the café a final glance, but it was impossible to identify whoever might have them under surveillance. Someone was listening, or Porter had turned into a conspiracy theorist overnight. Based on what Mercer already knew about Trila's security team, he didn't expect to find Logan donning a tinfoil hat anytime soon.

Once they were in the confines of their car, Bastian did a quick scan with the RF reader for any bugs before speaking. Perhaps the team was just as paranoid as their client, but they'd seen a lot of shady shit. Letting their guard down never ended well. Julian had the scars to prove it.

"He knows she's alive," Mercer said. "How can he play the corporate stooge and act like everything's fine when they've threatened to kill her?"

"They probably warned him to act normal."

"That's normal?"

Bas shrugged. "I'd wager he knows what's on the USB drive. He must know we know."

"Do we have any other information on the limo from last night?"

"The plates belong to someone with diplomatic immunity. Frankly, the only way to get any information would be through the state department or asking our own embassy, but it'll take time and cutting through much red tape. I've tried to find nearby traffic cams that might divulge the identity of the occupant or his final destination, but I haven't had much luck. This place might be a business mecca, but it's not up to the security standards to which we are accustomed."

"Porter needs to talk to us. We won't be able to get his wife back until we know exactly what we're dealing with. Doesn't he understand we aren't the authorities? We are the negotiators. We don't pose a threat to the kidnappers, and since most kidnappings are orchestrated by professionals, they should know that too."

"What are you thinking, Jules?"

"Trila wants us in the dark."

"But they hired us on Porter's behalf. Why go through the ruse if they weren't being supportive?"

"To appease Logan. To keep him from going to the authorities." Mercer looked out the window. "Kidnappings are commonplace in this part of the world. Surely, someone with Porter's means would seek help."

"Funny thing about Porter's means," Bastian

interjected, "it looks good on paper, but his bank account is practically empty. His residence and vehicles are paid for by Trila."

"Where does his salary go?" Mercer asked. "They must pay him handsomely if they give him all those perks."

"Charitable donations?"

"That seems doubtful."

While Bastian drove, tossing out other unlikely suggestions, Julian considered what they knew — two men, one missing woman, a threatening video delivered via USB, a missing kitchen knife, and some clandestine meeting with the aggrieved husband. The missing piece was painfully obvious. There had not been a ransom demand.

"Call the morgue and the hospitals and keep monitoring police communications." Julian swallowed. "She might already be dead."

"I know. Does that mean you want to give up?" Bas asked, aggravating Mercer who let out a disgruntled growl in response. "I'll keep digging into Porter's financials, but first, let's finish our dossier on Sarina. It'd help to know our victim better."

The car came to a stop outside a small building that looked like a house. The sign indicated it was a consulting firm — Marketing Experts: Sarina Porter, MBA.

SIX

Sarina Porter was thirty years old. Despite the fact she looked like a trophy wife, the woman had spent her time cultivating a career. She only had a handful of clients but always kept busy. Any one of them could be her big break. In addition to a flat fee, Sarina also earned commissions on her clients' earnings based on the lucrative nature of the marketing campaigns she devised. After some cajoling, Brie Dawson, the assistant, allowed Bastian to access Sarina's records and computer.

However, Sarina's daily schedule was anything but routine. She worked from home on occasion. She met clients in many different locations, sometimes via teleconferencing or e-mail instead of ever meeting face-to-face. While Sarina's advanced degree would indicate she was a hard worker, it was obvious she only liked to work on a few projects at a time.

"Does she have anything in the works now?" Mercer asked, hoping to distract the assistant while Bastian made fast work of checking the office for surveillance devices or signs of foul play.

"Not that I know of." Brie played with the end of her ponytail which was bright pink. "I can double-check if you really want to know."

"That would be lovely," Mercer replied, edging her toward the doorway. He caught Bastian's eye, nodding.

Brie checked the appointment book and deadline calendar, but everything was blank. "Mrs. Porter finished her last project a week ago. It was for a local artisan jam and jelly company. A new logo, catchy slogan, some billboards and flyers, and they were all set." She shrugged. "Nothing earth-shattering." She hid a look of disgust. "Why are you asking these questions?"

"I thought Mrs. Porter missed an appointment the day she disappeared."

"Right, well, she did. It was for the follow-up." Brie held out a two-page questionnaire. "It's to determine how happy the client is with the service."

"Were they pleased?" Mercer asked.

"I guess." She offered the same annoying shrug again. "I called the printers and had the smaller materials delivered. The billboards are getting put up by a local sign shop, but they aren't ready yet." She shrugged again. "It was too soon for the survey, if you ask me, but that's the day Mrs. Porter scheduled."

"Did she normally schedule her own appointments?"

"Sometimes."

Before she could shrug again, Julian grabbed her shoulders. As a second thought, he offered a smile, hoping to be charming. Frankly, the shrugging was irritating him, along with the bobbing pink tip at the end of her bleach blonde hair. It was a good thing there were no scissors in sight.

"May I have the client's contact information?" If Sarina scheduled the appointment herself, that might mean something.

"I guess. You did say Mr. Porter sent you, and he pays to keep this place open. Hell, he paid to have me open up the shop for you on a Sunday." She scribbled down some information and tore the sheet off the notepad. "Do you know when Mrs. P will be back?"

"Hopefully, soon," Mercer replied.

* * *

"Do you ever feel like our job is to wrestle a bag full of kittens?" Bastian asked. He was simultaneously working on three different computers. One was analyzing Sarina's work files. The other was running background checks on the Porters and their close acquaintances, and the last was dedicated to decrypting Trila's security protocols.

Julian snorted and dialed Hans Bauer. The other half of his team was set to arrive in a matter of hours, and Julian wanted to make sure they took the appropriate measures to avoid any unwanted attention at the airport. Granted, the former SAS had flown in and out of numerous locations with an arsenal packed in their bags, but it never hurt to double and triple-check. At least, that's the way Julian saw it.

"You're not our schoolmarm." Hans sighed, answering the incoming call. "You've got some bloody control issues to work through, mate."

"ETA?" Mercer asked, ignoring the dig.

"Sooner than I'd like. Didn't you promise us an extended holiday after we completed our last job?"

"Bastian will send you our coordinates. Don't dawdle and don't cause trouble." Mercer disconnected.

"Are they almost here?" Bas asked, still mesmerized by the screens in front of him.

"I suppose. It's hard to tell with Hans being mouthy."

"Ease off of him. Maybe he's got a bird stashed somewhere." Bastian chuckled. "Actually, he probably has a whole henhouse. At last count, there are twelve different pubs Donovan and Hans are banned from visiting for screwing one or more of the barmaids, and that's only in Australia. I don't think mathematics is advanced enough to calculate the number of establishments they have to avoid in the EU." He laughed. "At least we have the decency not to hit on the help."

"Speaking of..."

"That wasn't a suggestion," Bastian warned.

Mercer glanced at the time, knowing Logan would be leaving the office soon. The fact that he was working on a Sunday was suspicious enough, but to continue working after his wife's abduction was practically sinister. The only way Mrs. Porter would be returned was if Logan told them the truth. It was clear their client wanted help. Unfortunately, he was too afraid to clue in his best chance of saving Sarina.

"If you are planning to speak to him again, we'll have to find a secure location. I've identified a few possibilities, but we'll have to make sure he isn't followed," Bastian said, reading Mercer's mind. He leaned over, selecting a folder off the floor and handing it to Julian. "I don't understand any of this. We were hired to retrieve Sarina, but no one wants to share. If a demand has been made, we are unaware. We don't even know if negotiations have started."

"We know someone took her. We know Logan is afraid to divulge any information, so it seems imperative that the first thing I do is persuade him to change his mind." Mercer checked the clip in his Sig and slipped into a suit jacket. "Maybe the blokes at Trila will be able to shed some light on our current predicament."

"Don't call me if you end up in the clink," Bastian warned. "I'm too busy to bail you out."

* * *

On his way to Trila International, Mercer reviewed the intel they possessed. Frankly, it was nothing but contradictory rubbish that served as fodder for a dozen different conspiracy theories. Something about Logan rubbed Mercer the wrong way, but people reacted strangely to stress and threats. Although, Logan's actions or lack thereof were more indicative of an accomplice rather than a frantic husband. Of course, the nature of Trila fueled the fires of mistrust. The armed guards and security measures weren't typical of most corporations, especially when it seemed routine to have an after-hours meeting with some foreign dignitary, or so Logan wanted him to think.

"Bugger." Mercer rolled down the window a few centimeters.

The guard tapped against the side of the car with a nightstick and gestured that Mercer step out of the vehicle. Apparently, it was high treason to park this close to the garage. Mercer tilted his neck from side to side, loosening up just in case things turned ugly, and obliged. Noting the automatic weapon at the man's side and the earpiece, he decided it was best to let this play out before acting.

"Mr. Mercer, you are not authorized to be on the premises today," the guard said in a cordial but authoritarian tone. "Sensitive corporate matters could be compromised if we allow the public inside. Please vacate immediately."

"I'm here to discuss sensitive matters of a much more urgent variety," Mercer responded.

"That's doubtful."

"Trila security is aware of Mr. Porter's situation, are they not?"

"Yes, but now is not the time."

"When will be?"

"If Mr. Porter wants you to have access to the building during non-business hours, he'll put in a request. Until such time, you are not welcome here."

Mercer held up his hands, stepping backward toward the car. He could practically hear the smug superiority in the man's voice. Someone ought to teach the bastard some manners. Turning his back to the man, he caught the briefest glimpse of a black limousine in the side mirror. Spinning around, he noted the same diplomatic plates. The guard moved closer, annoyed by the delay, and shoved Mercer into the car using the nightstick like a horizontal bar.

That action removed whatever resolve Mercer had, and he grabbed the baton. Catching the man by surprise, he kneed him hard in the stomach and followed through with an uppercut to the jaw. The guy stumbled backward, said something that was relayed through his comms, and came at Mercer again. This time, the guard wasn't caught by surprise, and he moved like a man trained in close-quarters combat. It had been some time since Mercer faced off against a worthy adversary, and a part of him, the twisted, sadistic part, was pleased.

The two circled and fought like bare-knuckled cage fighters. Before permanent damage was delivered, the other guards arrived and ripped Mercer away from their comrade. It took three men to subdue him, and as Mercer remained on the ground, breathing heavy beneath the weight of two of Trila's guards while they decided what to do with him, the limousine pulled out of the garage.

Some clipped remarks were made, and the guards eventually let Mercer stand. They held him at gunpoint until someone escorted Logan Porter outside. From Porter's expression, it was obvious he didn't enjoy finding his negotiator in this condition. It was also apparent Porter had little choice in what he said based on the prodding he received from the man standing next to him.

"Mr. Mercer, this is not the time or place for us to discuss my private matters. If you have something for me, please call ahead. My associates do not appreciate being told there is a security breach when it is simply an overzealous employee."

"I thought Trila wanted my team to help you."

"They do but not on their time. Please," Porter jerked his chin at the car, "go on your way. We will meet later at my home."

Mercer eyed the man beside Porter, but he didn't look familiar. Memorizing the man's features, Julian would have to go through the Trila employee database later to determine the man's identity. However, gun barrels were deaf to protests, so Mercer saved his breath. He gave one last look to Porter, hoping if the man was in some sort of danger he'd signal or say something. Instead, Porter turned and marched back to the main entrance of the Trila building.

"You win, for now," Mercer mumbled, getting inside the vehicle. The guards didn't return to their posts until he was half a block away.

SEVEN

"What the hell are you doing, Jules?" Bastian asked, exasperated. He'd been half-listening while Mercer gave the abbreviated version of what happened. "You loathe coppers. We aren't investigators, but for some reason, you've gotten it into your thick head that we should investigate. Meanwhile, you've pissed off our client. If Porter says we're done, we're out of here."

"You don't decide that," Mercer said.

"Yes, I do. I've been handpicking our assignments since we started this endeavor. And there's no reason to stick around and make enemies when they don't want our help."

"Something else is going on at Trila."

"Since when do you care, Julian?" Bastian shot back. The words came out of anger, but they were true enough. He licked his lips. "You don't care. You haven't given two shits about anything in the last couple of years. No one blames you for that. I know it's been hard since Michelle."

"I care," Mercer said, his voice low and even.

"Is it really about the recoveries and asset retrievals or is it the proper avenue for your violent outbursts that you care about?"

"Stop psychoanalyzing me."

"Since we've arrived, our client has been toying with us. We've been left in the dark, denied access to pertinent information, and been subjected to an utter breakdown of communication. They don't want our help. They just wanted negotiators on-site in order to ensure the ransom insurance was forthcoming. We're here. They got it. It's done. We've been used, but at least they had the decency to buy us the metaphorical dinner first."

"Explain." Mercer's anger had shifted from Trila to Bastian.

"I finished the preliminary analysis of our client, his assets, and the potentially involved parties. Logan's bank accounts are sparse. Trila provides a salary, most of which is spent on the necessities, paying off student loans he and his wife have incurred, and paying the utilities and rent on her office. Their savings are considerably small given the luxury accommodations we've seen, but like I told you, Trila's footing the bill for those things. Actually, most things."

"Your point?"

"My point is Sarina Porter is a shitty target. After running through the Trila employee database, the parts I can access, there are at least two dozen executives who actually have substantial personal assets. It stands to reason if someone at Trila was involved in Sarina's disappearance, he would have picked his target more carefully."

"It could be personal, particularly since there hasn't been a demand."

"Well, not one we've been privy to, but that's another thing," Bastian continued. "I've concluded the background checks on the two sentries, the maid service, the car service, and the groundskeeper. It's highly doubtful any of them are involved. I'd say the system was accessed remotely by someone with technical expertise."

"But how could they get in and out without the two guards at the front gate noticing?" Mercer asked.

"Because they didn't enter the property through the front gate." Bastian pointed to a satellite image of Porter's estate that he'd printed from the day of Sarina's disappearance. How he'd managed to come by such a thing wasn't worth asking. "The house is accessible from the back. The thick brush cover isn't impenetrable, but it would be slow going." He pointed to a parallel street. "They could have had a car waiting, and once they made it through the dense foliage, they would have been able to take off with no one being the wiser."

"It's speculation."

"The point I'm making is I don't think this is an inside job. Porter's staff looks clean, and it wouldn't make sense that someone at Trila would target him. The man's in charge of rubber-stamping projects for the R&D division."

Mercer sat stiffly and stared at his second-in-command. "I'm tired, and I don't see the point."

"The point is they don't want our help. It isn't some conspiracy you need to unravel. More than likely, it's Porter's way of securing a nice payout while he keeps his wife stashed away somewhere."

"Did you watch the video on the USB? Did you see the way Porter's hands shook this morning?"

"It's called acting, Jules. It's the same thing you're doing right now by feigning interest."

Mercer picked up the mug Bastian had been using and threw it across the room, watching it shatter into a dozen pieces when it hit the front door. "I let those bastards best me, but I won't let you do the same."

"Then tell me what the bloody hell is going through your mind? Why this case? Why the mistrust? Why the need to investigate?"

"Someone has to protect Sarina. Her husband surely didn't." Julian let out an exasperated breath. "Forget it."

Mercer stormed out of the room, slamming the door to one of the bedrooms. Flipping the mattress off the bed and positioning it against the wall, he took out his anger and aggression until his knuckles left a bloody pattern on the sheet. Finally calm, he sat at the desk and unlocked the drawer, removing the file he'd compiled that detailed his wife's murder. The reason he wanted to investigate Sarina Porter's disappearance was he needed practice. Like Bastian said, they had never been detectives or trained investigators, but maybe those were skills he could pick up, like interrogation techniques, combat training, and precision shooting. After all, he'd learned how to aptly negotiate, most of the time.

Unfortunately, now was not the time to review the file he'd read hundreds of times or the recently acquired new information he'd already examined a couple dozen times. Today, he needed to focus on the task at hand. It was the entire reason he became a kidnapping specialist — to have something to focus on besides his own tragedy.

A slight knock sounded at the door, and then Bastian cautiously turned the knob. "Not to bloody bother you, your majesty, but Logan Porter's on the phone. He wants to speak to you."

Nodding, Mercer held out his hand, taking the

phone from Bastian. "Yes?"

"Mr. Mercer, I'd like to apologize for this afternoon. Hopefully, there are no hard feelings."

"Fine."

"After our breakfast this morning, I didn't expect to see you so soon. Have there been any new developments?"

"You tell me."

"Now's not the time," Logan said cryptically. "What I said this morning is still true. I'll contact you tomorrow to arrange our next meeting."

"Mr. Porter, if you refuse to assist us, then there's no reason for our continued presence here."

"No, please, just wait until tomorrow. Okay?"

"Fine." Disconnecting, Mercer handed the phone back to Bastian who was surreptitiously eyeing the file on top of the desk.

"You know you still owe me an apology. I'm not your punching bag." Bastian cast his eyes at the mattress. "And neither is the furniture. But maybe I was rather harsh." He went to the door, smirking slightly. "Deal with it."

EIGHT

"See if you can establish a trace." Mercer eyed the unknown number on his ringing cell phone.

"Two seconds." Bastian double-checked that the equipment and software were operational. "Do you think it's the kidnapper?"

"I don't know, but the only person with access to this number is Logan Porter and whoever he gave it to." Mercer waited half a second and answered.

"Don't say anything. I don't have much time. I snuck away for a minute, but I don't know if it's safe to talk. I'm not sure if my house is bugged. Did you check?"

"Your security system is functioning normally." Mercer recognized Porter's voice. "We didn't find any other devices during our preliminary walkthrough."

"Okay, then I guess that's okay." The sound of a toilet flushing sounded in the background. "I want to avoid another incident, but the people here are untrustworthy. I thought they'd help. They called you, but it seems to be for naught."

"Where are you?" Mercer asked, making eye

contact with Bastian who appeared just as flummoxed by the call.

"At work."

"Stay there. I'll see what I can do."

"No, please, I don't want another incident," Porter said hurriedly. "I have to go."

Mercer's protests were met by the sound of dead air. Hitting end call, he slammed the phone down and blew out a breath. "I'm not the conspiracy nut."

"It doesn't appear you are." Bastian clicked through the information they obtained from the call. "Porter used a burner phone to ring us. The GPS interface shows he's at work, probably in the loo from the sound of it." Bastian chewed on his lower lip while he entered more commands into the computer. "I can't get access to Trila's security system. They have too many firewalls in place." He blew out a breath. "Do you think they have him under surveillance?"

Mercer gave him a look.

"Stupid question," Bastian muttered. "So what do we do?"

"We get him out of there. I need to know the exact route his car service takes."

"I don't think I like where this is headed. I'm opposed to hitting the help, remember?" Bastian went to the wall and pulled down a few of the city maps. He had marked the garage location and most likely path the driver would take based on mileage, traffic, and time of day. "It's just a guess, but it's a start."

"Better than nothing." Mercer glanced at his friend. "It might get messy."

"In that case, I should probably come with you. You might need my assistance, and if not, Porter's driver definitely will." He gave the computers a final glance. "Just a friendly reminder, we aren't in the business of shooting people." Despite his words, his hand moved to his hip, feeling the reassuring weight of his holstered weapon.

"So you say, but we shoot an awful lot of people."

"Only when it's absolutely necessary," Bastian reminded him, "and I don't think the driver is a necessary casualty."

"It'd be easier."

"But much messier."

It was the same argument they had during every mission, but as Bastian insisted, they weren't mercenaries. Wet work wasn't a service that could be ordered. It was only a side dish occasionally required in fulfillment of an asset retrieval. Mercer knew this, and there were times he appreciated having the reminder, except when that reminder became a hindrance to finding answers and saving the lives of innocents.

"Do you have a plan?" Bastian asked as he climbed into the passenger's seat.

"Yes."

"Would you like to tell me what it is?"

"Intercept and replace. It should ensure access to Trila's garage and a way to get Logan out of there without anyone being the wiser."

"We'll need a diversion and an identical car to perform the switch." Bastian keyed something into his phone. "The service has two garages. Based on location, I'd guess the driver comes from the western lot. I might be able to disable the vehicle remotely, and if we intercept the driver's outgoing calls, no one will know anything's amiss. Can you score another car from the lot without causing an international incident?"

"Yes."

"Great. We can add grand theft auto to our résumé."

"It should already be included. After all, this isn't the first time we've had to borrow a ride," Mercer mused, enjoying the cross look on Bastian's face.

*　　*　　*

Stealing a car wasn't difficult. Normally, it took little more than a miscreant in tattered clothes. Car thieves didn't wear suits like professional chauffeurs, walk onto a lot, go directly to a vehicle, and get inside the car without batting an eye. It was even less likely they'd be able to start the car or drive away in broad daylight, but that's precisely what Mercer did. The joys of keyless entry and remote engine start.

Bastian created an app that could hack into almost any vehicle. Mercer used it to open the door. He climbed inside, opened the glove box, disabled the GPS tracker, and started the engine. After driving away from the garage, he turned down an alley connected to a parking lot. Bastian seamlessly entered the vehicle, and the two found an out-of-the-way place to wait for Logan Porter's driver.

The former SAS were situated on a side street near the garage exit. A few vehicles had already left, and Mercer was getting antsy. He wasn't convinced they hadn't missed their opportunity. For all he knew, Logan Porter's driver could already be halfway to Trila International. He let out a gruff sigh and focused on the car and driver who had taken them to Logan's home two days before.

"They told you the drivers rotate. What makes you think Porter's driver today will be this Appleman chap?" Mercer asked.

"Trust me." Bastian winked. "The car service doesn't bother encrypting their servers. It's the same vehicle and the same guy."

"Who drove the day of Sarina's abduction?"

"Kyle Culchek, the relief driver. Based on what I've uncovered, there are only a handful of men who drive for Logan either because he's too persnickety or because of security issues. It appears Trila International keeps tabs on each of their employees, particularly those closer to the top."

"Any reason they would think someone would target their rank and file?"

"I'm not sure yet. According to Trila's mission statement, they manufacture tech to build a better world, but according to their financials, their main source of revenue comes from government contracts. And not just one particular government either. Their designs could have military or espionage applications. I haven't been able to get deep enough into their databases to find out."

"That explains the diplomatic plates on the limo," Mercer mused. "We should ask Logan." He squinted, watching Stan Appleman get inside a car a few dozen meters away. "That could be the kidnapper's motivation for snatching Logan's wife. Perhaps the ransom demand is of the corporate sabotage variety instead of monetary."

"And it would explain why Trila's footing the bill for our services," Bastian said, "and why they don't want you snooping around."

"I'd wager a guess that those wankers are inadvertently responsible for Sarina's abduction, if they aren't behind it themselves."

Turning the key, Mercer waited for the car to pass, made sure no one else was following, and then pulled into traffic. While they waited for the driver and town car to move away from the more populated areas and into a less trafficked region, Bastian reached into the back seat and removed a black duffel bag. Inside was a gun specially modified to shoot a dart that would release an electromagnetic pulse that would temporarily disable the electrical circuitry of the target vehicle.

"Are you sure you'll be able to intercept the driver's call?" Mercer had seen Bastian work technical magic, but it never made sense how any of it actually worked.

"Yes, once that's done, I'll stay behind to monitor the situation with the driver, and you can go ahead to Trila and pick up Mr. Porter."

"From there, we'll head to our secondary location. It is secure, correct?"

"Affirmative."

They stopped at a red light, and Mercer caught a glimpse of another black sedan a few cars behind them. It continued on its path, keeping its position behind Mercer's town car. As traffic diverged, breaking away the farther they traveled from the main thoroughfare, the sedan closed the distance. Suddenly, the town car they were following hit the brakes. Mercer followed suit, and the sedan closed the gap, boxing them in.

"Bollocks." Bastian dropped the duffel and stuffed it beneath the seat. He glanced at Mercer, expecting the commander to open the door and start shooting. "Let's see what they want."

"I intend to."

Mercer opened the door slowly. No other vehicles were traveling on the road in either direction, and Mercer spotted an SUV blocking the street entrance behind them. This had been the location Mercer intended to use to his advantage, but clearly, someone else had the same thought.

Two men exited from the rear car, holding automatic handguns with extended magazines. They watched, staying within the cover provided by the open car doors, but they didn't make a move toward Julian. The rear door to Logan's town car opened, and another two men stepped out. Unlike their counterparts, they didn't brandish the weapons visible underneath their open jackets.

"Who are you?" one of them asked. "Why are you following us?"

Mercer remained silent, assessing the situation. Before he could answer, Bastian stepped out of the car with his palms raised. He offered a conciliatory smile to the men in front and a brief glance to the men behind them. The term ambush came to mind.

"We're not asking again," someone said from behind.

"Julian Mercer. I work for Logan Porter."

"You are not on the list of approved drivers."

"That must be an oversight."

"No, it isn't." The men who exited Porter's car stepped away, tapping on the side, and sending the driver and town car on its way. The two armed men continued their approach. Once they were a meter from Mercer, he spotted Trila security badges clipped on their belts. "You have been granted access to Mr. Porter's home and his wife's place of business. You are free to meet him anywhere else, but Trila International is strictly off-limits. You were warned about this earlier."

"Trila's paying our fee," Bastian interjected. "Shouldn't we notify your supervisor of our progress?"

"Consider him notified." The guard sneered. "Next time, we won't be so cordial."

"Neither will I," Mercer replied.

"By the way, stealing is a crime." The guard glanced pointedly at the Sig on Mercer's hip. "So is carrying a weapon."

"And you're the police?"

"No," the man smiled, "but they are." He jerked his head at the patrol car that had pulled up behind the rear sedan. "Enjoy yourselves in our prisons."

"You'll regret this." Mercer weighed his limited options. Unfortunately, a firefight wasn't ideal.

The man laughed and climbed into the back of the rear sedan with his cohort by his side. The two men with the automatic handguns waited for the police officers to approach before nodding and getting back inside their car and driving away. At the very least, it was obvious Trila controlled the police force and probably had the entire municipality in their pocket. It would make Mercer's job harder, but at least they now had some idea with whom they were dealing.

"From now on, I'm not going on any more of these outings with you," Bastian said as an officer pressed him against the side of the car and frisked him.

"No one asked you to come." Mercer explained the unfortunate misunderstanding to the officers, taking some creative licensing concerning the stolen vehicle being in his possession, but as the guards predicted, it didn't take long before Mercer and Bastian were arrested and thrown into a holding cell. "Any brilliant ideas on how to get out of here?"

"Hans is on his way. I turned on our cell phone tracker and told him to come forthwith." Bastian grinned. "Do you think one of those chaps would be so kind as to lend me a cigarette?"

"You quit."

"Details." Bastian sauntered across the cell to the dangerous looking men, offering a contrite smile. Within a few moments, he was shooting the shit with them, gathering as much intel on Trila and the local authorities as possible since their job had a few new kinks.

Mercer took a seat on the uncomfortable bench,

listening intently while considering the newest developments regarding Sarina Porter's abduction. Once he and Bastian were released, he'd have to find another way to free Logan from Trila's clutches and get his client to a secure place in order to speak freely. Sarina had been gone for five days. If they didn't get her back soon, he feared they never would.

NINE

"Explain again why you thought you would help yourself to an automobile," the detective said. He narrowed his eyes and leaned back in the chair, crossing his arms over his chest. It was posturing. "Grand theft auto is a serious crime. We take felony charges very seriously. You should do the same."

"I didn't steal the car." It was a lie but a reasonable one. "My client uses that car service. I was misinformed that I was to pick him up. When I entered the lot, no one questioned my presence." Mercer had used lines like this often enough. Typically, giving one-word responses was a better way to go, but since he was, in fact, guilty and caught red-handed, he had to put a polite spin on the situation. Bastian was much better at this, but Mercer would just have to make do in the meantime.

The cop sighed heavily. "We'll see if your accomplice will shed some light on this matter."

"He won't."

"Two armed men in a stolen vehicle doesn't bode

well, buddy."

"You have my permit, my passport, and my documentation. In my line of work, it is necessary to have defense measures in place."

"Or you strong-armed your way to get the car. Maybe you planned to do your own kidnapping."

"Preposterous." It was time to stop talking.

"Trila's security personnel informed on you. If you work for them or one of their employees like you claim, why would they call the police and report your actions?"

Mercer shrugged. The real question was how did they know what Mercer planned to do. They were prepared, and they tailed him. Had the safe house been compromised? Were he and his team also under surveillance, just like Logan Porter? He glanced at his phone inside an evidence bag on the detective's desk. They must have known about Porter's burner and traced the call. Mercer was deep in thought and no longer listening to the continuous questions or theories the detective continued to spout.

The detective slammed his palm on the desk. "How about you be real with me? You tell me the truth, and things will go a lot easier."

"That is the truth."

The two remained locked in a battle of wits, neither wavering. After fifteen minutes of tense silence, the cop stood up. He grabbed Mercer's arm and escorted him back to the holding cell. Bastian was gone, and Mercer figured it was because he was being asked the same questions by yet another incompetent, possibly corrupt, authority figure. So much for staying under the radar.

Before Bastian returned, another officer came to the cell, accompanied by Hans Bauer. The door unlocked, and Julian was let out. Once free from the cell, Mercer was handcuffed.

"Is that really necessary?" Hans asked, obviously enjoying every minute. "He's not a threat, at least not to you."

Mercer looked irate and bit his lip to keep from lashing out.

"Sorry, it's protocol. We can't do anything until he's officially released." The officer led the bound Mercer and Hans to the bullpen and into an open office. "The sergeant will be with you shortly. An officer will be outside if you need anything."

"Thanks, mate," Hans replied. The man left, and Hans glanced out the doorway. "I'm sure I could come up with a few things I need." He smiled brightly. "It seems like just yesterday when I was fetching you from a different holding cell."

"Shut it."

"This one is rather lovely. Did you see the receptionist? A lovely blonde bird with legs that go on for miles. That's what I call a help desk."

"I see jetlag has made you even more insufferable. Where's Donovan?"

"He's running recon." Hans leaned closer and lowered his voice. "Word is the car company isn't pressing charges. Trila's been in communication with the bobbies, and they're backing your story. It was scare tactics to keep your snooping to a minimum."

"How do you know that?"

Hans tapped his ear. "Bas left a present inside the car and routed the communication to my comm. Want to listen?"

Before Mercer could answer, a man in a white uniform entered the room. He took a seat behind the desk. "It looks like you're making a mess out of my city, Mr. Mercer. Is there any particular reason why?"

"We muck about. It's what we do," Hans offered,

earning a glare from the man.

"You're a personal security specialist, which means what exactly?"

"Kidnappings and ransoms, mostly," Hans piped up before Julian could respond.

"I haven't been notified of any such event. Who's been kidnapped?" the sergeant asked.

"That's none of your concern," Mercer replied. Maintaining his client's privacy wasn't a precise science, but the less outsiders knew, the better.

"Kidnapping is a crime. That makes it my business."

"No."

"I could throw you back into holding. Charge you with obstruction."

"Fine." Mercer waited, but the man didn't move.

"Forget it," the sergeant finally said. "You're a foreigner which means we would have to get the embassy involved and the state department, and since the car service and Trila don't want to press charges, you can go just as soon as someone vouches for your claim of being a private contractor for Trila. So do you want to tell me who to call on your behalf?"

By divulging a name, Mercer would lead the police to discover the abduction, but he didn't have much of a choice. Plus, it seemed plausible to assume Trila already controlled the authorities and the way they dealt with such information. "Logan Porter."

"See how easy that was?"

Mercer ignored the remark and remained silent, waiting for the call to be made.

An hour later, Bastian and Mercer were released from police custody, given warnings not to commit any other crimes, and strongly encouraged to discuss the real reason they were hired by Trila on Logan Porter's behalf. The former SAS team remained silent as they left the station, following Hans to a tiny subcompact. Bastian flipped the seat down and climbed into the back.

"Were they out of clown cars?" Bas asked.

"You said to come forthwith. I didn't have time to find a more suitable alternative," Hans replied.

"Drop us off." Mercer glanced at his phone which had been in police custody. He removed the battery and SIM card and watched Bastian do the same. "We'll need new gear." He held his hand out. "Give me your phone."

Hans handed him the phone, muttering something about ungrateful bastards. Mercer phoned Logan, setting up an impromptu meeting at the closest pub. It wasn't ideal to meet in public, but until Mercer and Bastian had time to sweep their belongings for tracking and listening devices the police might have planted on them, it would suffice. Porter sounded panicked, but he remained professional on the phone, agreeing to a rendezvous within the hour.

"Contact Donovan. I want eyes on our meeting and backup nearby," Mercer said. "Bas, do what you can to disable any surveillance Porter might be under."

"It'll be hard without my equipment."

"Make it work."

"Aye, sir." Bastian turned around in the seat, glancing out the back. "What are we going to do about the bobbies tailing us?"

"Nothing." Mercer knew the police would follow. It didn't matter what country or city they were in. The police always acted in the same fashion. "They want to find out more about the kidnapping. With any luck, their presence will spook whoever might be following Porter."

"And Donovan can follow them back to their hidey hole," Hans said.

"Precisely. Or at the very least, they'll tip their hand so we can begin the process of identifying who they are and what they want." Mercer looked at the phone he procured from Hans, knowing they'd have to replace that eventually if Trila's security was monitoring Logan Porter's personal number, which surely, they were.

They'd need new phones, new tech, and a few more vehicles stashed in various locations around the city. As Mercer continued to work on his mental list and compose the beginnings of a plan, Hans pulled the car to a stop. Mercer stepped out, pushing the lever down so Bastian could exit as well.

"Lose the car. The tail will probably stay with us but be careful, just in case. And make sure Donovan knows where to meet us. You know the address of our flat, but it might be compromised. If nothing occurs, we'll meet back there later this evening."

Hans nodded, putting the car back into drive. Julian slammed the door and scanned the area. As he predicted, the police vehicle parked a block away. They had an audience, but it didn't matter. The only thing that mattered was getting Logan to talk.

"What do you want to do first?" Bastian asked.

"Scope out the pub and get a drink."

TEN

"Mr. Mercer," Logan Porter bellowed over the noise, "what are you doing? You're supposed to be looking for my wife, not getting arrested for grand theft auto."

"That's rubbish." But Mercer saw no point in arguing. It was a waste of time and energy. "You need to come clean, or we're walking away. Who's after you? Who took your wife?"

Porter looked torn. He gulped down a mouthful of whiskey and visually swept his surroundings. The three sat in a back booth with Porter's back to the crowd. It was loud inside. The pub just happened to have an amateur mic night going on, and it was hard to hear oneself think, let alone eavesdrop on anyone else's conversation.

"Trila security has been guarding me since this happened, but I think there might be others keeping watch too. I don't know. Maybe it's the assholes who took Sarina," Porter said. "I just don't know."

"If they're watching you, out in public is the safest place to be." Bastian pressed closer to Porter to keep his voice from traveling. "We know she was taken. We watched your home security footage, and we found the USB you had hidden. Have they made any other attempts to communicate with you?"

Porter swallowed. "They said they'd kill her. They have her, and they will kill her."

"What do they want?" Mercer leaned across the table.

"That doesn't matter. I can't get it."

"We'll negotiate for a reasonable price," Bastian interjected.

"No," Porter shook his head vehemently, "it's not money." He lowered his voice, looking around again. "This is a mistake. Trila called you to keep up appearances. They don't want the bad press, but you can't help me."

"You haven't given us a chance," Mercer said. "You don't know what you're doing. Fucking around will guarantee you never see her again. Tell the kidnappers you hired professional negotiators to work on your behalf. If they are professionals, they should expect it."

"The majority of kidnappings are conducted by pros," Bastian added. "Frankly, most of them prefer dealing with us. We make far fewer mistakes."

"I don't know." Logan blew out a breath to steady his nerves.

"You said you wanted us to save her." The brief pause in Mercer's words was only perceptible to Bastian when he said, "And we will save her." Logan didn't look convinced, but the negotiator pushed on. "Do you know when their next communication will be?"

"Tomorrow morning at seven a.m." Porter inhaled. "I...I don't want you involved."

"What exactly did they say?" Bastian asked.

"No authorities. They said if I give them what they

want, then they'll return Sarina, but I can't get it. I told them that. They said if I wanted to see her again I would find a way." Porter turned around, scanning the room again. He paled slightly, and his Adam's apple bobbed. "I shouldn't even be seen with you."

"We aren't the authorities, Mr. Porter." Mercer's eyes traveled to the three men in business attire hovering near the exit. They stood out like sore thumbs. "Who are those blokes?"

Porter shook his head, edging as far away from Bastian as he could. As if the few extra centimeters of space would somehow indicate they weren't conversing. Since the question remained unanswered, Mercer stood. He had two options. He could introduce himself or pretend he hadn't noticed their unrelenting gaze. Frankly, Julian was sick and tired of playing dumb and succumbing to the pushy bastards from Trila. Striding across the room, he bumped into one of the suited men.

The suit glared and gave Mercer a shove. "Watch yourself."

Mercer smiled wickedly. "My apologies. My friend thought he recognized you. He was afraid you were following him. I hope he's mistaken."

"What's it to you?"

"You see, I'm working on behalf of the family," Mercer began, unsure if this could be one of the kidnappers or someone from Trila, "and it's important you understand that simple fact. I don't like people getting in my way. And right now, you sir, are in my way."

The man stepped to the side, away from the door. "I'd encourage you not to get in my way either."

Without taking his eyes off the group, Mercer gestured for Bastian and Porter to join him. A moment later, Bastian appeared behind Mercer with his arm slung around Porter's shoulders. It was the only way to get their client to comply. Mercer brushed past the suits and held the door for his two companions as they left the pub. It was dusk, but the area was adequately lit so Mercer was able to evaluate their surroundings.

"Let's continue this conversation at your place." Mercer forced Porter toward his waiting town car. "I don't think you should be alone in your current state."

"What did you do?" Porter asked, but Mercer shrugged it off, sending a quick text to Donovan.

Backup would be nearby, but it seemed unlikely the kidnappers would make a move against Porter tonight. Unfortunately, with this many unknown players on the scene, Mercer couldn't risk compromising another secure location. They'd simply play along and utilize Porter's driver and his estate for their meeting.

"I'm handling the situation the best way I know how." Mercer wondered if the driver harbored any ill will toward him.

"You're going to get her killed. They won't understand. They'll think this is a trick, or I'm not doing as they said." Porter paled. "Oh god, they'll realize I can't give them what they want."

"Sit down," Bastian opened the back door on Porter's waiting town car, "and shut up. This isn't polite conversation for mixed company."

Somehow, they managed to keep Porter quiet and his emotions in check for the remainder of the ride. A chauffeured car wasn't secure, but it ensured anonymity for Donovan and, hopefully, Hans too. The less the kidnappers knew about Mercer's team, the better.

Once they were locked inside Porter's meticulous estate, Bastian did a quick visual sweep for bugs. Even though none were discovered, Mercer turned on the stereo and forced Porter to keep his voice low. He didn't know if the home security system was spying on its owner.

"Tell us everything and start at the beginning. If you don't believe it's safe to talk here, we will arrange for a secure location, but time is of the essence." Mercer gave him a hard stare. "It's your choice."

"We should be safe here." Logan snorted. "Well, at least I thought that before Sarina was taken." For the first time, he dropped the act, giving up the appearance of being in charge. "I don't know how they knew, but they did. And they took Sarina, and there's nothing I can do."

"Knew what?"

"The protocols. I was in charge of overseeing the security protocols on the new computer systems. There's a backdoor. Obviously, that's pretty fundamental with software. Some way for the administrator to check functions and perform tasks without disrupting the user interface."

"What does this have to do with Sarina?"

"Everything. They want access to the systems and the override codes. That's what they want in exchange for Sarina."

"Okay, that's a start."

"No, that's the end. I can't give them the codes. First of all, I don't have them. I don't know them. I checked the software and monitored our progress. I'm not a programmer. I don't write code. I can barely read it."

"Maybe Bastian could assist," Mercer suggested.

"No. You don't get it." Logan began pacing in a tiny circle. "The first thing I did was go to upper management. I told the head honchos at Trila what happened. Of course, they were sympathetic. They hired you. They said this is a kidnapping, so there will be a ransom and I needed a specialist to deal with the negotiation. The company has insurance for this sort of thing. It was a clause in my employment contract. God knows I never expected to need it. I don't even remember reading it. It's in there I guess, but how insane is it that they make insurance for this type of situation?"

"Mr. Porter," Mercer cut in, hoping to get the conversation back on track, "I've done this before. Most of the time, both sides agree on a price, especially when insurance is involved."

Logan laughed, a deep bitter sound. "They made it very clear they have no interest in money. Trila knows it, but they refuse to help get Sarina back."

"Because they won't let you walk off with their intellectual property," Mercer surmised. Corporate espionage was a lucrative business, and if these systems were as grand as Porter made them sound, it made sense why this was the ransom demand. Trade secrets could sell for millions. "You can't blame them for that, but that's why Trila's security has been up your arse. You're a risk."

"I'm not going to steal it. I wouldn't even know how."

"It doesn't matter. You're in a jam, and you're desperate. Desperate men are known to do just about anything." Mercer had been there, and he had watched it happen. It was possible his team possessed the capabilities to gain the information the kidnappers wanted, but that was a line he wanted to avoid crossing if possible. "What else have the kidnappers said? Have they provided proof of life?"

"The only footage of Sarina is on that USB. They won't let me speak to her. I just..." The words caught in his throat, and he looked away. "I believe they will kill her. I told them it would take time to get what they wanted. They expect answers in the morning."

"Then we'll have to make sure they are asking questions we are able to answer."

ELEVEN

By seven a.m., Mercer's skull was pounding. He and his team had spent the night playing catch-up. The first two days had been a total waste. Little had been accomplished, aside from preliminary background information and investigation. Neither of which would lead to bringing Sarina Porter home alive. Now, the team had some idea of motive, and they needed to determine who had access and opportunity.

Bastian had borrowed a car and made various trips to one of their equipment lockers in order to properly wire the Porter estate. Every incoming message, whether it was phone, internet, or personal delivery, would be monitored and recorded. He split the Porters' security system feed, filtering one set into a computer with an expanded hard drive to save any new information that was recorded. Another computer analyzed the system for glitches, updates, and any changes that might have been made in the last month. And while this was going on, Logan had provided Sarina's tablet for them to review. Even though this information had already been analyzed, Bastian checked it again for signs of hackers.

Whoever took Sarina had to be intimately involved with the family. While Bastian worked the tech angle, Mercer reviewed the employee list with Logan. Painstaking hour after painstaking hour, each employee was rigorously assessed. The slightest tiff or inappropriate comment meant deeper scrutiny. Even those who appeared perfectly professional needed further evaluation. But with the clock ticking, the possibility of pinpointing the party responsible was unlikely.

"Are you aware a knife's missing?" Mercer asked.

It was five a.m., and he leaned back in the chair to rub his eyes. The racket from the stereo would have driven most men crazy, but he and Bastian were used to it by now. Logan was another story. He had changed the music selection every hour or so, tired of hearing the droning lyrics over and over again.

"Yeah, I thought it might have dropped down the drain, but I haven't bothered to check." For someone so persnickety, that was odd.

Mercer narrowed his eyes. "Rubbish."

"What?"

"That is utter bullshit."

Logan didn't deny it. He simply shrugged. "It's a steak knife. There's nothing special about it, and I have something more important to occupy my thoughts."

"When did it disappear?"

"I don't know." Logan held Mercer's gaze. "Honestly, I don't remember. Why does it matter? Are you planning to buy me a new set?" The hours had made him combative and sarcastic.

"No. It matters because everything about Sarina's abduction is professional. However, if the knife was used, that indicates the kidnapper's needed a weapon of convenience and something unplanned occurred."

"Maybe she grabbed it to defend herself," Logan suggested.

"Perhaps." But questions swam through Mercer's head. "Your security footage from that day leaves everything to the imagination." He stood and stretched his legs. In one corner of the room was a surveillance camera. "Did your wife object to such a blatant disregard for privacy?"

"How did you know?"

"Trila owns your home. That's a matter of public record." Mercer glanced at Bastian who hadn't moved from behind the computer screens. Bastian's lips were tinged blue from chewing too vigorously on the end of an ink pen. "According to my associate, the information from your security system is stored on-site, and your personal employees are provided by Trila. That includes the two guards at the front gate."

"I wouldn't call them guards. They just monitor the system and open the gate. The cameras and sensors are here to prevent break-ins. Despite the lovely accommodations and classy perks afforded by my job, this isn't a part of the world that boasts much wealth. Trila installed the system and the two sentries as a theft deterrent, and Sarina hated it. She thought they were spying on us." Logan swallowed, reconsidering what he had just said. "After these last few days, I think she was right."

"At least they splurged on the kidnapping insurance, mate," Bastian said, joining them. "The good news is the footage can only be accessed via your network. The bad news is getting onto your network isn't too difficult. However, it would require physical proximity to your home. One hundred meters, give or take." He shrugged, focusing on Mercer. "Someone particularly crafty might have used a drone to hover overhead and remotely access it, but the range on those isn't particularly great unless we are dealing with military tech."

"If they had that type of access, wouldn't they be able to gain access to Trila's protocols without using a middleman?" Mercer asked.

Bastian considered the point and returned to his position behind the computer. Mercer rubbed his eyes again. All-nighters weren't uncommon. However, being unprepared for his first interaction with the kidnapper was. Going in blind had never been beneficial to the former SAS, and something told him today wouldn't be any different.

"You should get some sleep while you can," Mercer said.

Logan looked bewildered. "How can I possibly sleep? I'm not sure I've really slept since Sarina's disappearance."

Bastian made an amused grunt but didn't speak. Mercer knew what his friend was thinking. Porter hadn't faltered from his routine since her abduction, and despite the fact he appeared distraught, that didn't mean he really was. It irked Mercer that it had taken nearly three days to get a straight answer out of their client, forcing them to stumble into the situation practically blind.

"Give it a try," Mercer said. "I'm sure you'll manage." Frankly, he wanted some time alone to think and prepare. The late hour and the previous day had drained his limited patience even further. "I will wake you in time for the call in case you are needed."

Grumbling, Logan went up the steps to the bedroom. Once he was gone, Mercer turned off the stereo, no longer needing the blaring sound to mask their voices. He was tired of the music. Frankly, he was just tired. He took a seat at the kitchen table and field stripped his Sig Sauer, cleaned the parts using one of Porter's fine linens, and reassembled his firearm. Once it was holstered, he took a deep breath and cleared his throat.

"You should call it quits for the night, too," he said to Bastian. "We're less than an hour away. Turn that off for now. I want you sharp."

"How sharp can I possibly be?" Bastian retorted, but he pushed away from the table. "You do realize this wouldn't be a problem if I still smoked."

"Do what you want, but those bloody things will kill you."

"And this job won't?" Bastian cocked an eyebrow and went to the fridge. "It's a disgusting habit anyway." He opened a Tupperware container and gave it a sniff. "And so is whatever's in here." He shut the door and searched the cabinets. "What do these people eat?"

"The shit Trila feeds them," Mercer replied. His words earned a warning glance, but he already knew the tech company had probably bugged the entire house and was eavesdropping on their conversation using the home security system as a guise. "They provide everything, don't they? I mean they hired us. They gave Porter an insurance clause in his contract. This house, the car, everything is because of them. Maybe they do the grocery shopping too."

"Jules, stop being ridiculous." Bastian settled on a spotted, overripe banana from the fruit bowl on the counter. "They aren't evil incarnate. If they were, they'd pay better."

"I don't like being jerked around. Getting set up by those pompous security wankers and arrested was just their way of asserting dominance, and they need to know we do not fall into their chain of command. We are not their subordinates. We do not owe them anything. We are private contractors, hired to perform an asset retrieval. They do not dictate the terms. Is that clear?"

Bastian finished the banana. "Right-o, but that point has always been very clear to me. Now it should be bloody clear to absolutely everyone." He focused on the camera in the corner of the room. "But for the record, Trila isn't our enemy. No one is. We don't have a horse in this race. We were hired to perform a service, and that is it."

"Always the diplomatic one," Mercer muttered under his breath. His diatribe had been a dig at the eye in the sky that he wasn't under their jurisdiction and he would do as he pleased. But as usual, Bastian was working to keep the peace. After all, someone had to foot the bill for their toys and gear.

TWELVE

Seven a.m. came and went. The phone didn't ring. The post wasn't delivered. Nothing happened. Logan Porter stared bleary-eyed out the kitchen window. His cup of coffee remained half full, but his optimism was another story.

"Why haven't they made contact?" he asked.

"Are you sure they didn't?" Mercer countered, but the same question was the only thing on his mind.

There were three possibilities. The kidnappers realized Porter wouldn't deliver on the ransom, so they cut their losses and moved on, in which case Sarina's body would eventually be discovered or she'd return home unharmed. Second, someone prevented the communication. The police and Trila's security goons were at the top of Mercer's list of unwanted meddlers. If they interfered, there was no telling whether future negotiations could ever salvage the situation and lead to a positive recovery.

"Did they say they would speak to you here?" Bastian asked.

The third possibility was the kidnappers planned to

communicate with Porter at Trila International. Maybe the unannounced arrival of their team inside Porter's home had spooked the kidnappers.

"They didn't say," Logan replied. "I just assumed."

"Don't." Mercer examined the security feed on the laptop, watching it scan the exterior and interior. "Why seven a.m.? They know your routine. The car service should be arriving momentarily. It leaves a small window." The realization crashed through his thoughts. "You canceled the bloody car."

"Of course." Logan looked indignant. "It's not like I could go to work when I have to talk to them."

"You bleeding moron." Mercer left the room, knowing it wasn't wise to berate. He needed sleep. He was getting agitated which wouldn't help anyone, particularly Logan if he ended up with his head through the wall. After a few moments, Mercer returned to the kitchen. "Go to work. If you hear from them, contact me immediately."

"How can I possibly go to work now?" Logan squawked.

"Your position at Trila is the only thing useful to them." Bastian kept his voice even. "They probably know Trila is monitoring your movements. If you start acting suspicious, it practically guarantees you won't be able to deliver the protocols. You need to be at work to prove to them you're trying. Do you understand?"

"Yes, but how can they expect me to act normally at a time like this?" Logan asked.

"Because you have been doing exactly that. They took your wife, and nothing changed. Now negotiators arrive. Trila's tracking you. And you cancel the company car with no plans to go to the office. They know you told your bosses about the abduction," Mercer said.

"Oh my god." Logan slapped his palm over his mouth. "I *am* a moron."

"Go to work," Mercer repeated. "And get my name put on the freaking approved list in case I need to stop by."

Logan continued to sputter out questions, but Bastian ushered him to the garage. The man could drive himself today. Hopefully, the kidnappers would conclude that after the grand theft debacle yesterday, Porter was too embarrassed to ask for a ride.

Once he was gone, Mercer turned the stereo back on full blast and placed a piece of tape over the camera lens in the kitchen. The idea of shorting out the entire system was appealing. But Bastian was piggybacking off the surveillance, and it might prove just as useful to them as it was to Trila. Picking up a pen, Mercer wrote on a sheet of paper: *The kidnappers have access to the car service.*

Bastian nodded. It made sense. They had always been suspicious of the drivers. Perhaps this was a lead, not that they were in the business of identifying the culprits. More often than not, it simply helped to have as much background information as possible in order to aid in negotiations. However, when negotiations failed, it was also nice to know how much firepower would be necessary to subdue the kidnappers.

"Let's pack up," Bastian said. "We've been compromised. It's a new day. Time to start fresh."

The storage locker he'd visited the previous night was no longer secure which is why he'd unloaded everything from it. The burners they'd been using would have to be destroyed. The flat they had occupied was questionable, and if they returned, they'd have to be extremely vigilant.

"We'll reconvene at our hotel rendezvous point,"

Mercer said.

Donovan was somewhere in the city, but he hadn't made contact. And Hans might have something to add about what he'd witnessed last night. In the event either of them had compromised their location, Mercer didn't want to walk into a trap.

After their equipment had been removed from Porter's home, the phone rang. Mercer glanced at the security camera in the hallway. "Son of a bitch." Two rings later, he answered.

"Don't try to outsmart us or outthink us. You are outmatched," a mechanical voice said.

"I'm Mercer. To whom am I speaking?"

"Alpha," the same voice replied. No additional words were wasted. "You are the negotiator." It didn't exactly sound like a question, but Mercer answered anyway.

"Yes. Logan Porter hired me."

"Don't lie again."

"Trila hired me on his behalf. However, I work for him. The safe return of Sarina Porter is my primary concern." Normally, Mercer was in control of the conversation, but this time felt different. "Is she alive?"

"Yes."

"I need proof."

"You'll have to earn it." The odd spacing between the words caused Mercer to pause. Initially, he suspected a voice modulator was being used, but this sounded more like a type and talk program.

"That's not how this works," Mercer warned.

"It is now."

"Without proof, you'll get nothing."

The voice remained silent, so Mercer counted to fifteen and hung up the phone. It was the worst part of the job. Potentially, it was the most devastating moment. Normally, it was his way of reasserting control over the situation, but it could easily backfire and lead to serious injury or death of the abductee. So far, he'd been lucky, but it was only a matter of time before his luck ran out.

Bastian stood in the doorway. He was in one of the surveillance blind spots and didn't want to move back into the picture. Already, he had the time and number down and hoped to trace the call just as soon as he was behind a computer screen. Silently, the two men waited.

After what felt like an eternity but was actually closer to ten minutes, the phone rang again. Mercer swallowed. Turning his back to the camera, he took a moment to regain his composure before answering.

"Proof is on the way," Alpha declared. Before Mercer could say a word, the call disconnected.

He put the receiver back in its cradle. "Go," he said to Bastian. "I'll stay here. See what you can find."

"Jules, I don't think—"

But Mercer silenced him. "Hurry. I'll see you at the rendezvous."

"You better be there." Bastian gave the commander a final glance and headed out the door. Unfortunately, he now had the task of finding transportation. "What I wouldn't give for an Uber right about now."

With Bastian gone, Mercer was alone. He stared at the closest security camera. There was no reason to believe Alpha was monitoring the feed, but something told Mercer that was the case. The call didn't come in until they were no longer prepared. Surely, that couldn't be a coincidence.

Going into the kitchen, Mercer searched the drawers for a rolling pin. Then he went from room to room, knocking out every camera inside the house. So much for using the surveillance system to his advantage.

While he waited for proof of life to be delivered, he evaluated the house and the various rooms for tactical advantages. Deciding the landing on the staircase provided the greatest vantage point but the least amount of cover, he moved on to other parts of the house. The kitchen and living room had ample cover but were prone to multiple entry points. Frankly, a gunfight inside would come down to the element of surprise and who was a better shot.

"Fantastic," Mercer muttered.

He remained on high alert, watching and waiting. Alpha provided no insight into how the proof of life would be delivered. It could be an e-mail message, a phone call, or even a delivery. Most were done via e-mail or phone, but Alpha wanted to send a message.

The doorbell rang, and Mercer went to the window. Outside was a delivery truck from a flower shop. He memorized the truck's details and went to the door with his Sig in hand.

"Whoa." The man stepped backward, almost dropping the arrangement.

"Who are you? Who sent you?" Mercer's gaze swept the exterior of the house, not seeing anyone else.

"Here. Just take it. Okay?" The man continued to step backward until he had cleared the porch, then he ran back to the truck and drove away.

Attached to the flower arrangement was a thick envelope. It had red blotches on the outside that didn't look intentionally decorative. Mercer carefully reached down and opened it. Inside was a finger with a perfectly manicured nail and a wedding ring.

"Fuck."

THIRTEEN

"You have your proof," Alpha said.

"I said she should remain unharmed," Mercer replied. His voice was devoid of emotion. There was nothing left but the cold, surgical precision needed to properly execute a negotiation. "Damage to the package is unacceptable."

"I say what is unacceptable." A slight clicking sound resonated inside the receiver. "Logan Porter is aware of our demands. We want the protocols ready for delivery in forty-eight hours."

"That's impossible. We are prepared to provide a different form of payment."

"No."

"They have no determined value. What are they worth to you?"

"What is a hand worth to you, Mercer? Or an ear?"

"Doing further harm to Sarina will only decrease the value of the ransom."

"I think you should ask Logan about that. I will make contact again in twelve hours. Be prepared to provide the protocols."

The call ended, and Mercer slammed the phone down. Then he picked it up and slammed it a few dozen times. Eventually, it shattered into pieces. Taking a breath, he sifted through the shards, locating a small listening device. Obviously, Bastian must have missed it. Unsure if it was still operational, Mercer wrapped it in a few thick layers of aluminum foil in an attempt to block any possible transmissions before shoving it inside his pocket.

After locking up the house, he did a quick check of the perimeter. Briefly, he spoke to the sentry at the guard post, Thomas Redding, who had waved the delivery driver through. It didn't take long to obtain a screenshot of the truck and driver from the exterior security feed. Once that was done, Mercer headed in the direction of the rendezvous point. There was much to discuss, and he wanted his team clued in and prepared before he spoke to Logan again. No one paid any heed to Mercer, and he continued at a quick march toward the hotel. They were now on a deadline, twelve hours and counting.

Inside the lobby, he spotted Donovan. The younger man looked utterly bored. He flipped through a magazine, absently drumming his fingers against his thigh. Mercer didn't acknowledge him but instead took the lift to the seventh floor. He stepped outside, walked to the end of the corridor, nearest to the stairwell, opened the door to check for any uninvited visitors, and then unlocked the adjoining door to the neighboring room. A few minutes later, he heard the corresponding latch on the other side open, and Donovan stepped inside.

"Really, mate? Did you think it was the bogeyman?" Donovan rolled his eyes at the Sig pointed in his direction. "You've got to get over your hang-ups.

Maybe get a massage or find a hooker. You need to do something to blow off steam."

"Have you spoken to Bastian?"

"He'll be here. He's updating our tech. I swear you're making him just as paranoid as you tend to be." Donovan sunk onto one of the beds in the room. "This is comfy. How about we don't speak for the next six hours?"

Mercer reached into his jacket and removed the envelope and listening device. Without a word, he handed the envelope to Donovan and sat on the adjacent bed. Reaching across to the table, he picked up the pad of paper and began jotting down notes on Alpha, the delivery truck, and their brief communication.

"Did you see anyone last night?" Mercer asked.

"Nope. No one followed you back to the client's house, and the street traffic seemed normal." Donovan placed the envelope on the nightstand. "I'll get a bucket of ice." He shook his head. "I hate it when things go this way."

"This was the result of our first contact."

"What do they want?"

"Computer protocols." Mercer stopped writing. "He's called Alpha. That was his proof of life."

"Doesn't ring any bells, but he's done this before. And he must know you have too. A novice wouldn't cut off a finger as proof of life or expect a negotiator to be smart enough to realize that it better damn well be bloody."

"No blood, no heartbeat," Mercer stated.

"Precisely."

Donovan returned with a bucket of ice to preserve the finger. Mercer removed the wedding ring to show to Logan since the aggrieved husband didn't need to see the extent of the damage. Ideally, the finger would be printed and compared to Sarina Porter in order to confirm identification, but in this instance, that would likely be an unnecessary step.

"Julian," Donovan said, "it's not your fault." He nodded at the ring that Mercer had yet to put down. "This is some sick, twisted bastard who wants to play mind games with you."

"Where's her engagement ring?" Mercer wasn't listening. He was thinking.

"Maybe she didn't have one, or she didn't wear it out." Donovan raised an eyebrow. "This isn't exactly a place to flaunt your wealth." He squinted. "From what I've seen, shouldn't she have had her own security detail? Frankly, Logan ought to as well. Doesn't Trila pay for everything else?"

"Who knows?"

Placing the ring on the table, Mercer rubbed his face, feeling two days' worth of stubble scratch against his palms. He needed sleep, a shower, and something to eat. The order wasn't important. He studied Donovan, who upon closer examination didn't look much better.

"I could go for a hot and a cot," Mercer admitted. "Try to get some rest while we wait for Hans and Bastian. Then we'll update them and trade out." He looked at the clock. "We have ten hours until the next communication with Alpha."

"Any idea what you're going to do?" Donovan asked, edging back toward the adjoining room.

"Not yet."

For the next forty-five minutes, Julian Mercer twisted and turned. He was exhausted, physically and mentally, but sleep didn't come. Too many things were in the works, and he knew he didn't have the luxury of resting. Instead, he took a shower, did a few dozen push-ups and sit-ups, and watched the news.

Trila owned this city and everyone in it. They probably controlled the local media outlets, so it wasn't surprising there was no mention of anything pertaining to them or their workers.

By the time Bastian and Hans arrived, Mercer had mentally evaluated the three separate phone calls with Alpha. All of which had been brief. Whether that was by design was undetermined. After briefing the other two members of the team and hearing Bastian announce the calls were untraceable since the phone number originated from an unregistered internet number that had been run through a proxy, it was obvious they were dealing with professionals.

"I'll make some calls and see if anyone has dealt with this Alpha bloke," Hans offered. Thankfully, their former service to the Crown afforded them friends in various international intelligence communities. Surely, someone would know something. "You could always ask the local bobbies. They're particularly fond of you."

"What'd you discover after dropping us off last night?" Bastian asked.

"Not much. The coppers stayed behind to watch the two of you. I double-backed after a time, but they were dispatched." Hans shrugged. "I can't tell you where they went, but I know they weren't waiting at that pub or Porter's."

"What about Trila?" Mercer asked.

"Security is tight. They've been trained," Hans exchanged a look with each of the men, "like we have."

"What's some tech company doing with a bunch of special ops military personnel?" Donovan asked.

"Their international dealings and government contracts might have something to do with it, but I'll ask Porter," Mercer said. "In the meantime, Donovan will sit on Trila. Bastian, see what you can dig up on this shit." He gestured to the notepad he'd filled with data and the photo of the delivery truck and driver. "Hans, ask your friends about Alpha, Trila, and the Porters. We're missing something. I want to be prepared for our next conversation instead of standing around with my dick in my hand. Got it?"

"What are you planning on doing?" Bastian asked.

"Finding a way to get Alpha what he wants."

"Jules, do you understand what that entails?" Bas inquired. "We'd be breaking dozens of laws, sacrificing our position and reputation, and jeopardizing countless corporations."

"We need leverage. A good bluff works just as well." Mercer sighed. "I'm going to Trila to have a talk with someone in charge. Since they got Porter into this mess, they ought to help get him out."

"Make sure you ask nicely," Bastian warned.

"I'll go as backup," Donovan said.

"No, you will remain a ghost," Mercer ordered. "I don't want to tip our hand and let them know our team is larger than they expected. Regardless of their generosity, I don't trust them."

"Fairly certain that feeling is mutual," Bastian said.

"I'll need a ten minute head start to get set up in the shadows." Donovan returned to the adjoining room and left from that door. Hopefully, it'd be enough to prevent any potential onlookers from realizing the four men were together.

"Be careful," Bastian watched Mercer check the clip in his gun, "and try not to shoot anyone."

"We'll see."

FOURTEEN

Mercer made it inside the lobby of the Trila International building before he was stopped by security. It was an improvement from being chased away by the guards inside the parking garage. Although, Julian had avoided them this time by being dropped off by a taxi near the front entrance of the building.

"Remove your weapon slowly, sir," one of the security guards said.

"No."

"Sir?" The momentary surprise was replaced with anger over Mercer's insolence. Apparently, the guards weren't used to being told no. Then again, they weren't used to dealing with this particular kidnapping negotiator either. "I won't ask again."

"Good because the answer will be the same." Mercer kept an eye on the four men. "I want to speak to someone in charge."

"You work for Mr. Porter. You do not have clearance to speak to anyone else."

"I work for this company. Now ring your boss."

The guards didn't want to budge or give in to Mercer's demands. The five men remained locked in a battle of wits, waiting for the other side to concede. The lobby grew silent as others began to notice the commotion. One of the guards reached into his jacket and pulled out a radio. He whispered something and returned it to its previous position. A few seconds later, the man pressed his fingers against his ear, obviously receiving a message over his earpiece.

"If you do not willingly disarm, we will be forced to subdue you," the guard said.

"You're welcome to give it a go." Mercer shifted his stance.

The mouthy guard stepped closer, reaching for Mercer's holstered gun. Mercer turned sideways, grasping the man's wrist and placing his other hand on the man's elbow. Before Mercer could follow through, the man shifted his momentum, spinning toward Mercer and attempting to land a left hook. Mercer ducked, releasing the guy's elbow and twisting his wrist at a ninety-degree angle, forcing the man to drop to his knee. The guy fell to his side, sweeping out with his left leg. Julian went down, landing an elbow to the man's shoulder.

Bouncing back up, Mercer narrowly avoided another guard's right jab and the darts from a third guard's taser. The fourth guard keyed his radio. Any minute, the rest of Trila's security personnel would appear, brandishing automatic weapons, or so Julian imagined. Oddly, he wondered how many Donovan would kill with his long-range rifle before they could gun him down.

"Stop," the fourth guard shouted. "That's an order." The guards withdrew, wary of Julian who remained still, shifting his eyes cautiously to see if this was a trap. "There is no need to fight with a private contractor. We are on the same side."

Mercer studied the guard. He didn't appear to be in charge. He was dressed like the others, but he might be the only one with a brain. Obviously, he had radioed for orders, and they'd just come from on high.

"Side?" Mercer asked, hoping to gain information.

"We both want to protect Trila employees." The man paused, cocking his head to the side and making it obvious someone was speaking through him. "However, your unconventional methods will not be tolerated on Trila property. Consider this your final warning."

Before Mercer could say anything else, the lift doors opened and Logan stepped out. "Mr. Mercer," he called, unaware of the fracas that had occurred, "do you have news?"

"I was hoping to speak to your boss," Mercer replied coolly, his eyes never wavering from the guards.

"Don't be foolish," the puppet guard said, "you are only here for Mr. Porter." He held out his hand. "If you plan to leave this lobby, I'll need your weapon."

"Forget it," Mercer muttered.

Logan pushed his way into the center of the group. He looked exhausted and panicky. "They haven't made contact. No messages or e-mails." Logan turned to see the guards hadn't moved. "Is there a problem?"

"He's in violation of building security," the nearest guard said. "We can't let him pass with a weapon on his person."

"Can't you make an exception?" Logan asked.

"No, sir."

"Mr. Mercer," Logan jerked his head toward the guard, "if you'd be so kind."

"Turncoat," Mercer muttered just loud enough for

Logan to hear. The previous night Porter had bashed Trila security, terrified they were tracking him, and now the same man wanted Julian to willingly hand over his gun. "You better bloody well be careful with it." Unloading the weapon, he ejected the chambered round, hearing the bullet hit the floor with a resounding metallic clink.

"Happy?" Logan asked the annoyed platoon of guards. They grumbled a response and escorted Mercer and Porter back to the proper office. "This may take a while."

Once the door shut, closing out Logan's assistant, Mercer pulled the wedding ring from his pocket. He placed it on the desk and took a seat.

"She's alive. They will make contact again this evening."

"Have you negotiated a price?" Logan picked up the ring and examined it. He gave it a sad little smile and put it back on the desk.

"Not yet. I hoped to speak to your boss."

"Why? What good will that do? They won't give us the protocols."

"I wanted to update them on the demands. Perhaps an alternative solution would be presented, but I'm persona non grata here." He narrowed his eyes. "Why do they find my presence inside this building so disconcerting?"

"I guess you pose a safety risk, being armed and everything," Logan said. "When are the kidnappers making contact again? How did you get Sarina's ring? Are you sure she's alive? Did you talk to her or see her? How'd she look? Is she okay?"

"Stop," Mercer held up a hand, "this was delivered as proof. That was it."

"What kind of proof is it?"

"It's enough to know she's alive. We're working on

the rest." Mercer reached into his pocket and pulled out a note with an address. "It might be wise to discuss these matters later." He passed it to Logan, who studied it for a moment.

"Then why did you come here now if you won't answer my questions? Aren't you supposed to be helping me? This isn't helping." He shook his head and grabbed his jacket from the hook behind the door. "I'm calling it quits for the day. We will deal with this now."

"Remember what I said," Mercer warned. "It's important you stick with a routine."

"But they have my wife."

"And we'll get her back if you do precisely what I say. Meet me there at seven." Mercer pointed to the address, making sure Logan read it one more time before shoving it back inside his pocket. "Don't be late." Seven was extremely close to the deadline which meant it wouldn't give Trila too much time to interfere if they overheard what was happening, but it also left a narrow window for the former SAS.

Julian went to the door, opening it to find two of the four guards waiting. Silently, they escorted him back to the lift. Once the doors closed, the one on the left unexpectedly turned and kneed Mercer in the stomach. Mercer doubled over in pain, and the two men laughed.

"You're not so mighty after all," the guard scoffed. "Now stay the hell away from Trila and stay out of our business or you'll be spending the rest of your visit inside the local prison. And trust me, it's not nearly as friendly as the police department's holding cell." He kicked Mercer hard in the ribs, but the former SAS operative didn't retaliate. Sometimes, it was best to let someone think he'd won.

The other guard grabbed Mercer by the shoulders

and hauled him to his feet just as the door opened. The other two men were waiting in the lobby. One shoved the Sig into Mercer's grasp, and the four men practically dragged him to the door, pushing him outside.

"Bastards," Mercer muttered, selecting a direction at random to throw them off his scent.

The trip to Trila accomplished very little on the surface, but despite that, Julian had accomplished what he planned to do. Sure, it would have been nice if everyone had been civil and offered to share information in order to ensure a quick and easy resolution to Sarina Porter's kidnapping, but the company that hired the negotiator didn't want to help. Frankly, they didn't want Mercer's assistance either. They simply contracted him to appease Porter which meant they didn't expect Sarina Porter to come back alive. *What the hell are they hiding?* Mercer wondered.

FIFTEEN

Mercer studied the bruise in the mirror. He'd been hit plenty of times, so he was no stranger to cuts and scrapes. He wasn't a stranger to bullet holes or shrapnel either. His body was littered with scars to prove it. However, this stupid bluish bruise that ran along his ribs was an irritant.

The bathroom door opened, and Mercer caught Bastian's reflection in the corner of the mirror. The steam from the shower wafted into the room as Bastian towel-dried his hair. At least his team was starting to look more like themselves and less like zombies.

"Amazing what a change of clothes and a power nap can do," Bastian mused.

"Did you determine who planted the bug inside Porter's phone?"

"Our pals at Trila International. Perhaps you should have asked if they want it back."

"Fucking bastards." They must have heard Mercer's promise to get the protocols to Alpha. No wonder they'd given him such a warm welcome.

"I thought I told you to play nice," Bastian said, emerging from the bathroom. "Fractured or bruised? Or can you even tell anymore?"

Mercer shrugged. "Your trackers better be worth it."

"They aren't trackers. Well, they are, but they're also much more. We have GPS location, some low-quality audio, and this." Bastian tapped a key on the monitor. "I like to think of it as being bloody brilliant. It's practically SONAR, except it uses a low frequency, undetectable laser to map dimensions and create a virtual blueprint of the offices."

"Good. How long until the building is mapped?"

"Where'd you put the devices?"

"On the guards, while they were taking a few liberties. They provided their own distractions."

"Assuming they follow a route throughout the building, we'll get the information as they make their rounds. For the record, this is a bad idea."

"The tech is untraceable, right?" Mercer had placed an almost clear, sticky circle on the back of a collar and near the bottom of a shoe.

"They might find it, but it's my own concoction, using our Majesty's tech. I highly doubt they'd think it was anything. Don't forget, I added a corrosive to the adhesive which will eat through the device in forty-eight hours." Bastian smiled. "I've learned how to cover my tracks. It's a shame though. Those buggers cost a pretty penny."

"Charge it to Trila's insurance."

"Right, should that be before or after we burglarize the place?"

Bastian had made it clear he was not in favor of stealing the protocols from Trila. Donovan and Hans hadn't weighed in, but they probably thought the plan was rubbish. Unfortunately, they were in the business of negotiating, and that was difficult when Alpha was a sadistic piece of shit. He'd already cut off Sarina's finger, so there was no doubt in Mercer's mind the threat of a hand or an ear wasn't far off. This negotiation would require finesse and a lot more give on the part of Logan Porter than most negotiations. Violence always precipitated more violence.

"Things will get brutal," Hans said, entering the room. He gave the two men an odd look. "Should I come back? You look like you're about to get friendly."

"Jealous?" Bastian asked.

"Explain." Mercer winced as he stretched to put his shirt back on.

"Y'know, a little how's your father," Hans replied cheekily. "Although, that would explain Bastian striking out with the birds. You've always had much better luck, Jules. Michelle was stunning."

The mention of his late wife soured Mercer's already horrid mood. "Speak, Bauer. Now."

"Sorry." Hans squeezed the bridge of his nose, realizing his joking had gone too far. "Alpha's been flagged by New Scotland Yard and MI5. They've encountered him before. One instance involved mass casualties. And in the other case, the entire body has yet to be found."

"Any positive recoveries?" Bastian asked.

"I don't know. I have contacts at Interpol doing an international search. It'll take a while to see what else Alpha has done."

"Who were the previous victims?" Mercer asked.

"A duke and duchess and their staff were held hostage for almost three days. When the estate was breached, the tactical team found a dozen bodies."

"What did Alpha want?"

"He wanted a formal pardon and release of a few

prisoners. The full file has been e-mailed, but the prisoners were alleged weapons dealers, wanted for trafficking to areas involved in private wars."

"Terrorists?" Bastian asked.

Hans shrugged. "Perhaps. The demand was refused, and Alpha retaliated and escaped."

"What about the other case?" Mercer asked. Things had gone from bad to worse.

"The victim was the son of a computer mogul. I don't have the details. Most of it was dealt with privately, but the authorities discovered a torso and head belonging to the boy. From what they've pieced together, the man responsible went by the moniker Alpha."

"It could be a coincidence," Bastian said. "It's a common enough call sign. The first letter of the Greek alphabet. It's probably as common as John Smith."

"Until we know otherwise, let's assume the worst," Mercer replied. "As soon as you know something more, let me know."

"Aye, sir," Hans said.

Mercer folded his arms across his chest and rested his hips against the dresser. In the stillness, he processed this new information. They had to work under the assumption the only way to recover the asset intact would be to placate Alpha until they could determine a location and safely rescue Sarina. Stealth would be better than going in hot, but it would depend on how many men were working with Alpha.

"She has to be close," Mercer said. "From the time we disconnected until the delivery driver arrived was roughly two hours. In that time, Alpha had to remove her finger, place it in an envelope, deliver it to the shop, and the driver had to make the delivery."

"I ran the plates on the truck. They are registered to the shop owner." Bastian picked up his phone and scrolled through a few images. "That's the delivery guy. The man's name is Denis Reeham. He works at the shop. From the intel I've collected, it looks legit. I don't think they're involved."

"Did the bloody computer tell you that?" Mercer asked.

"No, but they haven't had any serious scrapes with the law. The shop is eight kilometers from the Porters' estate. Calculating traffic patterns from this morning, I'd estimate the delivery route took roughly forty-five minutes. That puts Sarina's location somewhere in this vicinity." Bastian marked a ten kilometer radius on the map. "That, of course, assumes the arrangement was premade. If it wasn't, the search area would be limited to this." He pointed to a smaller circle. "And before you ask, I've already started a search for possible locations. The information is being sent directly to Donovan. He's running recon."

"Good." Mercer stared at the map. "What about trace evidence that might be on the finger?"

"Nothing. It was wiped with a disinfectant," Bastian said. "Did you leave the ring with Logan?"

"It belongs to him," Mercer replied absently. The walls of the hotel were starting to close in. He inhaled deeply and shut his eyes. *Relax*, he thought. The answers were close. They had a lead on the kidnapper and were hoping to have a solid clue as to the location soon. In the meantime, plan B was well under way. The interior of Trila was being mapped, courtesy of the clueless security arseholes. One way or another, a bargaining chip would be brought to the table. This wasn't a no-win situation. Sarina wouldn't be killed. He wouldn't let it happen. "Be prepared to do whatever is necessary."

Bastian nodded. "This time, I'm not opposed to doling out justice."

Normally, Bastian served as the moral compass, insisting violence wasn't the answer. He'd declined numerous offers to provide wet work, proclaiming they were not assassins or mercenaries. However, these were desperate times.

"It's time." Mercer pulled himself away from the dresser. "When you're finished with this, clean the room, and let's get everything moved to one of the secure flats. I don't like being exposed."

"Fine. Next time, I'm asking for professional movers as a clause of our contract," Bastian retorted, annoyed to have to move again. Before all was said and done, they'd probably relocate a few more times. It was paranoia. Most of the time, it was unnecessary, but there was no way of being sure. "Better safe than sorry, I suppose." He glanced into the adjoining room. "Hans, you're in charge of your own shit."

"Bite me." Hans held up his fingers in a v. How he managed that was impressive since he had the phone pressed to his ear and was jotting notes with his other hand.

"Do you know what you're going to tell Logan this evening?" Bastian asked.

"That I will do everything in my power to bring Sarina home safely." Mercer concealed a few more weapons on the off chance Alpha made a surprise visit.

"Hans is an arse. Don't get stuck in your head because he mentioned her. You have to be on your toes."

"I am." Mercer left, doing his best not to think about his own wife's wedding ring locked securely in a safe deposit box at a London bank. It was the only part of her he was able to keep safe, and he didn't want the same fate to befall Logan Porter.

SIXTEEN

"What's with the clandestine meeting place?" Logan asked. "You waltzed into Trila like you owned it, pissed off the guards, and demanded a secret rendezvous point." His eyebrows scrunched together. "You do realize I was tailed. It defeats the purpose, don't ya think?" Aggravated, he rubbed his forehead. "Do you think he'll let me speak to her? I can't remember the sound of her voice, which is stupid because it's only been six days. But for the life of me, I can't remember it, and I'd give anything to hear it again. Please."

"It's not up to me." Mercer turned his head and gulped down some air. *Stay focused.* "Do you have any enemies who might have a military background or some fondness for the alias Alpha?"

"None."

"We believe he's done this before. He's familiar with negotiations."

"That's a good thing, right? You said that professionals respond better, making positive outcomes more likely." Logan read the expression on Mercer's face. "What aren't you telling me?"

"I'll get her back," Mercer promised, "but you need to prepare yourself." He pushed out a chair for Logan. "Sit." Once Porter was seated, Mercer glanced around the empty dining room. He'd booked a private room inside a restaurant for the meeting just to make sure no one could spy on them. "Alpha wants the computer protocols. My team is prepared to make it happen." Mercer held up his hand to silence Porter's question. "You should be aware the ring was still attached to Sarina's finger when it was delivered."

For a second, Porter couldn't comprehend what he'd been told. Then his face grew ashen, and he made a brief choking sound. He didn't ask any other questions or speak, which was a relief to Julian. Instead, he stared at his own ring finger, pondering how it happened.

"Since Alpha is escalating to pressure us to comply, it's imperative we play along. Emotions will hinder our communications, so if you must speak to him, remain calm." Mercer hoped they'd both be able to follow that advice.

"Why would I have to speak to that piece of filth?"

"It's just precautionary. I will do what I can to handle the situation, but occasionally, kidnappers want verification from the family. It's not customary, but it could happen."

"Why didn't you just tell me this at home?"

"He has access to your home security network." Even though Bastian hadn't verified this as true, Mercer's gut knew it was. "The call didn't come until you had left, seconds before I planned my own exit. He was watching on surveillance, waiting to catch us unprepared."

"So you don't know anything? You didn't trap and

trace or whatever it's called."

"We'll find him. For now, he needs to believe he's in charge and we are following his orders. Is that understood?"

"Yeah, I guess." Porter sounded uncertain. Mercer knew his client was irate. It was the primary emotion with which Mercer identified. He just hoped the anger would not be to their detriment. "Shouldn't we be waiting for his call? He'll know if we're late getting back."

"No, he won't." Mercer opened the door to the dining room and glanced outside. The suited men from the other night were at a corner booth. "I disabled your system."

"You what?" Porter's angry voice drew the attention of many customers.

"It's done. Let's go." Mercer led the way toward the door, keeping the men in his periphery. Their identities hadn't been determined, but chances were they worked for Trila.

Outside the restaurant, Mercer led Logan to a rental car. Unlocking the doors, he opened the passenger's side. "Get in, Mr. Porter."

"I have a car."

"Get in." The men hadn't emerged from the restaurant yet, and Mercer wanted a head start to avoid the tail. When Porter moved too slowly, Mercer gave him a shove and slammed the door. Sliding behind the wheel, he put the car into drive and peeled away from the restaurant. "It's your show."

"What?" Porter asked, bewildered, angry, and possibly frightened.

"Delay, detain, just take care of it." Mercer glanced at the man next to him and tapped his ear to indicate he was speaking to someone else.

A few moments later, Hans's voice responded,

"Affirmative, tracking now. Planning to intervene in five. Stipulations?"

"None," Mercer replied, clicking off the earpiece. He trusted Hans to take care of this matter.

"Who the hell are you?" Porter asked.

"A man doing his job."

The rest of the ride was in silence. No one followed the car, and Mercer relaxed slightly, removing his death grip from the steering wheel. He had no way of knowing what waited for him at the house or what new scare tactics Alpha planned to initiate. Until they had solid footing beneath them, Mercer would be compliant. It was the best way of ensuring Sarina's return.

Arriving at Porter's estate, Mercer parked on the path and scanned the area, checking for signs someone had been there. In the growing darkness, it was difficult to tell, but Julian felt certain no one was there now. Walking into a trap would be an amateur mistake. Carefully, Mercer went to the back door, opened it, and entered the house. No one waited inside. He conducted a thorough sweep before opening the front door and gesturing for Logan to join him.

"Do you have to leave the car there?" Logan asked, annoyance dripping from every syllable.

"Yes." There was no reason to waste words. "Now we wait."

Porter's jaw dropped when he saw the smashed electronic pieces in the hallway and the corners of the room. "You're going to pay for those. Who do you think you are to come into my house and destroy it? How do I know you aren't one of them?"

"Should I go?" Mercer asked.

"Dammit." A long string of expletives followed, and then Porter slumped into a chair. "They shattered my world. My perfect world. And now you're here with a baseball bat smashing cameras and getting oil on the driveway. I want my life back. Sarina and I should be at dinner now, not waiting for a phone call from some psycho who maimed my beautiful bride."

The outburst wasn't surprising, but Porter's depiction of perfect was. Deciding not to ask questions, Mercer let the man rant while he prepared himself mentally for his next battle of wits with Alpha. The priority would be to delay Alpha's timetable for delivery as long as possible. The only flaw with that plan was it meant Sarina would remain a pawn, subject to his will until the exchange. Mercer had seen a lot, serving in wars and performing black ops missions. He knew cruelty and evil, and leaving someone defenseless in this situation was never good.

"If you cannot remain quiet, you *will* not be here when he makes contact," Mercer said. "Do you understand?"

"I thought I had to talk to this asshole?"

"Perhaps. Hopefully not."

"Fine." Logan removed a bottle of tequila from the cabinet. "Can I at least have a drink?" Mercer didn't answer, and Logan poured a shot and downed it. "Maybe it'll take the edge off."

He had another while Mercer hooked a splitter to the new phone he was installing. It would send the data to Bastian's computer. With any luck, a remote trace would be possible.

Once everything was set, Mercer took a seat. It was an exercise in patience, best to conserve energy in preparation for the unknown. Pacing or anxiously waiting would only speed up the fatigue, and he couldn't afford to be functioning below his best. The lack of sleep took enough of a toll without exacerbating it with pointless worry and impatience.

The communication would come when it did. However, that didn't keep his mind from wondering what would happen if no further communication occurred.

Logan aimlessly rummaged through the fridge. He reorganized the already pristine cabinets and swept up the electronic shards. Finally, he went upstairs to change out of his work attire. He was gone less than a minute when the phone rang. Running down the steps, he stared at Julian who hadn't moved from the couch.

"Answer it," he screamed.

"Silence." Mercer waited for the next ring and picked up the receiver.

"Time's up," Alpha said.

SEVENTEEN

"Do you have the computer protocols?" Alpha asked.

"Not yet, but I will."

"Honesty. That's very good. You catch on quickly, Mr. Mercer. I'm pleased. Did you enjoy the gift I sent this morning? Am I correct to assume you've verified the owner as Sarina Porter?"

"Yes, but I'd suggest you refrain from inflicting further damage. Sarina is valuable as long as she remains unharmed. You've already done damage. Please consider this before acting again."

At those words, Logan lunged for the phone, and Mercer shoved him hard in the chest, causing him to lose balance and hit the ground. It was an effective way to keep the man quiet and from botching the communication.

"You do not dictate my actions," Alpha said. The emotionless voice made it difficult to determine if Mercer's words had angered the kidnapper. "I dictate yours."

"What do you want?"

"You know what I want. The only way Sarina will be returned is when I have the computer protocols in my possession. Is that clear, or should I snap off a few more digits to make my point?"

"That won't be necessary." Mercer glanced down at Logan who was rubbing his wrist. "I need to reassure my client of her well-being."

"Go ahead."

"May I speak to her?" Mercer asked. Logan pulled himself to his feet and cautiously stepped closer.

"No," Alpha paused, "but I'll see if she'll give you a nice loud scream." Something shuffled around in the background, despite Mercer's protests and backpedaling. A bloodcurdling shriek cut through the phone, and Mercer flinched. A door slammed, and then Alpha said, "Did that make you happy?"

"No." Mercer wouldn't grovel or beg, which appeared to be Alpha's goal. "Don't hurt her."

"You can't stop me. I am in control. I determine what happens to her. If you want to persuade me to stop, then give me what I want."

The line went dead, and Mercer cursed. Forcing his hand to gently place the phone back in its cradle, he clenched his jaw so hard he thought his teeth would break. Logan was speaking to him, frantic and animated, but Julian didn't hear him. It was accusatory nonsense, and he had other things on which to concentrate. When the phone rang a few minutes later, one look immediately silenced Logan, and Mercer waited two rings before answering.

"You have thirty-six hours," Alpha said. "If the item is not delivered by then, Sarina Porter is dead. It will not be quick. And it most definitely will not be painless. Do I make myself clear?"

"Yes." Not waiting for Alpha to respond with additional threats and demands, Mercer added, "But I don't know if we'll have it by then. Can we negotiate a postponement?"

"You expect me to fall for that trick? It's a stall tactic."

"No, let's work something out. It'll be a show of good faith."

"Interesting. I will consider your proposal. In the meantime, you better work on procuring payment and stop wasting precious time. Sarina doesn't have long to live."

Mercer remained impassive. "It's in the works as we speak."

"Very good. Stay by the phone. I'll get back to you."

Alpha disconnected, and Mercer took a deep breath. Dialing Bastian, he wanted to know if the kidnapper's call had resulted in a location. Find Alpha, and they'd find Sarina, it was kidnapping 101. Unfortunately, the first call ended before an exact location could be identified. Alpha had hung up by design. It was planned and removed any lingering doubt that Alpha had done this many times before.

"Now what?" Logan asked. He was smart enough to realize his hopes for being reunited with Sarina lay with the man before him. "What can I do? What does he want? Money? We have it. The insurance will pay. Just give me an amount."

"He wants the protocols."

"I can't get them. I'll give him anything else. Tell him that."

"He knows. Until he rings again, my hands are tied."

"Okay. Okay." Logan kept repeating this while he paced the living room. Suddenly, he stopped. "What should I do?"

"Wait."

"Not like I have a choice." His eyes darted around

the room. "How did this happen? How did he find us? Why us? Why her? How did he get access to my home? To my security system? How dare he do this. How dare he take her away."

"Mr. Porter," Mercer swallowed his pride, "I need you to trust me. I need you to help us get her back. Tell me about Trila. What do they do? When did you start working there? How long have you lived here? Who has access to your home? I need to know everything."

"I already gave you the dossier on my background."

"You gave my associate a file of rubbish. That was shit. What's the truth?"

"That is the truth. We've been through this." Porter pressed his lips together, thinking. "No more deceit. I do believe you're Sarina's only hope." He looked away, focusing on a framed photo of the two of them. "The other night, everything I said was true. I'm sorry." He choked, swallowing uncomfortably. "I should have told you everything the first time we met. If I had given you the USB and told you about the men following me, then maybe she wouldn't have been hurt." He removed the ring from his pocket, placing it on the table next to the photo.

"Start at the beginning," Mercer said softly.

"I was recruited out of MIT to work at a software company. It was a dead end job, and within a few weeks, I knew I was out of my depth. However, I managed to bluff my way into a different position that wasn't quite as tech-centric. It was focused on business expansion, more dollar signs, less ones and zeroes. Needless to say, the company went bust."

"You bankrupted the company?"

"It wasn't me. Our tech couldn't keep up. We were drowning." He licked his lips. "Trila bought it out. Almost everyone was canned, but for some reason, they kept me on. They offered a promotion, gave me a moving bonus, and sent me to this godforsaken place. They didn't bother to mention the risks involved."

"When was this?" Bastian had done the research, but Mercer liked to hear things firsthand.

"Almost five years ago, I guess."

"Did Trila ever realize you were a fraud?"

"I'm not a fraud. I can do the job, but I'm not a developer. I can check the systems and review the reports our guys file. We have professional hackers who find weaknesses. My job is to determine the degree of risk each weakness presents and whether it's within a reasonable limit."

"Meaning you perform cost-benefit analyses," Mercer surmised.

"Sort of, I guess."

"What did you determine concerning the latest security protocols?"

"They're practically impenetrable. It's the most secure system Trila's designed since I've been there. The risk of a breach is negligible. Even our hackers couldn't crack it without access to the administrator function and backdoor. That must be what makes this so valuable." Porter's eyes grew dark. "Valuable enough to kidnap my wife and cut off her finger to prove a point."

Mercer's mind twisted around the facts, contemplating what the value of unhindered computer access might be. "What does the program or system do?"

"What?"

"It's a system, so it runs something. What does it operate?"

Porter opened his mouth to answer, but a puzzled look erupted on his face. "I have no idea. We design. We don't implement."

"Who bought the operating system?"

"I don't know."

"Dammit," Mercer cursed. "Alpha desperately wants it. We have to figure out why."

"Why does that matter?"

"We might be able to leverage it to get Sarina back." He narrowed his eyes. "Can you find out?"

"I can try. The information has to be at Trila. Either a paper trail or someone must know. I'll ask."

"Does Sarina know what you do for a living?"

"Of course, she's my wife."

"I mean the exact project you were assigned. Do you tell her things like that?"

"Sometimes, but she didn't know about this. Plus, why would anyone think she'd be able to give them access? You don't think she was taken because they thought she could get the protocols, do you?"

"No, but if she shared this information with her acquaintances, it might have attracted the kidnappers to her."

"Now you're blaming Sarina for this? Un-fucking-believable."

"I'm not. I'm trying to figure out why the kidnappers decided to target you."

Before Porter could ask any other questions, the phone rang. It was time for round three.

EIGHTEEN

"What can I do for you?" Mercer asked, unable to hide the sneer from his voice. *Maybe you'd like my balls on a silver platter,* he thought bitterly.

"Thirty-five hours and forty-seven minutes remain. Tick tock," Alpha replied.

"I'm not sure that's enough time."

"Then I'd suggest you find a way. If not..." Alpha didn't say a word, letting Mercer's imagination fill in the blanks with his own horrific scenario.

"Fine. Where will we make the exchange?" It was best to move on. The more information plied from Sarina's captor would aid in formulating an adequate recourse.

"You must think me a fool. Contact will be made two hours prior to the delivery time."

"Wait," Mercer said, hoping to keep him on the line as long as possible, "how will the next communication be made? I don't want to miss it."

"Do you really want to play games with me?"

"This isn't a game. A woman's life hangs in the

balance. I do not want to jeopardize her safety because I missed your instructions."

"I'll have a courier deliver the instructions to Logan Porter's office at Trila International." The voice paused for a second. "But I know this is part of your playbook, Julian, and you should be warned I can play too."

"What is that supposed to mean?" The fact that Alpha had just used Mercer's first name was not lost on the K&R specialist.

"Julian Mercer, a young lad from England. Privileged upbringing, attended Eton, then Cambridge, devoted to Her Majesty's service, but forced into early retirement for mental instability following a gruesome killing." Despite the computer-generated voice, it was obvious Alpha was taking pleasure in this. "Did you tell your client you murdered your own wife? He might want to hire a different negotiator in light of that fact."

That was it. Mercer hung up the phone. He'd given Alpha too much power, and now he had to right that mistake. This psycho thought he had control over the situation and had just attempted to prove his dominance by making this personal. Negotiations should never be personal. It meant mistakes would be made because emotions clouded judgment and rationale. Alpha knew this, and he'd just thrown Julian off his game.

"Is Sarina okay?" Logan asked, horrified by Mercer's pallor and abrupt action.

"She will be." Mercer moved toward the door. "He shouldn't make contact again for another thirty-four hours. You'll receive a message at work, if he does what he said. In the meantime, my team will be in touch."

"Wait. What do I do if he calls again? Where are

you going?"

Mercer was in no mood to deal with these infernal questions. "Bastian will handle it. We have the situation under control."

Once he was out of earshot, Julian phoned Bastian. "Alpha knows who I am. He wants to intimidate us. I hung up. Can you reroute Porter's calls in case that bastard rings again?"

"Of course. How quickly did the negotiation break down?"

"We are awaiting delivery instructions which should arrive in thirty-four hours. He wants the protocols in his possession in just under thirty-six hours. We can't wait. We have to move on this. He'll kill her."

"Jules, if he does, he knows he won't get what he wants."

Opening the car door, Mercer waited to be locked inside before speaking again. "Bollocks. You and I both know he's going to kill her regardless of what we do. The only reason she's alive now is because he needs her to incentivize us." Mercer stared out the windshield at the house. Alpha couldn't harm Logan because he was the only person capable of getting the protocols out of Trila. "We're spread thin, and time's running out. I'm leaving Porter's estate. I'll meet you at the secondary flat in thirty minutes."

The drive gave Mercer time to compartmentalize. The Porters' blight had nothing to do with him. The only reason that sick son of a bitch brought up Mercer's private life was to distract. It was nothing but smoke and mirrors. It also demonstrated Alpha had the upper hand. Frankly, it might even mean he'd underestimated the former SAS team.

Turning off the engine, Mercer studied his surroundings, recalling the cars and lights that had been nearby when they first arrived. Nothing had changed. Ever vigilant, he watched traffic patterns on the quiet street for another five minutes before going up the steps to the flat.

"It's about time," Hans greeted. He was leaning over Bastian's shoulder, staring at the computer monitor. "We need a third to break the tie." He pointed at the screen. "I say we leave them incapacitated. They didn't want to talk, so solitary confinement ought to break their resolve. But this one's worried about common human decency. It's rubbish, if you ask me."

"Why aren't you interrogating them?" Mercer asked, the annoyance evident in his tone. "I gave you a green light."

"They didn't answer my questions. In case you forgot, they're trained mercenaries, just like we are."

"So the two suits are Trila security guards." Mercer took a seat next to Bastian, vexed by this hiccup. "Why are they following Porter?"

"To protect him," Bastian said. "They were told to keep an eye on him by the head of Trila. Interfering is going to make things worse for us. We need to release them, apologize, and chalk it up to bygones."

"That's ludicrous," Hans argued.

"Silence," Mercer said. Answers would be nice, but drawing additional scrutiny from Trila's security team now wasn't ideal. "Alpha possesses information about me, probably all of us. How did he get it?"

"Internet search, hacking into a government database, a random newspaper article, or a possible security leak at Trila." Bastian reached for the slobbery pen he left on the table and chewed thoughtfully. "You have to keep in mind the reason Logan's being followed is because Trila fears he'll abscond with their tech. Before he went to his boss for help, no one was following him."

"Or they did a better job of hiding it," Hans suggested. "Don't we owe it to the client to find out?"

Mercer chuckled. The situation didn't merit that response, but normally, Mercer was vying to conduct an interrogation, not Hans. The laugh elicited a bewildered look from Bastian. Shaking it off, Mercer stood and went to the wall, studying the surveillance photos they'd taken of the Trila building and Porter's estate.

"Mr. Porter wants to know why he was targeted. How did Alpha know to choose him?" Mercer didn't bother to turn around to gauge his teammates' responses. "I'd like to know the same thing. Hans, go ask the gentlemen what they know. If Alpha bribed them, we ought to be able to do the same. The good thing about soldiers of fortune is they work for the highest bidder."

"You want to pay them to talk?" Hans asked. "How do you know they're even crooked?"

"Everyone has a price." Mercer spun around, seeing a slightly relieved look on Bastian's face. "We don't have the time needed to break them, and they know it. Get whatever you can and then tag and release. It'd be nice if they could lead us to Sarina."

"Optimism doesn't suit you," Bastian said. "What's your real plan?"

"We figure out how to infiltrate Trila and remove the protocols. It might be our only way to get close enough to save the woman," Mercer said.

"So the exact same plan we've had since the beginning. Bloody hell." Bastian didn't say it, but they felt it. This was an assignment they might not win. "The computer isn't finished processing the building schematics, so until that happens, I'll continue to focus my efforts on narrowing possible locations."

"Good," Mercer said.

Hans ducked out of the flat to return to the cargo container they were using as a holding cell. Bastian continued to narrow locations, accessing satellite imagery and checking for suspicious activity.

Alone with his thoughts, Mercer's ever-present rage bubbled a little closer to the surface. Alpha's words were meant to cause a reaction, and Mercer had denied giving that bastard the satisfaction. But it still hurt. Mercer didn't kill his wife, but many nights he'd been unable to shake that thought. Somewhere deep down, he knew she died because he hadn't been there to stop it. It was his fault. He didn't protect her. Logan Porter would probably feel the same way if Sarina didn't make it home alive.

"Why is this happening?" Mercer asked, but the photos on the wall didn't give him an answer. Maybe one of his teammates would.

NINETEEN

The night dragged on as Mercer fell deeper into an endless chasm of despair. Alpha had screwed with his head, and no matter how hard he tried to concentrate, he couldn't. Around two a.m., Bastian sent him to bed. No one had slept, and it was taking a toll on their leader. The nightmares were worse than ever, but Mercer stayed locked in the dream, waking with a start at the sound of the front door slamming. Picking up his Sig, he opened the bedroom door and watched an exhausted Donovan drag himself inside.

Bastian had been asleep on the sofa, a few meters from the computer array. He too lowered his handgun and sat up. Donovan's gaze shifted from Bastian to Mercer, and he snorted.

"I might have found it." Donovan rubbed his eyes, flexing his fingers a few times when he noticed a slight tremor. "Bloody caffeine." He patted his pocket, making sure he had some diazepam in case he needed to counteract the jitters and steady his aim. "There's a condemned building within our suspected radius." He went to one of the maps and pinned the location. "It's quiet, secluded, and not susceptible to foot traffic."

"So are half the buildings in this city," Bastian remarked.

"But unlike those buildings, this one has power. I saw a light on. It was faint. At first, I thought it was from a torch or lantern. So I called the power company to complain about interrupted service, and they verified the power was on and suggested I check the circuit breaker. Fancy that."

"It's too soon to jump to conclusions. Anyone could be squatting inside." Mercer focused on Bastian. "Find out who's being billed." He turned back to Donovan. "Anything else to report?"

"Negative." Donovan pushed past them and into an empty bedroom. "Night."

Before Mercer could utter a word to the contrary, the door slammed shut. "Guess he's earned some downtime." Mercer rotated his shoulder, which often got stiff following a recent dislocation, and hovered near the computer screens, studying the images and intel displayed. "Did Hans return?"

"Not that I'm aware." Bastian rubbed his eyes. "He might have snuck in while I was passed out, but I'd wager he's questioning our captives or scouring the city for an ATM that will dispense thousands of dollars." Bastian cleared his throat and went into the kitchen. "We need to talk about this. Are you intent on nicking the protocols and delivering them to some tosser in exchange for the girl?"

"If that's what it takes," Mercer said.

"Since when do we join forces with the other side?"

"We aren't, but Alpha won't bend, so something has to break. If Donovan's wrong, we won't be able to get close enough to save the girl without the protocols."

Bastian took a deep breath, not wanting to cause

another argument. "How many times have we compromised ourselves for this job? How many laws have we broken? How many times have we been behind an abduction of our own? This isn't the proper way to conduct business. We are supposed to rescue captives, not play capture the flag with the other team's men." He returned to the room with a piping hot mug. "Ninety-nine percent of the time we don't even know if the people we snatch are involved."

"They are always involved," Mercer said, but it was obvious he wasn't listening. "Trila's involved in Sarina's disappearance, but I can't pinpoint the connection. Surely, they wouldn't sabotage their own program or leak their own corporate secrets. Is there a disgruntled employee or displaced CEO with an axe to grind against Logan Porter?" Mercer studied Porter's dossier plastered on one of the walls. "Alpha has an inside connection at Trila. He must."

"Jules," Bastian put the mug down, "what are you talking about?"

"Porter explained how he came to work for the company. He was moved here. He works here. But he's a small fish with a nice office. He lacks know-how."

"The merger." Bastian nodded. "I read about it. He was a decent employee, so they kept him on. Nothing sinister there. He does his job. He gets some perks. That's how corporations work. Maybe you'd know that if you ever took a moment to look around and observe normalcy."

"It sounds like they planted him here. They put him in the perfect position to become Alpha's puppet."

"Ahh, another of your conspiracy theories. Haven't we been through this before? There isn't an evil overlord behind every bad thing that happens in this world."

"I'm not so sure." Mercer didn't bother to say anything else. This was where the two disagreed. His obsession, as Bastian called it, started when Michelle was murdered. The police blamed him. No evidence ever pointed to someone else, but the timing had been perfect, so perfect he was convinced it was orchestrated.

Mercer had returned from a clandestine mission a few days earlier, and he and his wife had been practically inseparable. That morning, he'd gone to the market to pick up some supplies, and when he returned less than an hour later, she was on the floor, gasping. He'd held her as the life left her body, and he was still holding her when the police arrived to find him covered in her blood. Since then, he'd reviewed the case file and done everything he could to determine who was responsible. Recently, he'd received some new information, but they hadn't had time to properly evaluate it due to occupational demands.

Bastian snapped his fingers in front of Mercer's face. "Did you hear what I said?"

"That I'm certifiable?"

"No, that we have a problem." He pointed to the flashing *scan incomplete* on the monitor. "Something went wrong. Maybe they found our devices, or we're experiencing technical difficulties. Either way, the interior mapping of Trila didn't finish, and the transmission has ended."

"How much did we get?"

"I don't know." Bastian typed in a few commands and scrolled through some options. "The entire lobby and Porter's floor are complete. Other than that, it's piecemeal."

"Fine." Mercer checked his watch. They had twenty-six hours until Alpha delivered instructions.

"It's not fine. We have to scrub the plan and come up with a viable alternative that will appease Alpha until we can get Sarina back."

"There's not enough time. Either we find Sarina, or we continue as planned. First, we need to scout the building Donovan found and follow up on every lead we have. If all else fails, I'll march into Trila tomorrow morning and get what we need."

"That's suicide."

"Then Donovan better know what he's talking about." Mercer picked up the phone and dialed Logan Porter to make sure nothing had been delivered to the office. Once Logan was reassured the call was cautionary and the original timeframe was in place, Mercer disconnected. "I want to make another pass at Sarina's office. Maybe we missed something. What did her computer files show?"

"Important meetings with clients. Dates and times for appointments. A reminder to pick up an anniversary gift for some friends. Nothing useful."

"What'd you find on the assistant, Brie Dawson?"

"Squeaky clean. She's a nobody."

"Do we have anything of actual use?"

Bastian hit a few keys, scrolling through Sarina's work files. "Sarina missed the meeting with the jam people. According to the phone records, they called her office to ask where she was."

"Meaning she wasn't meeting them at the office. Is that relevant?"

"It might be." Bastian's brow furrowed. "She was at home when she was taken. If she had a meeting scheduled, shouldn't she have been on her way out?"

"Maybe it was an internet meeting. Did she make any notes concerning location?"

"She has some notes saved on how to improve their marketing campaign by joining a network of small businesses, but nothing about where they were meeting. It's odd her assistant doesn't know anything about it."

"Or so she says."

"Aside from the potential bio we have on Alpha and the building Donovan discovered, I'd say everything else is a dead end." Bastian narrowed his eyes, staring at one of the satellite images pasted on the wall. "He'd have to have a way in and out to pick up food and other supplies. Let me see what I can do."

"Get to it. I'm going to Sarina's office." Mercer checked his watch again. "Wake Donovan in two hours and have him meet me at this building." He flicked the pinned location on the map. "Tell him to be prepared."

"Who's going to monitor Trila and Porter?" Bastian asked.

"Trila has no issue monitoring Porter, and we don't have the manpower to spare. He shouldn't be in danger, unless you think Trila plans to kill him before he can compromise their corporate secrets."

"Let's hope not."

"Either way, we weren't hired to protect Logan. He's on his own."

TWENTY

When Mercer arrived at Sarina's consulting firm, he was surprised to find the place boarded up. A note on the door said they were closed until further notice with a contact number for current clients. Mercer dialed, but the number went to the assistant's voicemail box. At least it'd give him free rein to examine the office for anything they might have missed the first time.

Breaking the lock, he let himself in and pushed the door closed. First, he scanned the area with an RF reader, checking for transmissions. The wifi network was active, but based on the low output, it didn't appear to be in use.

Convinced the building was secure, Mercer went into Sarina's office and conducted a thorough physical search. Her desk, the bookcase in the corner, and the closet proved pointless. Moving the computer to the floor, Mercer flipped the desk on its side to check for hidden compartments.

"Dammit." He righted the desk and shoved the

drawers back in place. He picked up the calendar and flipped through the pages, even though Bastian had scans of the information. Nothing new surfaced. Alpha was a pro. It didn't appear he had made previous contact with his victim. That thought stopped Mercer in his tracks. He studied the writing, finding something eerily familiar about it. If Alpha hadn't made contact with Sarina, he must have made contact with someone close to her. There was no other way to explain how seamlessly the abduction was orchestrated.

Ringing Bastian, he barely waited for his second-in-command to answer before blurting out, "Find Brie Dawson, now."

Hanging up, Mercer felt incompetent. He swore at his own stupidity. Instead of waiting for Bastian to phone back with the information, he called Logan again. After too many unanswered rings, he hung up. Something was wrong. On his way to the door, he dialed Hans. No answer. What was going on? Why hadn't the team remained on comms this entire time? Fearing the oversight would cost them dearly, Mercer hastened his departure.

A second later, the phone rang, startling him. "What?" Julian asked.

"She's gone," Bastian said.

"What do you mean gone?"

"She's off the grid. I did some checking. No activity on her credit card or phone. I'm guessing she's in the wind. She probably disappeared or," Bastian swallowed, "the less pleasant alternative. I'll start checking with hospitals and the morgue. Logan might be able to get in contact with her faster, assuming she's okay."

"He didn't answer either. Something's gone awry." Mercer ran to the car, put it in gear, and drove down the street before realizing he needed a location. "What's Dawson's address?"

Bastian relayed the information, glancing at a map. "I'm closer to Trila, so I'll check on Logan. You get to the apartment and see if you can find Sarina's assistant."

"Get Hans on the line. He's gone radio silent. Is his comm active?"

"Negative. I have GPS enabled on his phone." There was an uncertain pause. "I'll handle it."

"Handle what?" Mercer asked, ignoring the blaring car horns and profane screams shouted at his speeding car.

"Just check on Brie." Bastian hooked a bluetooth to his ear, stuck his cell phone in his pocket, grabbed a spare nine millimeter which went into his ankle holster, and went out the door. "How close are you?"

"Eight minutes. Maybe less." Slamming the brakes, Mercer expertly maneuvered the wheel, stopping the car from skidding into the side of a building. "When did she drop off the grid?"

"Monday night." Unlike his counterpart, Bastian observed some of the traffic laws while he made his way to the Trila International building. "It could be nothing. Was there any hard evidence to support your hunch?"

"Aside from the obvious?" Mercer scanned the addresses as they flashed past.

"Yeah, like blood or detached fingers lying about?"

"No."

"She might be fine."

"I'm here," Mercer said. "Going silent."

He turned off the speaker and secured the phone in his breast pocket. After removing his handgun, he held it against his thigh as he walked swiftly to the apartment building. Hitting all the call buttons on the outside wall, he waited for someone to buzz him in. Once the door opened, he gave the lobby a quick scan and headed up the steps.

Three floors later, he cautiously stepped out of the stairwell. No one was in the corridor, and he went to Brie's apartment. He knocked, but there was no answer. Waiting three counts, he stepped backward, took a deep breath, and kicked the door open, splintering the wood frame.

Moving from room to room, he cleared the one bedroom apartment in under a minute. The place was messy. He shut the door, ignoring the gawking stares of a few nosy neighbors. The authorities would probably be notified momentarily. Assuming a break-in wasn't a top priority, he had roughly ten minutes to determine where Brie was and if she went of her own volition.

Picking through the scattered items on her bedroom floor, he wasn't sure if the assistant was a slob or if the room had been tossed. *Think*. Mercer hoped to determine what she might possess that the kidnappers or someone at Trila would want. Sarina's day planner, a key to the office, something that would give them access to Logan Porter and Trila's protocols. It could be anything or nothing. Realizing he had no idea what he was looking for or what had been taken, he returned to the main living area. A woman screamed, and he pointed his gun at her, half a second away from firing.

She screamed again, louder this time, and a man from the hallway burst through the door with a shotgun. Mercer shifted his aim, relieved the man hadn't fired. The shotgun wielder stepped in front of the girl and yelled at Mercer to lower his weapon.

"You first." Mercer saw the woman peek around the man's shoulder. The annoying pink tips of her hair were unmistakable. "Ms. Dawson, there's no need to be alarmed."

She stopped screaming, recognizing the man before her. "The hell there isn't. You broke into my house." She looked around the room. "You. Broke. Into. My. House."

"I'll take care of him," the shotgun goon mumbled. "I'll teach this foreigner some manners."

"Shut it." Mercer wished he could simply make the guy vanish. Forcing himself to speak softly, he focused his attention on Brie. "I was under the impression something happened to you."

"Something? Like what?" She curled a strand of hair around her finger. "Does this have to do with Mrs. P?"

"Your phone and credit activity ceased Monday night."

"I've been staying with Brick." She hugged the shoulders of the man in front of her. "He was worried about me after the kidnapping crap." She looked around her apartment again. "As you can see, someone else was here. When the neighbor said some man just busted through my door, I thought whoever it was had come back." She narrowed her eyes. "You didn't do this the first time, did you?"

"No." Mercer shifted his gaze. "You can lower the gun, Tex."

"It's Brick." The man dropped the barrel to the floor. "Answer the lady, or I'll make you."

Mercer had seen lots of tough guys and guys who wanted to be tough. It would be easier to do as the guy said. "No. Was anything taken? Did you have any valuable information here?"

Brie shrugged. "Like what?"

"Information on Sarina or her husband or a key to her house? Something like that?"

She shook her head.

"Okay." Mercer holstered his weapon. "You need to tell me everything about Sarina's missed meeting and when you first realized she had been taken."

TWENTY-ONE

"You're insane," Brie concluded. "Why would I collude with a kidnapper?"

Mercer sighed. As soon as the questions started, she had become defensive, and the lug sitting beside her exacerbated the situation. Standing, Mercer glanced around the room again. He didn't notice any surveillance equipment anywhere inside the building or in her apartment. That didn't mean it wasn't bugged, but he assumed not.

"Sarina made the appointment with the jam company on her own. She wrote it on the calendar, and she didn't need your help. Correct?"

"Yep." Brie popped a piece of gum into her mouth and snapped it loudly. "I already said that. It's why I don't know where she was meeting them."

"How did you discover the meeting?"

"The guy called to ask where Mrs. Porter was. He thought she was going to meet him at his office, but she didn't show up. He thought he had the time wrong." She blew a bubble, popping it with her finger and pushing the gum back inside her mouth. "I found it written on the calendar and told him their signals must have gotten crossed and Mrs. P would call to reschedule. When she didn't come to the office, I gave her a call, but there was no answer. Like the phone didn't ring. It just went straight to voicemail." She shrugged. "I thought it was strange. I found out later something happened. I wasn't entirely sure what it was until now." She looked pointedly at Mercer. "I don't have anything to do with this, so you can't arrest me."

"I'm not with the police," Mercer said.

"Then why are we talking to you?" Brick asked.

"Look," Mercer said, "stay out of sight. If anyone else shows up, call me. Is that understood?"

"Yeah, whatever," Brie replied.

"And if I ring you again, make sure you answer." Mercer pulled out one of his cards and handed it to her. It was the only static number the team possessed. "Right now, I need to know if there is any way of discovering who spoke to Sarina about scheduling the meeting. I'll need office records and access to any private line or e-mail she might have."

"I thought Mr. P gave you all that." Brie chewed thoughtfully on her gum.

"What about that other account you told me about, babe?" Brick nudged her in the ribs. "Would there be something on that?"

"I don't know. Maybe." Brie reached for the pen and scanned the room for a piece of paper. "Give me your hand." Obediently, Mercer held out his hand, and she wrote a username on his palm. "That was her little secret. I don't think Mr. P knows about it. I teased her that she used it to meet men online."

"Did she?" Mercer recalled the kinkier items in Sarina's lingerie drawer.

"I'm not sure. She said it was just business, and she wanted it separate. No one knows about it. She only accessed it on her smart phone, never on her desktop."

"Then how do you know this?" Mercer held out his hand.

"She left her phone on the desk one day, and I was bored." Brie shrugged. "What? I'm her assistant. It's how I assist."

"Did you read her e-mails?"

"I scanned some subject lines. They sounded boring, but Mrs. P came back to get her phone and tore into me for snooping. She kept a closer eye on her phone after that."

Shaking his head, Mercer went to the door, regretting his earlier level of concern for Ms. Dawson. Frankly, he should have realized a kidnapper of Alpha's caliber wouldn't risk his operation by leaving loose ends. Had he gained access to Sarina through Brie, the woman would have been killed immediately. No, Alpha had created the perfect opportunity with Sarina's help. Either she had inadvertently given him access, believing he was a client, or he had used surveillance and hacking to his advantage. The question that remained was how he happened upon her, and the best way to determine that would be to track Logan Porter's movements.

Returning to the car, Mercer took the phone off mute, hearing Bastian's voice through the earpiece. Obviously, his second-in-command was at Trila, deep in conversation. It sounded polite, like the bulk of Bastian's conversations, so Mercer drove to meet Donovan. His concern over Hans hadn't abated, but Bastian said he'd handle it, which meant their sharpshooter mustn't be in any real danger.

At the conclusion of Bastian's conversation, Mercer

spoke up, providing an update on Brie Dawson. The lack of response meant Bastian wasn't alone, so Mercer didn't share his current location or the information he had gleaned concerning Sarina's private e-mail account in case the overzealous guards were listening in. Like his teammates had said, the Trila guards had the same training as special operatives which made things a lot trickier.

Bastian cleared his throat in acknowledgement of Mercer's update, but unfortunately, he didn't think the commander would recognize it. They had a list of code words to explain hostile situations, but Bastian's current whereabouts didn't exactly fit the bill. He was seated in a conference room with Logan Porter, Hans Bauer, the head of Trila's security team, and the two men Hans had attempted to bribe.

"Pardon me, chaps, but this truly is a misunderstanding," Bastian said. He had already spent the last half hour explaining who he was, who Hans was, and why they had temporarily detained two guards. "Come on, you can't possibly think one man could wrangle these burly blokes." Bastian relaxed his posture as if it were all in jest and focused on Logan. "You're pulling our leg. You set this up to have a little fun with us."

"What?" Logan had that panicked look on his face. "I would never do anything to jeopardize Trila." He focused on the head of security, George Browne. "Mr. Browne, I've never seen this man before." He pointed at Hans. "And this guy," he turned his gaze to Bastian for half a second, "is assisting Mr. Mercer in finding my wife. I don't see why they would do any of the things they're accused of."

"Precisely." Bastian smiled again, resisting the urge to wink. "We wouldn't do anything untoward. We simply believed these gentlemen might have insight into Mrs. Porter's disappearance since they are extremely thorough in their protection of our pal, Logan. Isn't that right?" He looked at the three men, who not only looked annoyed but also confused. "You are protecting him to the best of your ability, aren't you?" No one spoke, so Bastian raised an eyebrow at them. "That is why you're following him, isn't it?" Still, no response was forthcoming. "Why else are you following him?" Bastian narrowed his eyes, focusing on Browne.

"It's like you said." Browne gave the men a stern look. "However, we aren't able to assist in your recovery since we only began shadowing Mr. Porter after his wife went missing, not before."

"Ahh," Bastian nodded as if this made perfect sense, "that explains it. And it clears up any confusion and misunderstanding that might have taken place. You see, my associate was told to offer a reward for pertinent information. I apologize if that was somehow misconstrued, as were his intentions when he approached these lovely chaps."

Browne returned the saccharine smile. "Clearly." He stood, extending his hand. "Glad that's been cleared up. Now if you wouldn't mind vacating the premises, we do have sensitive matters that need to be addressed."

Bastian shook his hand and waited for Hans to lead the way out of the room. "You won't mind if I just have a brief word with Mr. Porter, will you?"

"Not at all," Browne said, but Bastian saw the glare just beneath the surface.

"Excellent." Bastian waited in the corridor for Logan, who was smart enough to keep his mouth shut. "Mr. Porter, when we phone, you will answer. We don't have time to play games."

"Did Alpha make contact?" Porter shifted his gaze

from Bastian to Hans. He involuntarily squinted at the sight of Hans's bloodied eye but didn't ask how it happened.

"Not yet. Jules needed your assistance." Bastian hoped the commander hadn't disconnected their call. "There was something he wanted to ask you. Go ahead, Jules."

"Does Logan know where Sarina's cell phone is?" Mercer asked.

Bastian relayed the question, and Logan furrowed his brow. "I haven't seen it. Did you check her purse?" He pressed his lips together. "Come to think of it, I haven't seen that either. It's usually in the kitchen."

"It's gone along with her bag. Maybe the kidnappers took it with them," Bastian restated for Mercer's benefit. "You must know her phone number."

"Sure," Logan scribbled it on the back of a business card.

"Is that the only line she had? Nothing else dedicated to just business?" Bastian asked.

"Not that I'm aware." Logan glanced at the office behind them. "I need to get going. Thanks for clearing things up." He shifted his gaze back to Hans. "Did you actually do what they said? On second thought, I don't want to know."

"We'll see you tonight at your home," Bastian said. "Seven o'clock. Don't be late."

TWENTY-TWO

"Is Logan unharmed?" Mercer turned the speaker back on while he sat inside the parked car, waiting for Donovan to arrive.

"Affirmative," Bastian replied. "Trila had detained him, hoping he'd clarify the situation with their guards."

"Situation?"

"It's fine." Bastian looked at Hans. "By the way, I found Hans. He's a bit worse for wear, but he'll live. So will Trila's men. However, they didn't buy into your brilliant scheme. Instead, they turned the tables and reported us to their boss. I have resolved the matter. Everything's copacetic."

"I doubt that." Mercer sunk lower in the seat, monitoring the area. He was situated a few blocks from the condemned building in a dilapidated garage. A few skateboarders were performing tricks on the ramp leading to the next level, and a couple was getting stoned in the corner. "I don't recall seeing a woman's handbag anywhere inside Porter's home.

Perhaps it was taken during the abduction in order to cover their tracks. Sarina's private e-mail account must be how Alpha initially made contact and discovered enough personal details to abduct her. Brie provided the username. Do you think you can hack into the account?"

"Probably, let me have it." While driving one-handed, Bastian pantomimed taking notes, and Hans withdrew a pen and scribbled down the information. "As soon as we're back at the flat, I'll get started on this. We have twenty hours or less to go. If this doesn't pan out, I don't think you can risk another run-in at Trila. I'm under the impression George Browne, which is most definitely not his real name, will shoot us on sight."

"I don't have time for this when there's a clock on procuring the protocols." Mercer spotted Donovan slide into the garage with the stealth of a shadow. "I'll deal with that later. Right now, we're going to investigate the building. If we need you, we'll call. In the meantime, do what you can. Sarina needs a miracle."

"Talk to god because I'm a mere mortal, and I've already used my allotted miracle today," Bastian replied, disconnecting.

"What did I miss?" Donovan asked, slipping into the back seat. "I woke up to find the place empty. Were there additional demands?"

"No, just a hitch in plan B."

"Shall we move on to plan C?"

"Absolutely."

Silently, the two men left the car. Mercer stopped at a water fountain and washed the markings off his palm. Then they took a circuitous route to the abandoned building, paying close attention to the area. It was rundown. The foot traffic consisted of fringe members of society. Some were lawbreakers. Most didn't want to be found. Mercer's suit would have stuck out like a sore thumb had he not left the jacket in the car. He partially untucked his shirt to conceal his weapon, and at the first opportunity, he rubbed dirt down the front to blend in better. Donovan had dressed appropriately in a dark colored hoodie and jeans. Grunging down, they did their best to blend in and camouflage themselves.

"That's it." Donovan jerked his chin at the building coming up on their left. It looked like an old housing project that had been condemned for the better part of a decade. "I noticed lights in the second and third windows." They continued around the building. "Did Bastian determine who's paying the electric bill?"

"It's under a corporate listing that covers most of the public buildings. It's no use." The time crunch had made Mercer more of a defeatist than usual. "Were none of the other buildings in our estimated radius viable?"

"Alpha could be keeping her anywhere, inside a house or a storefront. There are too many possibilities, but given our assumptions, this is our best bet." Donovan met his eyes. "It's the type of place we would use."

"Take the south entrance," Mercer instructed after they circled the building once. "I'll go in from the north. If you meet resistance, take them out."

"Right-o." Donovan checked his earpiece, making sure it was turned to the same frequency as the one he brought for Mercer before sticking it back inside his ear. Then he disappeared to the left, leaving Mercer to climb the rickety stairs.

Julian internally cringed at the creaking of the metal staircase. From the shrieks and groans it emitted beneath his weight, anyone inside would know they had uninvited company. Checking the rusted latch on the door, he broke it with one hit from the butt of his gun and ducked inside.

The room was dark except for the few traces of light that filtered in through cracks in the ceiling. Dust motes floated in front of his face, but he resisted flipping on the torch. Instead, he pressed against the nearest wall and inched his way across the room, checking for any signs of life.

From the other end of the building, he heard a loud bang. Holding his breath, Mercer waited, but nothing happened. Continuing through the first room, he entered a short corridor that led to another similar room. This one was practically identical to the first, and Mercer continued on his way.

The building layout continued in the same pattern. A dormitory-esque room that opened into a corridor that led to another empty room. It reminded him of a few hostels or the setup on certain refugee camps. The building could have been used for anything, and without furnishings, it was hard to determine its intended purpose. When he entered the next area, he found someone.

Aiming at the lump inside the sleeping bag, Mercer inhaled, calming the rush that accompanied this unexpected discovery. He edged to the corner of the room, strategically placing his back against the wall so anyone who might enter from the opposite side would not see him immediately.

"Stand up," Mercer said, "slowly."

The lump on the floor didn't move. Keeping his aim steady, he reached into his pocket and removed an LED light. Flipping the torch on, he pointed it at his target. From this angle, it was impossible to tell who might be underneath it.

"Get up. I won't ask again." He edged his way

closer, prepared to fire at the slightest sign of danger. However, in the dim light, there didn't appear to be any movement. If someone was underneath the blanket, it was unclear if she was breathing. "Bugger."

After kicking the bag, Mercer realized there was some give but not much. No one moaned or groaned or moved. *She's dead*, Mercer thought. *Alpha killed her and didn't expect us to find the body this soon.* Swallowing, Mercer prepared himself for the worst. He put the small torch back into his pocket, kept his gun trained on the sleeping bag, and reached out with his left hand to pull the blanket away.

He inched the zipper down a centimeter, recognizing a familiar stench. The chemical odor covered the bag, growing stronger as the inside was exposed. Mercer's brain was half a second behind his hand, and before he realized it was a trap, he heard the zipper strike against something inside the bag. Diving to the left, Mercer barely cleared the blast zone before the bag ignited in a flash, casting blinding light throughout the room.

The explosion momentarily disoriented him, and when he looked up, Donovan was hovering over him. Julian squinted and shook his head, watching his friend's lips move but unable to hear anything over the ringing inside his own head. He pushed himself to his feet and reached for his dropped handgun. The bag smoldered, but the blast had burned itself out. It wasn't meant to maim or cause serious destruction.

"Jules," Donovan said, "there's nothing here. Let's go." He tapped Mercer's shoulder and made hand signals that they pull back.

Julian brought up the rear, blinking at the odd green glow that had temporarily entered his peripheral vision. He turned his head, but nothing was there. "Did you see that?"

"What, mate?" Donovan stopped, checking behind them. He asked something else, but Mercer didn't hear him. Continuing on course, they exited from the door Donovan had entered, having swept the building and finding nothing else of interest.

Outside, a small group waited. They exchanged whispers and stares, disbanding when Mercer and Donovan emerged from the side door. Mercer focused on their faces, catching a few words here and there. At least his hearing was returning. No one looked familiar, but he knew any one of them could be Alpha.

"What the bloody hell was that?" Donovan asked.

"A homemade flash grenade," Mercer said, unable to wrap his mind around its intended purpose.

"Yo," a man shouted, making his way toward them, "what were you doing inside?" He had a large revolver tucked into the front of his pants, and from the way the onlookers avoided him, it was obvious he was someone they feared.

Mercer shrugged, worrying he'd caught that condition from Brie Dawson.

The man's mouth opened ever so slightly, a sign he was surprised by the lack of response. He puffed up his chest, straightening his posture to bring himself to his full height. He stood in front of Mercer, staring into his eyes, but Mercer didn't flinch.

"I'd step back," Donovan said. His tone was firm, and the man glanced at him, noticing the laser sight pointed at his chest. "Is this your place?"

"Nah, man. I use it to stash some of my shit from time to time," the drug dealer said.

"Is that it?" Mercer asked.

"Yeah," the guy took a step back when Donovan shifted the laser from the man's chest to his forehead. "Look, you're not from around here. So you don't get that causing trouble is a bad idea, but it is. I told your pal the same thing the other night."

"Pal?" Mercer raised an interested eyebrow.

"Yeah. Some blond guy. I made him clear out and set the trap in case he came back. He was cozying up inside with my TV and heater like this is the freaking Motel 6."

"Trap?" Mercer stepped closer, his fists clenched. The rage bubbled inside of him. This entire endeavor was a waste of time. This drug dealing tosser decided to squat inside a building and nearly blew them all to kingdom come because some homeless guy wanted a warm place to spend the night.

"Don't." Donovan grabbed Mercer by the shoulder. "We can't afford to waste more time." He pulled Mercer away, sprinting back to the car. "I'm sorry. I should have gone inside. I should have checked last night."

"The possibility of a positive resolution now rests entirely with those protocols."

"We'll find a way to get them." Donovan swallowed. "We will."

TWENTY-THREE

"What'd you get from Sarina's e-mail address?" Mercer asked.

"Shite." Bastian sighed. "Newsletters, ads, spam, hundreds of unread messages. Do you think Sarina was in the market for penis enhancement? Because there are two hundred and seventeen e-mails offering her a miracle product."

"Ask the bloke she married," Hans retorted as he entered the room.

"You okay?" Mercer asked.

"Fantastic." Hans opened his mouth wide, causing an audible crunch.

"Can you shoot?" Donovan asked.

"My trigger finger's fine, but my depth perception is a tad iffy." Hans held an ice pack against his face. "Shouldn't matter at normal range."

"Okay." Mercer leaned over Bastian's shoulder, scanning the e-mail addresses and subject lines. "What about read messages and sent messages?"

"They've been deleted, and with Sarina's settings,

the only way to recover them is with the actual device she used to initially open them. I hate to say it, but this isn't promising. I'm searching the internet for this e-mail address, just in case there are sites or message boards she frequents, but I haven't hit on anything yet. I take it the building was a bust," Bastian said.

"Apparently, a local pusher was using it for his business," Donovan said. "He booby-trapped the center room with a homemade incendiary. We caused quite the ruckus."

Julian circled the room, rehashing everything he knew. "Alpha's better than us. He prepared for this. He took his time. He knew precisely how Trila International would react to the news and how they would treat their employee."

"It could be an inside job," Hans said. "Trila's men don't pull their punches, and they wanted nothing to do with the money I offered them." He narrowed his one good eye. "I'd wager they let me trap them to find out more about us, rather than the other way around." He cursed, kicking the bottom of the table hard enough to scoot it a few centimeters.

"Security is intent on protecting those protocols with everything they have." Bastian chewed on his lip for a moment. "Whatever that program runs must be extremely valuable, and Mr. Browne knows it. That must be why they bugged Porter's home phone. They want to keep tabs on Porter and us and make sure we don't get any crazy ideas."

"Trila knows we're planning something." Mercer recalled his conversation with Alpha prior to the discovery of the listening device. "The computer protocols are Alpha's only ransom demand, and we're out of options. So how are we going to steal them?"

"We aren't thieves," Donovan mumbled. Regardless of that assertion, he would follow orders. "Have we considered everything else?"

"We've exhausted the possibilities." Mercer folded his arms and leaned against the wall. "If you have a bloody better suggestion, I'd love to hear it."

Donovan shook his head and fell silent. Bastian didn't look up from the computer, and Hans suddenly found the condensation forming on the outside of the ice pack fascinating.

"Alpha won't settle. He won't compromise. He knows us. He knows how we work. He knows how Trila works. Frankly, it appears the only unknown is Logan Porter," Mercer said.

"He's not unpredictable. He acts the same way every grieving target acts," Bastian said.

"Which is emotional, irrational, and terrified," Mercer said, "but Porter was never compliant. From the beginning, Logan knew he wouldn't be able to get the protocols, so he asked his boss. Then he reluctantly told us his dilemma."

"Alpha must realize we're his best shot of getting the ransom," Donovan added. "It's why he won't negotiate."

"Why can't he just get it himself?" Hans asked. "He abducted a woman from her home in broad daylight. He has the resources. He's done this before. He must have his own team. Why involve a middleman?"

Julian listened to his teammates theorize. Slowly, the pieces began to fit together. "He's been to Trila International. That would make him recognizable to them. It's probably how he initially learned about Logan Porter. It's why our client was targeted. From there, he must have researched the mark, finding Sarina. He made his approach, compiled his data, and abducted her." He let out an exhausted sigh. "The bloody good that does."

"If only I could get around Trila's firewalls."

Bastian went into the kitchen and rummaged in the pantry for a bag of pretzel rods. Crunching on his bounty, he returned with a second laptop. Powering on the device, he entered a number of commands. "What are these people hiding?"

After ten minutes, the laptop let out a shrill beep. "That doesn't sound good," Hans said.

"It isn't." Bastian slammed the lid closed. "Bollocks." He threw his half-chewed pretzel across the room. "I've broken into the encrypted city surveillance feeds. I've had the ability to change traffic lights. I've gained access to Porter's finances, his e-mails, his wife's secret account, but I can't get into Trila." He stomped around the room. "Balls."

"Relax," Mercer insisted.

"Relax? Relax? For god's sake, Julian, you are not someone who can say that, least of all to me."

Without another word, Mercer walked out of the room. He and his team were wound too tight. They were feeling the pressure, and it was releasing itself in the worst possible way. It had happened before on their uglier missions. And while staying inside and arguing, possibly even throwing a few punches, held a certain appeal, it was a waste of valuable time.

Dialing Logan's cell phone, Mercer waited for the man to answer. After three rings, Logan picked up, sounding just as nervous as ever.

"We need a list of visitors who have been to Trila within the last month, possibly longer," Mercer said.

"Okay, how do you propose I get that?"

"Find a way." Mercer thought about his own introduction the first time he entered the building. "There's a list of approved guests in the lobby. The receptionists have access to it. Just get it."

"Mr. Mercer, is everything okay?"

No, Julian thought. "We're working on it."

"He's supposed to call in the morning, right?"

"In roughly fourteen hours." Mercer looked at his watch.

"And then what?"

"Then we bring Sarina home." Hanging up, Mercer took a breath and punched a hole through the drywall. He was wiping the dust and blood off his knuckles when someone cleared his throat.

"Jules, there's an incoming call to Porter's home," Bastian said.

"Patch it through." It was too soon for Alpha to be making contact. Something had gone wrong.

TWENTY-FOUR

Mercer followed Bastian into the living room. He took a seat next to the computer and put the headset on. Briefly, he made eye contact with Hans and Donovan. Blowing out a breath, he waited for Bastian to nod his approval before answering the call. As usual, they were attempting a trace, but Mercer knew it was fruitless.

"My, my, my," the computer-modulated voice said, "you made quite a scene today, Mr. Mercer."

"What can I do for you?" Mercer asked, forcing himself to remain professional.

"I want the protocols."

"We're working on it."

"You might already have them if you weren't wasting your time trying to find me," Alpha said. Mercer looked at Donovan, who was equally perplexed. "Are you denying it?"

"No," Mercer replied. "You could make this easier and tell me where you are."

"When you get the protocols, I'll tell you exactly

- 145 -

where to go."

Pressing his lips together, Mercer fought off the desire to vocalize his opinion, instead shuddering under the pressure of containing his anger. "How is Sarina?"

"Alive, but she won't be if you fail to deliver." The voice made an odd sound which Mercer interpreted as a sign of disapproval. "Since you have ample time to waste, I'm moving up the deadline. You will deliver the protocols by oh-eight-hundred and not a minute later. If you fail to comply, Sarina's dead."

"Alpha, we need more time."

"Then you shouldn't have been wasting time."

Abruptly, the call ended, and Mercer threw off the headset. "Bas, pull up the blueprints for the building. I need an overlay of whatever data we collected off your tech. Hans, work some magic and see if there's ever been a break-in reported at the Trila building. We'll need police reports and any information they might have."

"On it," Hans said, obediently moving into the next room.

Mercer narrowed his eyes, shaking a wayward thought loose. "After the explosion, on the way out of the building, I saw a green light."

"You think Alpha recorded us?" Donovan asked, recalling the drug dealer's story of a blond man who had taken up refuge inside the building. "I'll run through the city's CCTV data and see if I can pinpoint the guy."

"Facial recognition will take too long." Bastian's hands flew over the keyboard, and within seconds the two-dimensional blueprint became an interactive three-dimensional rendering with distances and alarms marked from the data his trackers had transmitted. "Even if you find him on the feed, by the time we identify him, we'll have missed the deadline."

"Do it anyway," Mercer insisted. "We know his alias, and I want to know what he looks like. I'd hate to kill the wrong man by mistake." Shifting his focus to the model on the screen, Julian pointed at the server room in the basement. "They would expect us to go directly to the source, so we need to find an alternative."

"The server room might be nothing more than a decoy. The protocols operate a computer program," Bastian said, "or a program to run within a program. They're protocols. Trila must have a hard copy of the actual data."

"So it isn't a program?" Mercer asked.

"It's code." Bastian shook his head, not wanting to explain something this technically complicated. "I'd assume it's stored on various devices. USB drives, hard drives, disks. Hell, with the amount of hacking that's been happening lately, some companies have printed out their code in order to keep it offline and secure."

"So where do we look?" Mercer asked.

"Logan says he reviewed the reports and checked the protocols. He can tell you about their format." Bastian pointed at the screen. "But given the amount of security surrounding this specific protocol and the ridiculous firewalls that protect Trila's information, it has to be on their system. The access terminals on their R&D floor are protected by fingerprint and keycard scan. I wouldn't be surprised if they didn't have a retinal scanner on the actual computer."

"How do we bypass it?"

"This is theoretical, but I don't think we can. However," Bastian skimmed the blueprints until he located Porter's office, "they're watching him. Just to get into his office is like entering Buckingham Palace.

You remember the security measures in place."

"Your point?"

"They didn't like it when we were on that floor or inside his office. They escorted us to and from the door." Bastian cocked his head to the side, assessing the diagram. "If he reviewed it on his office computer, the data might be on his hard drive."

"They would have deleted it. They don't trust him."

"They don't trust us either, but it could still be on his computer. Even after a deletion, information lingers. It'd be the easiest way to access it."

"Will you be able to copy it?" Mercer asked.

"I can't say for certain but probably. I need to see it in person which will be far more complicated now that Trila's head of security has banned me from the building."

"I can handle him." Julian looked at the computer rendition. "We'll have to go after hours with Logan in tow. He can get us inside." Cognizant of the need for an alternative plan, Mercer posed the next question. "What if it's been wiped off his system or he didn't review the data on his computer?"

Bastian pointed at the screen. "This room has a palm scanner, keycard mechanism, and according to the trackers you planted, not a single guard entered that room. I'd wager they don't have access."

"So what?"

"Based on the blueprints, it consumes a lot of energy for such a small space." He toggled the images to show heat signatures. "It's slightly colder than the other areas of the building. It must be temperature controlled and is roughly the size of the server room."

"It's a backup."

"That'd be my guess." Bastian pulled up the power usage for the building. "That room runs hot, just like the basement. No other parts of the building use that kind of energy, and they wouldn't waste time with the high-tech security measures if it was of no consequence."

"Assuming the protocols are stored on their internal servers, can you access them?"

"I'd have to do it in person, and the files might be encrypted, corrupted, or otherwise unreadable, depending on the level of security. It's Trila, so I'm assuming something topnotch, like a kill program that destroys the information when it's not accessed properly."

"That won't help us," Mercer said.

"I thought the plan was to buy time to rescue Sarina. Alpha is going to kill her either way, Jules. Frankly, I'm pretty sure he plans to kill us too. I don't think we should give him what he wants."

Mercer stared at the computer screen. "What if we fake it?"

"The end result would be the same as giving him a steaming pile of rubbish," Bastian said. "I could probably borrow some code from a program or two, but if we don't know what it's supposed to do, it won't look real. And you know he's going to check it at the exchange."

"Then we need a convincing bluff."

"Trila had one attempted break-in two years ago," Hans said, returning to the room. "The intruder was killed on-site. The police ruled it a justified shooting, and the report doesn't detail anything else."

"Trila paid off the authorities," Bastian said. "They can do whatever they want which means they'll use lethal force to deal with us as well."

"Since when does a gunfight scare you?" Hans looked at the printed photos of Trila's exterior. "Employee entrance is inside the parking garage. That's why they monitor the area around the clock.

There's also an emergency exit. It's a stairwell that opens up at the back of the building." He flipped through the photos, finding one of the back. "They have another guard station there, but those guards are too busy jacking each other off to pay close attention. At least that seemed to be the case when they dragged me inside. I yelled bloody murder and didn't get a reaction out of any of them."

"What's the security on the door like?" Bastian asked.

"FOB scanner. Two guards," Hans replied. "I wasn't impressed."

"I could probably overwrite it," Bastian muttered. "What do you think, Jules?"

Mercer clasped his hands together, realizing his knuckles were swollen from his earlier outburst. He went into the kitchen and returned with a bowl of ice. Taking a seat, he looked at the photos, the three-dimensional blueprint, and the array of information pasted on the wall.

"We know he's a pro. We know he leaves a trail of bloodshed in his wake. And we know he desperately wants access to a computer program. We don't know what it does, and we can only postulate why he is unable to get it on his own. So we need a way to get it, and we need a way to keep it from him until Sarina's safe. Let's get to work." He pointed at the photos. "This is where we begin."

TWENTY-FIVE

The team of kidnapping specialists had devised a plan of action that included two contingencies. Negotiations weren't an exact science, and neither was breaking into a heavily fortified, tech-savvy building. With any luck, the simplest plan would work. Of course, the crux of it rested on Logan Porter, and Mercer had trouble believing their client was capable of performing the necessary feats. Frankly, if Porter was ballsy enough to do anything, he would have figured out a way to get the protocols on his own and would have told Alpha exactly where to shove them. Then again, that might have led to Sarina's swift execution. It was better Porter wasn't the heroic, macho type, or so Mercer had convinced himself.

"I don't like this," Bastian whispered. They had just arrived at Logan's estate. The two guards on duty, Will and Thomas, waved them through without so much as a second glance. "Shouldn't they be more proactive, particularly in lieu of what has already happened?"

"Now you're paranoid." Mercer parked on the

cobblestone path in front of the house. He took a perverse pleasure in knowing it would irritate Logan and make the man more likely to agree with their plan just to get them to move the car.

"No, I'm being pragmatic." Bastian glanced in the rearview mirror. "For all they know, we could have a trunk full of C4."

"We have some det cord." Mercer smiled. "But no one would believe we're about to storm the house."

"No, just Trila International." Bastian sucked in some air. "Is this really the best we can do?"

Without responding, Mercer exited the car and jogged up the steps to the porch. He rang the bell. A second later, the door opened, and Logan ushered the two of them inside, glowering at the car.

"I couldn't get the visitor list you asked for," Logan began, but Mercer cut him off.

"There's been a change of plans. This isn't that unusual, and we will adapt. Right now, I need you to stay put for a few moments."

Mercer turned, watching Bastian pull out an RF reader and scan the vicinity. They couldn't afford to let Trila overhear their plans again. Bastian looked up, turning the device so Mercer could see the faint glow of a signal somewhere in the room.

"Have you had company since my last visit?" Mercer casually asked.

"No, why?" Logan glanced at the gadget in Bastian's hand, unaware of what he was seeing.

"The flowers look fresh." Mercer glared at the arrangement that had been delivered along with Sarina's finger. "I thought those had been left outside."

"The groundskeeper must have brought them in. Is something wrong with them?"

"Flowers inside a house mean death, mate,"

Bastian said. "How about we go somewhere with better juju?"

Logan gulped. "Is Sarina...? Is she...?" He couldn't bring himself to say the words.

"Come on." Mercer didn't want to deal with hysterics. Cryptic was important at this juncture, and he dragged Logan out of the house and into the car. Once they were inside, Mercer turned to Logan. "Your wife is fine. However, your house is bugged. I suspect that is your employer's doing. This was the fastest way to get you outside without tipping them off. I'm sorry." Mercer's words were sincere, and Logan closed his eyes and pressed his lips together in a silent prayer of thanks. "Time isn't on our side, and I need you to tell Bastian everything you can about the protocols."

"What do you want to know?" Logan asked.

"Did you run the actual protocol within the program?" Bastian asked.

"Yes, after reading the report, I had to verify the data, so I ran the protocol, executed the backdoor commands, and made sure the system was responsive to the intrusion."

"Did you do that on your office computer?" Bastian asked.

"No, I did it upstairs in the lab."

"Dammit." Mercer shifted his focus to the guard post, but the sentries weren't paying attention to the parked car or the men inside.

"What about hard copies or digital copies of the code? Did you review them?" Bastian asked.

"Yeah, well, they were included in the reports I read and rubberstamped. I don't have copies. I never expected to need them. It's Trila's proprietary property. There are rules governing how the information is stored and filed. By now, any paper trail has been destroyed. The protocols are saved on the system, so the programmers can create updates and improvements after the operating system is released."

"So the data is somewhere on Trila's network." Bastian drummed his fingers against the seat. "That's the only place it exists?"

"As far as I know." Logan eyed both men. "Are you going to hack into Trila's network?"

"More or less." Mercer turned the key in the ignition.

"How? It's unbreakable. You'd have to be inside the building," Logan protested.

"Sharp as a tack," Bastian said. "That's good. You'll have to think on your feet."

"Why?" Logan looked like he might be sick. "Where are we going?"

"You left something of great importance in your office, and you need to retrieve it immediately. It's of dire consequence if you don't," Mercer responded.

"They'll never let the two of you inside with me," Logan said.

"That's precisely what I'm counting on."

A few kilometers from the Trila International building, Mercer pulled into an alleyway and flashed his lights. The vehicle in front of them returned the signal, and Bastian stepped out of the car. The darkness swallowed him as he headed deeper into the alley, toward the source of the returned headlights.

"What's he doing?" Logan asked.

"Throwing in the towel. You said it yourself, Trila won't let us inside. Bastian won't risk it after this morning, so it's just the two of us." Mercer put the car in reverse and backed out of the alley. He had monitored traffic the entire way and was positive no one had followed them. Regardless, splitting up would improve their odds.

"Isn't he your tech guy? Do you even know what to do?" Logan asked.

"Sure."

It was almost nine p.m. when Mercer parked in front of the Trila International building. Most of the employees had gone home for the night. However, the guards were on duty and making their way to Mercer's illegally parked car.

Mercer opened his jacket and took his gun from his hip. Holding it by the barrel, he offered it to the nearest guard.

"Logan Porter." Logan held out his Trila credentials. "This is Julian Mercer. He's my personal security specialist."

"We are aware," one of the guards said. "What are you doing on the premises at this time of night?"

"In the rush to leave today, I forgot an important item in my office. It's imperative I retrieve it tonight." Porter's words sounded rehearsed, and Mercer internally cringed. Hopefully, Porter believed Bastian had given up so he wouldn't accidentally compromise the rest of Mercer's team, who were waiting for a distraction before making their move.

The guard radioed ahead, listening to the response before saying, "You can go inside, Mr. Porter, but Mr. Mercer will remain here."

"I'm sorry," Porter said, "but he has to accompany me. It's of the utmost importance."

"Why?" the guard asked.

"He has to remain by the phone." Mercer held out the cell phone. "The kidnapper is supposed to be making contact any minute, and he expects to speak to both of us directly. If Mr. Porter isn't present at the time of the call," Mercer pressed his lips together and looked away, "I don't want to be responsible for that. Do you understand?"

The guard didn't look convinced.

"Please," Porter begged, "it is a matter of life or death."

"What do you need from the office?" the guard asked.

"Her wedding ring," Mercer replied, knowing Porter wasn't prepared to answer. "It's complicated, but it's in his office. And we need it. It's vital to the negotiation."

The guard radioed for further assistance, and soon a few more men joined the two guards at the front of the building. "We will escort you to the office and back again." They looked around. "Let's step into the lobby."

Inside, Porter and Mercer went through a metal detector, and then Julian was thoroughly frisked. It was nice to know they feared him. Once they were satisfied he was unarmed, four guards escorted them to the lift. The doors opened, and the group entered.

"It's a go," Mercer whispered.

"What?" the guard asked.

"I said let's go." Mercer smiled, a wicked, disconcerting expression that did nothing to ease the guard's suspicions.

The lift continued its ascent but stopped abruptly half a level below the desired destination. The doors opened, showing the elevator shaft and part of the floor above. One of the guards cast a sideways look at Mercer while two of them reset the elevator, forcing the doors to close and the lift to continue upward. When it stopped on the proper floor, the doors wouldn't open.

"What is this?" the guard asked.

"How the bloody hell should I know?" Mercer said. "It's your damn lift."

"If this is a joke or some kind of trick, you'll be

leaving here in a body bag," the guard threatened.

"And if you don't get the doors open, we'll all be stuck inside this metal box from now until kingdom come." Mercer stepped to the side and attempted to help the guards force the doors open. "Isn't there someone in the lobby who can manually override the lift?"

After another few minutes of trying to pry the doors open, a guard got on the radio to request a manual override. Meanwhile, Mercer exchanged a look with Porter and glanced at his watch. Things were moving according to plan. Bastian must have accessed the basement lift and triggered the shut off. Once the reset was initiated, it would give Bastian three minutes to get upstairs and inside Porter's office before the system came back online.

"Are we on schedule?" Mercer whispered, knowing his team would understand the question was meant for them. He covered his mouth and faked a cough, hoping the guards didn't hear him.

"Affirmative. We met little resistance. Two have been subdued," Hans said through the comms.

"I need more time," Bastian hissed. "How much longer can you hold the lift?"

"We should be out in another minute," Mercer said for Bastian's sake. "We need to hurry."

"I'm going as fast as I can, Jules," Bastian said. "Bloody hell. They're on the stairs."

"Get out," Mercer ordered, drawing attention from the men inside the elevator. He pushed one of the guards. "I said get out of the way. I think I can get it open." He clawed at the doors for purchase. "Just one good shove and we'll be out." Mercer hoped Bastian and Hans were clear and an army of guards wasn't waiting on the other side for them. The doors slid open, and Mercer held his breath.

TWENTY-SIX

"Claustrophobic?" the guard mocked, exchanging snickers with the three other men, amused by Mercer's actions. "We'll have to remember that."

Mercer cast his gaze down the corridor, finding the hallway empty. The stairwell doors opened, and two more guards emerged on the level. Immediately, they were waved away by the guards who had taken lead.

"Make it snappy," the mouthy guard insisted, "we shouldn't have even let him up here without approval. I don't want my ass in a sling because of it."

"Right, sorry. Thanks." Porter pressed his palm against the scanner, hearing the mechanism release. The red light flashed to green. "We'll just be a second."

Mercer opened the door and stepped inside. To the left, he spotted Bastian and Hans pressed against the wall, waiting to make sure the guards remained in the hallway. Once Porter entered, pulling the door closed behind him, they let out a collective sigh of relief.

"Holy —," Porter began, and Mercer clamped his

hand firmly over the man's mouth to silence him.

"Quiet." Porter nodded, and Mercer released the man. "Stay in here and stay quiet."

Hans and Bastian opened the adjoining door inside Porter's office. In the center of the wall, Bastian had drilled a small hole. He attached fiber optic cables and spliced through the cords, hooking a tablet to the apparatus. Entering a few parameters, he continued the data search he had been conducting before Mercer's arrival. Hans fidgeted in the corner, prepared to retaliate if the guards decided to burst into the room.

"Thought it'd be easier to go through the wall since we couldn't get into the other room," Bastian whispered.

"We don't have much time," Mercer said. "How long until they discover the intrusion?"

"Based on their patrols, we have five minutes until they find their mates unconscious in the rear guard station," Hans said.

Focusing on Bastian, Mercer asked, "What's taking so long?"

"I have to search the entire network to find what we need." Bastian wiped the back of his hand over his forehead. "Shit." He tapped a lengthy command into the tablet. "In thirty seconds, they're going to know the system's been breached."

"Can't you stop it?"

"If I knew how to stop it, I would," Bastian held out his hand. "Give me your cell." Mercer gave him the device, and Bastian input a few commands then plugged it in where the tablet had been. He ripped it from the wall and tossed it back to Mercer. "It's the best I can do, but it won't stand up once the encryption is broken." Bastian turned back to the tablet. A red warning beacon appeared on the screen.

"Go. I'll delay the system notification as long as I can. You have to get out of the building before they realize what we've done. We're out of options, Jules. Just go. We can handle this."

Mercer grabbed Porter and pulled him toward the door. He flipped the lights off, casting a final look at his team. It was unacceptable to leave them behind, but if they were all caught, no one would be able to negotiate Sarina's release and the entire mission would be for naught.

"Can I see it?" the guard asked as soon as Porter emerged from the office.

"What?" Porter asked, confused.

"The ring," Mercer said. "You put it in your pocket."

"Right." Porter removed the item he had been carrying around since Tuesday afternoon and handed it to the guard while the group of men made their way to the lift.

Mercer pushed the button, not wanting to waste any more time. The sooner they cleared the building, the better the chances were that his men would make it out safely. He held himself stiffly to keep from fidgeting, and as soon as the doors opened, he stepped inside.

"Aren't you afraid we'll get stuck again?" one of the other guards asked.

"Yes," Mercer said.

The guards exchanged snickers and looks, but it kept them from noticing anything else was amiss.

The doors opened again, and for once, the guard who asked Porter about the ring showed some compassion. "I hope your wife's okay," he said. "Good luck." He nodded at Porter and Mercer and led them to the security desk to return Mercer's weapon.

"Thank you," Porter said. "I know you've just been doing your job and trying to help. I appreciate it."

"We need to go," Mercer reminded him. "The call could come at any moment." He took hold of Porter's elbow and led him toward the front door. "Almost clear," he whispered into his comm.

They were two meters from the door when the warning claxons sounded. Rushing forward, Mercer pushed the door open. He saw the urgent looks on the guards' faces. Half of them were en route to intercept Mercer, and the other half were on their way upstairs.

"Company is on the way. Get out now." Mercer sprinted to the car with Porter at his side. They got in, and Mercer sped away from the curb before Porter even had time to close the door. "Donovan, do something to aid their evac. Bastian, report."

"We're a little busy, Jules," Bastian replied. A loud burst of static and shouts sounded in the background.

"Bloody fucking hell." Hans's voice was heard at the same time as Bastian's. His team was trapped, and Mercer couldn't stomach leaving them behind.

Mercer checked the mirror, finding two SUVs fast approaching from the rear. It took every ounce of willpower not to whip the car around and drive back to the Trila building. Instead, he executed a sharp turn, jumping the curb and scraping the side of the car against a building. The tires on the SUVs squealed, and the lead car missed the turn. The second vehicle closed the gap and took the lead. Mercer turned again, this time heading the wrong way on a one-way street.

Car horns blared as he darted around oncoming traffic. The SUV was forced to slow to avoid a collision, so Julian drove into a parking garage. Going straight to the second level, he stopped the car abruptly.

"Get out," Mercer said, already three steps toward a different car. He hit the unlock mechanism and climbed behind the wheel. "We have to move. Now."

"What's happening? Why are they after us?" Porter asked. "What did you do?"

"I got Alpha the damn protocols in order to save your wife." Mercer hit the gas, exiting the garage and driving past the two SUVs that were now entering the garage. They didn't seem to notice the departing sedan, and Mercer took a moment to breathe. "Bastian? Hans?" Normally, they used code names, but since Trila already knew who they were, it would have been a waste of time.

"They're alive," Donovan said.

"Are they with you?"

"Negative."

"I'm on my way."

"No."

"I'm on my way," Mercer repeated.

"You can't. You have to save Sarina. If you come back, we might all be compromised. I promise I'll get them out, Jules."

"How?"

"Remember Amsterdam?"

"Bollocks. Now you have to rescue them from Trila security and the freaking coppers."

TWENTY-SEVEN

Mercer rubbed the stubble on his cheeks and stared at the phone. Whatever information Bastian downloaded onto the device wouldn't hold up under much scrutiny, and without his second-in-command, he didn't know how long it would take Alpha to break the encryption or what information he would uncover. The shit hit the fan. Half of his team was incarcerated or worse. Donovan had been providing updates as often as possible, but no news was good news. Bastian and Hans were still inside the Trila building. The police were on-site, but as far as anyone knew, Bastian and Hans were unharmed. However, their comms were down, and Mercer suspected they'd been shorted out by a taser rather than having been discovered.

Logan Porter was a wreck. From the way he was acting, one would have thought he had personally infiltrated Trila International and sabotaged the entire company. Logan paced the room, taking a moment to sit down. Then he stood abruptly, went into the bathroom, returned a few moments later, fidgeted, paced, and lingered closer to the window.

"Sit down," Mercer said. "And stay away from the window."

"I thought you said this was a safe house."

"It will remain safe as long as no one knows we're here. Now sit down."

Reaching for the remote, Logan increased the volume and watched the reporter deliver breaking news on a burglary inside the Trila building. Mercer glanced at the television, knowing precisely what the talking heads would have to say. It was conjecture and a cover-up, but the flashing police lights and the magnitude of the building made for a nice dramatic backdrop to the dribble spilling from the woman's mouth. Apparently, the news station didn't care it was one a.m. and no one was watching. From the looks of it, they'd be repeating the story again on the morning show. Mercer idly wondered if Alpha was watching the coverage live or if he was enjoying a peaceful night's rest, content in the fact he'd be getting precisely what he wanted in a matter of hours.

"She makes it sound like we failed," Logan said. "What if he doesn't bother with a follow-up communication because he thinks we're in custody?" Mercer ignored the panicked questions until Logan grabbed his shoulders and shook him. "Are you listening to this?" He pointed emphatically at the screen. "You have to do something."

"Get your hands off of me."

"Authorities responded to a robbery in progress. The security on duty trapped the thieves inside. It is not yet clear what they intended to steal. More details will be provided as we uncover them," the reporter said, staring into the camera.

"Rubbish." Mercer turned off the television, slamming the remote down with enough force to snap the battery cover into pieces. He turned his gaze on Logan, and the man sunk back onto the couch. "In a couple of hours, the power dynamic will shift. That is our one chance to rescue Sarina. Until then, we wait."

"But what about the news story?" Logan asked timidly.

"No one gives a shit."

Frankly, Mercer figured the fanfare and notoriety of the break-in would help sell the legitimacy of the program. He focused on the cell phone again. Normally, it didn't matter if the ransom was legitimate or total bullshit. But his team sacrificed themselves for this, so it would have been nice to have some guarantee it would dupe Alpha long enough to get Sarina clear.

"Julian, my life will never be the same again. My job is over, and I'll probably be arrested. I might spend the rest of my life behind bars. You have to make sure this," he pointed to the cell phone, "was worth it."

Unable to hide the contempt, Mercer stood. "My team believed in this. So should you." He went into another room and slammed the door.

They agreed to the mission. They took payment to provide a service. They were always aware of the risks, and getting caught by some supposed 'good' guys was a better alternative than getting caught by Alpha.

"Donovan, report," Mercer said, glad their comms were operational.

"Some police brass have shown up. Trila has deep pockets, so only the best will do."

"Have you seen Bas or Hans?"

"Negative."

"Are you positive Trila's guards didn't open fire?"

"I've tapped into the police frequencies. Based on the radio chatter, two men are inside. No reports of gunfire. No calls for a coroner or ambulance have been made."

"Roger," Mercer said.

"Has the kidnapper made contact?"

"Not yet."

"Radio when he does. You'll need backup support."

"I can do this alone."

"You're daft. That's suicide."

"I will not sacrifice anyone else. Is that clear?"

"Commander," Donovan said, that smartass tone broadcasting clearly over the radio, "you fail to realize that unlike the Special Air Service, we don't have to follow your orders."

Mercer fumed over the comment, but it was something he knew to be true. Most of the time, he called the shots because he had the experience and rationale to back up his decisions. However, on a few occasions, when he had been off the rails, Bastian or someone else took over.

"Keep me updated," Mercer said.

"I trust you will do the same."

The two-way communication remained open, so Donovan would hear the call, just like he heard Logan Porter's meltdown.

Had he been so inclined, Mercer would have disconnected the comm, but he needed the connection with his team. He needed to know Bastian and Hans were okay. In some ways, he was just as powerless and frustrated as Logan. The only difference was Sarina had been unknowingly targeted while Bastian and Hans forced the guards to target them in order to give Mercer time to escape.

"I screwed up," Mercer whispered, hoping his mates could hear him. "I should have found a better alternative."

Grabbing a map of the area, he picked up a pen and

began to formulate ground rules for the exchange. The ideal location would limit entry points and the chances of an ambush. It would also delay Alpha's escape, potentially giving Mercer the ability to track him in the event Sarina wasn't brought to the drop site. Julian knew Alpha would have something up his sleeve, but allegedly having the protocols would give Mercer some leverage. It was time he used that to his advantage to dictate his own terms. Alpha wasn't the only one who could establish non-negotiable terms.

TWENTY-EIGHT

Several hours later, Mercer returned to the living room. Logan hadn't moved from the couch, and Julian did a double take to make sure the man was asleep and not dead. The events of the evening might have been too much for the out of shape computer tech to handle, but the rise and fall of his chest indicated he was breathing. At least someone was.

Picking up the cell phone, Mercer contemplated examining the data upload but decided not to risk it. Instead, he returned it to the spot on the table and sat in front of the computer screen. In his haste to relocate, he barely had time to grab the basics. The computer held the rudimentary trap and trace programs needed to identify and locate the caller. So far, Alpha had been careful, but with any luck, he'd slip up sooner rather than later.

Once the program was running, Mercer made sure the wires were properly connected and the satellite signal was strong. Then he waited. Bastian had made sure to redirect any calls received at the Porter residence to Mercer's phone. If Alpha was on schedule, the call would be made in forty-three minutes.

Taking a deep breath, Mercer memorized the maps. He wanted the exchange to be in a public place but not somewhere heavily trafficked. Bystanders could get in the way, or any Tom, Dick, or Harry could be a henchman working for Alpha. Normally, Mercer would have Donovan scout ahead and Hans would set up with a rifle on a rooftop. Since that wasn't a possibility, Julian had to improvise.

He selected the parking lot of a local restaurant. It wasn't on any of the main thoroughfares, and since they were closed on Thursdays, there was no danger to the public. Furthermore, it was located on a two-lane street, limiting the possibility of an ambush. However, if Alpha refused to meet at this particular location, Julian had mapped out three other possibilities.

The phone rang, and Logan bolted upright. He bit his lip and stared at the ringing phone. "Is it him?"

Mercer nodded, hitting a key to start the trace before answering the call. "Alpha?"

"Do you have it?" the modulated voice asked.

"Yes."

"Excellent. We will meet in two hours. Instructions will be delivered to Mr. Porter's estate."

"No." Mercer stood, needing to alter his position to make his words more forceful. "That is not acceptable. In order to receive your protocols, you will have to agree to a location of my choosing. If you fail to comply, you get nothing."

Porter turned puce, too overcome to speak. Mercer held up his pointer finger, hoping his client would remain silent and not botch the negotiation.

"Amazing. I didn't think you had a pair, let alone a

set of brass ones," Alpha said. "I thought you were a eunuch."

Not letting the dig goad or distract him, Mercer continued. "My demands are as follows: Sarina Porter will remain unharmed; she will be brought to the exchange; it will occur in a secluded, public area; no more than two men will be at the exchange. Is that clear?"

"Let me tell you what's clear, Mercer," Alpha said. "You have what I want, and I have what you want. For some reason, that makes you think I'm willing to do your bidding. It does not. Sarina's well-being is determined by me. Not by anyone else. You have a hacker's wet dream. I have a person's life in my hands. Which do you think is more valuable?"

"It depends." Mercer could play the game. He was as cold and calculating as any other son of a bitch. "Frankly, neither one means shit to me."

"Really?"

Mercer swallowed, knowing he'd misspoken. "This is a job. It is not personal. I'm negotiating an exchange. Neither bartering chip should be delivered in an unsatisfactory condition. Is that understood?"

"Spoken like a true negotiator." Alpha paused. "Fine, I'll accept the terms of the exchange, but you will deliver the item personally. And you will come alone. No wires. No trackers. No police. Is that clear?"

"Absolutely."

"I will call again in one hour with the delivery time."

"Okay."

"And one more thing, if you try anything, I'll kill her."

The call abruptly ended, and Mercer shut his eyes, allowing the information to process. Alpha agreed to his terms. Was it too easy? Something about the call didn't sit well with Julian, but he couldn't figure out why. Perhaps, it was the predicament of his team or the hysterical man peppering him with a million questions.

"We wait," Mercer said, ignoring everything Logan was saying. "Alpha has an hour to change the play. We can't count on any certainties."

Picking up the earpiece, Mercer slipped it back into his ear to update Donovan on the situation. As he suspected, Donovan had been paying attention and had heard the call come through via their comms.

"Where's the exchange taking place?" Donovan asked.

"It doesn't matter. I'm going alone."

"Bollocks."

"Alpha will call again in an hour. Until then, nothing is set in stone."

"Do you expect him to alter the meet or the terms?" Donovan asked.

Mercer stole a glance at Logan who was now in the kitchen, searching the cabinets for something hard to ease his apprehension. "Alpha likes demonstrating his power, so he'll do something to prove he's in charge."

"Jules, I don't like this."

"We have no choice. Focus your energy on Bastian and Hans." Mercer licked his lips and settled onto the couch. "Any updates?"

Donovan had maintained radio silence since the last time they spoke. Mercer didn't even hear background noise or static, so he suspected Donovan had silenced his microphone.

"They've been taken into police custody. They're being held in separate interrogation rooms. I can't get near them, but the police are pissed. Hans and Bastian haven't said a word, which is frustrating the shit out of the coppers."

"Okay."

"Should I contact a solicitor or the embassy?"

"Wait and see. Trila's likely to intervene. It depends on what they do." Mercer thought about Bastian's words concerning George Browne. "If it becomes necessary, do whatever it takes to get them out."

"First, we plan a heist. Now, you want to orchestrate a prison break. What's next? Overthrowing the government?"

"No, but killing Alpha has crossed my mind." Julian ran his fingers against the handle of his gun. Turning around, he made sure Logan was out of earshot before asking, "When do you think he plans to clean up his mess?"

"He has to make sure you deliver the protocols. He won't risk killing her before the package is in his possession. That'll give you a small window to get her and get out." Donovan exhaled. "You need me on-site."

"There's no guarantee he'll bring her to the exchange. Honestly, it'd be stupid if he did."

"You can't be in two places at once, mate." Donovan paused, thinking through their options. "I don't suppose you could convince him to make the exchange at one of the locations we've scouted for our use."

"Negative. I barely got him to agree to meet in a public place. Trila's data is on my cell phone. Bastian has a GPS tracker built-in. Can you monitor it from your location?"

"Aye."

"Okay, worst case, follow him. He should lead you to Sarina."

"I don't like the timeframe."

"We'll have to make it work."

"No one knows Alpha's true identity. Do you

believe he'll risk showing up to make the exchange himself?"

"Not unless he plans to kill me on-site, and that's what I'm counting on."

"Commander, take him down."

"I intend to."

TWENTY-NINE

"I'm supposed to wait here?" Logan asked. "What if he calls while you're gone?"

"The calls are routed to my phone. Stay here. Don't answer the door or the phone. Don't leave. Don't do anything." Mercer patted his pockets, feeling the weight of the cell phone in his breast pocket. He had another burner cell in his pants pocket. His Sig rested on his hip, and a backup was tucked inside an ankle holster beneath his pant leg. "I should be back shortly. However, if a wrinkle develops, Donovan will take control of the situation."

"Who the hell is Donovan?" Logan asked.

Mercer rolled his eyes. "Follow my instructions. The next few hours are crucial. Do not cause problems."

Logan nodded. He took a seat on the couch, like a wayward child attempting to behave. "Please bring her home."

"I will."

Pulling the door closed behind him, Mercer made

sure it was locked and stuck the key in the top corner of the doorframe. He couldn't risk leaving anything on his person that would jeopardize Logan or his team. Their safe house would not be compromised in the event Alpha searched him.

The sun had just broken over the horizon, and it looked like today would be sunny and clear. It was perfect weather for a sniper. Dismissing the thought, Mercer climbed behind the wheel of a plain white sedan. He switched the license plate with another vehicle to complicate matters. After all, he couldn't be too careful.

"En route," Mercer said, knowing Donovan was listening. "You have the address and the pertinent information regarding Logan Porter and our safe house. The key's above the door."

Donovan grunted, hating how the commander often went over contingencies based on his demise. It was downright morbid. "He agreed to your meeting spot. Fancy that."

"It's a good location."

"For whom?"

"That's to be determined."

Mercer took a moment to breathe. The adrenaline started to flow, and he felt the euphoria that came before every exchange. He identified it as hope. Anything could happen. A resolution was within reach. It could be peaceful, without the need for violence or cruelty. Alpha could simply hand over Sarina without comment as soon as the phone was within his grasp. It'd be nice, but Mercer knew how unlikely that was under these circumstances. He knew things would get messy, and the darker side of him enjoyed the danger and how it drew out his survival instinct. *To the victor, goes the spoils*, he thought. The truth was he felt alive when he was in the field. It was one of the rare occasions his mind didn't dwell on his own internal pain. It freed him, ever so briefly, from his torment.

"Are you positive Alpha didn't change the location?" Donovan asked.

"He left the terms in place."

"There has to be a reason."

"It's of no concern." Mercer turned onto the side street, watching the road ahead for danger. After spotting the large sign for the diner, he saw a black SUV parked at the side of the building. "I have to lose the comm."

"Godspeed."

Mercer removed the earbud and placed it inside the cup holder. Slowly, he pulled into the parking lot, leaving a fair distance between his vehicle and the SUV. The truck's windows were blacked out, making it impossible to determine who was inside. Mercer removed his handgun from his hip and stepped into the morning sun.

The SUV's occupant followed suit, cautiously opening his door. "Mercer, do you have it?"

"That depends." Mercer studied every aspect of the SUV and what little he could see of the man over the truck's roof. "Is Sarina safe?"

"See for yourself." The boot of the SUV opened, sending the rear windshield skyward.

"Bugger." Mercer would have to expose himself and enter the kill box — the open area between his vehicle and the rear of the SUV. There was no cover and no excuse not to comply.

Staying close to the car for as long as possible, Mercer gave a wide berth to the SUV while his eyes continuously swept the area. He had to maintain a visual on the SUV's driver, but he didn't want to encounter any other surprises either. The man laughed and strode to the rear of the SUV, coming to stand a few meters from Mercer. He was dressed in a suit with large aviator sunglasses to hide his face, and he spoke through a voice modulator to further disguise his identity.

"Open your jacket," the kidnapper instructed. Mercer obliged, holding one side open with his free hand. "Are you wired?"

"No."

"But you are armed." The man nodded at the gun in Mercer's hand. "Is this how you typically arrive at an exchange?"

"You didn't dictate those terms." Mercer forced his voice to remain neutral. However, he holstered his gun and focused on the vehicle before him. From his current angle, he could see a woman bound and gagged inside the trunk. "Is she alive?" A mess of blonde hair obscured her face, and she wasn't moving.

"I gave her a sedative. Her fate is yet to be determined." The kidnapper smirked. "The rest depends on you. I held up my end. It's time you show me the item."

"It's inside my jacket pocket." Mercer reached inside and removed the device. He kept his eyes trained on Sarina, watching for the slightest movement to indicate she was breathing. Unfortunately, escaping with an unconscious woman would be difficult given the SUV and the distance between the two vehicles.

"Excellent," the man held out his hand, and Mercer caught sight of a nine millimeter in a shoulder holster, "I'll take that."

"No." Mercer kept his grip firm and stood his ground. "This is unacceptable. She's not in any condition to travel. How do I know you didn't poison her?"

"You don't." The words turned cold and authoritarian. "Hand over the protocols, or I'll kill her." The man removed the gun and pointed it at her skull.

Without hesitating, Mercer removed his Sig and trained it on the kidnapper. "I'd reconsider."

"What's to stop me from shooting her, shooting you, and taking that phone from you?"

"Are you sure this is what you want?" Mercer asked. "It could be nothing more than a bloody cellular phone. Why don't you pull the trigger and find out?"

The man considered it for an agonizing moment. "Show me the protocols. Now. Or I start shooting."

Mercer watched him for a moment, believing Alpha would follow through on the threat. "They're encrypted. I'll give you the device, and you let me walk away with Sarina. Once we're clear, I'll give you the password to break the encryption. If you harm her, you'll never crack the code. If you kill me, you get nothing."

"Bravo. You think you've come up with a foolproof plan." He holstered his gun and held out his hand. "The device." Mercer handed it over, and the man stepped back, gesturing toward his captive. "Take her."

Having to carry Sarina would leave the two of them defenseless, but Alpha had given him no choice. Scooping Sarina into his arms, Mercer carried her toward the car. He slung her over his shoulder and opened the passenger's side door, laying the seat flat to safeguard her against gunfire. Then he shut the door, turning around to find Alpha's gun trained on him.

"What's the password?" the man asked. The phone was locked, so Mercer rattled off the four digit code that would allow the kidnapper to open the downloaded file. After inputting the code, the man scowled. "Now, how do I break the encryption?"

"You'll need a computer," Mercer said, hoping to provide enough of a distraction to neutralize Alpha or get into the car and drive away.

"It's a shame you aren't as smart as you think." The man signaled someone, but Mercer couldn't afford to turn. He needed an immediate escape route. "Your weapon and your backup," the man barked, but Mercer didn't move, "I want them now." He smiled. "And don't try anything or Sarina's dead."

"I don't think so," Mercer said, calculating his options. He pulled his gun, firing on Alpha. The kidnapper dove behind the SUV, and Mercer slid across the hood of the car. He opened the door, but before he could get inside, something shot through him, reducing him to a heap on the pavement.

THIRTY

The taste of blood was unpleasant, and Mercer spit on the man who had just punched him. He'd woken up in worse situations, but for some reason, none of them came to mind. Working his jaw, Mercer studied his surroundings. The room was dimly lit with a concrete floor, painted cinderblock walls, and a damp mustiness to the air. A single staircase stood in the far corner of the room. It was unfinished with slat stairs made of wood and metal. Mercer wagered he was in a basement, but frankly, he could be anywhere in the world.

The man that had thrown the punch stepped back and removed his jacket. He wore a typical dark colored suit, reminiscent of a bodyguard. Stretching his arms and back, he looked down at the saliva and blood on his otherwise perfectly polished dress shoe.

"Animal," he mumbled in a deeply accented voice. He stared at Mercer. "Where are the protocols?"

Mercer laughed, an amused, sardonic sound that caused the hitter to pause before delivering another blow. "You should have killed me."

"Don't worry, friend, that will happen soon

enough." The hitter's accent was strong and discernible. Despite the fact he wore a mask over his face, his pale blue eyes and blond hair were easily noticeable.

Mercer focused on the indicators, deciding the man was of Scandinavian descent. Filing that thought away in case it proved useful later on, Mercer knew the man who he'd spoken to at the exchange was not the same one currently using his face as a punching bag.

"Your boss needs me alive," Mercer said. "Shall you fetch him so we may continue the negotiation?"

The man hit Mercer again, hard enough that Mercer's entire body shifted to the right, pulling against the manacles that bound him to a support pillar in the center of the room. However, the assault didn't stop. The hitter shifted his stance and style, pummeling Mercer's torso utilizing the training and fighting techniques of the Jægerkorpset, the Danish equivalent of the SAS. Eventually, Mercer's stubbornness proved to be no match for the physical abuse, and he sagged, dropping to his knees while the metal of the restraints scraped loudly against the pillar.

The Dane snorted. "You are nothing like your reputation."

Mercer lifted his face to stare at the man. "I want to speak to Alpha."

"Omega," the familiar computer-modulated voice said from somewhere behind Mercer, "you're dismissed."

The Dane nodded, marching to the stairs and disappearing from sight. Mercer concentrated on the sound of locks being turned and the slam of the door before he struggled to maneuver around to face the kidnapper. The sudden movement made him dizzy, and he took a moment to assess his injuries.

Somehow, by being woken so violently, he'd forgotten how he arrived in this predicament.

"Where's Sarina?" Mercer rasped.

"You needn't worry about her." Alpha stepped around the pillar. "You should be more concerned about your own well-being."

"You can't break the encryption."

"I already have."

"Then kill me." Mercer stared at the man who still wore dark aviator glasses, even in the dim light. Hoisting himself to his feet, Mercer stood, noting the suit and the scent of expensive cologne. He narrowed his eyes. The wheels were turning, but he couldn't make sense of these observations. "Do it."

"Don't think I won't." But it was a hollow threat, and both men knew it. Instead, Alpha circled around, a decent technique that obscured him from view seventy percent of the time. "I've seen the news. Your men are in custody. You are alone. This doesn't need to be unpleasant."

"Then hold up your end of the agreement." Sarina might be dead, or she could be unconscious outside the diner. There was no way of knowing, but placing too much emphasis on her safety would lead Alpha to use her as a way to break Mercer. On the plus side, Mercer had no idea how to break the encryption, and even if he could, the protocols weren't contained on the cell phone. "Release us, and I'll give you the information," he bluffed.

"Stop lying," Alpha screamed, his real voice overpowering the modulator. He removed the cell phone from his pocket and held it in front of Mercer's face. "This is shit. Where are the protocols?" He threw the cell phone against the wall. The glass cracked, and the battery and exterior case broke free. "I am not a fool. You stole the protocols, but you didn't bring them to the exchange. Where are they?"

"Release Sarina."

Alpha disappeared from sight, and a terrified whimper sounded from the back of the room. Mercer pulled against the chains, helplessly watching Alpha drag a dazed and semiconscious Sarina Porter into the center of the room by her hair. Alpha removed the gun from his hip and held it against her skull. "Answer me."

"It's game over if you kill her." Mercer's heart beat like a drum, but he held firm, forcing the calm exterior to remain in place.

"Where is it?" Alpha asked again, the desperation becoming more apparent by the second.

"Let her go."

"Omega will break you. It's just a matter of time. But this should certainly be faster." Alpha flipped the safety off and cocked the gun. "You have five seconds."

"She goes free. That's the only way." Mercer hoped he could reason with the kidnapper, but Alpha continued to count down.

"One." Alpha pulled the trigger. Mercer didn't breathe. The gun clicked ineffectually, and Alpha smiled. "She matters to you. Next time, this will be loaded. I'm not playing a game. Consider your options, and when I return, I expect to know the location of the protocols. You went inside Trila and stole them. Now, I want them."

Alpha strode across the room and up the stairs. The door slammed shut, and Mercer sunk to his knees, his bound arms keeping him from falling face first to the floor. His heart raced, and he saw static bursts behind his eyelids.

"Sarina." He gasped at the sudden pain that he hadn't felt until now. "Mrs. Porter," he tried again. "Bloody hell."

Uncomfortably shifting off his knees, so he could lean back against the pillar, he knew he had a few broken ribs which were making it difficult to breathe. His shoulder was sore due to the bindings, and there was a pain in the back of his neck that burned and stung. They either drugged or tasered him before he could get inside the car. More than likely, Omega, the Dane, had been at the exchange, but Mercer missed him due to his preoccupation with rescuing Sarina. Dammit, Donovan had been right. He needed backup support at the meet.

"Sarina," Mercer hissed louder this time, "look at me."

The woman groaned, barely stirring from her spot in the center of the room.

"Sarina," Mercer shifted his gaze to the staircase, "open your eyes." She was three meters away, perhaps less, but it could have been three hundred for all the good that did either of them. He saw a bloody bandage covering her left hand, and he swallowed, blaming that monster for permanently maiming her. "Sarina."

Her eyes fluttered, and she looked at him. No fear or hope registered on her face. She was too dazed to process what she was seeing. Instead, she stared with dead eyes at him. Then she blinked in and out of wakefulness for a time. Finally, she cleared her throat and gathered her bearings. "Who are you?"

"Julian Mercer. Your husband hired me to negotiate your release."

She sat up. Her eyes began to focus, and she took in Julian's condition. "This is how you negotiate?"

"Not usually."

She squinted, rubbing her temples. "You can't help me. You can't even help yourself." Sniffling, she rubbed her nose with the back of her bandaged hand, turning away from the bloodstains. "This was because of you." She held up her hand. "Proof of life, that's what the man called it. They had to provide proof of life." Her chin quivered, but she fought the tears away. "You sick son of a bitch."

"That was unintended. Harming you was prohibited. Alpha's behavior is erratic. I couldn't predict he'd do that." Mercer glanced at the staircase again, knowing someone would be back soon enough. "Do you know where we are? Who these men are? What they want? Or why they want it?"

"They took me from my home. I've been kept in this dungeon for," she shrugged, "I don't even know how long. When they come down here, it's never good. Occasionally, they leave a tray of food or empty the bucket," she shut her eyes, "but mostly, they terrorize me. They want to know about my husband's job and our house." She shrugged again. "I don't know anything about them."

Mercer nodded. Donovan should have been tracking the cell phone. It was destroyed now, but it had been operational for quite some time. Surely, help was on the way. It was just a matter of time. Feeling the restraints with his fingertips, Mercer knew the chains were a thick iron that would require bolt cutters to remove. They had to be attached by a lock, but it was out of his reach.

"Can you move?" Mercer asked, and Sarina nodded. "Okay, I'll get you out of here, but first, I need your help."

THIRTY-ONE

"Julian," Sarina said, her voice a soft lilt, "what do they want?"

"It doesn't matter."

Mercer opened his palm, pressing his back against the pillar to gain as much give as possible. She placed the cold metal lock in his hand, and he ran his fingers over the surface, realizing it was a simple combination lock. The dial spun easily.

"It does," she insisted. "I want to know."

"Computer security protocols." Mercer turned the dial again and concentrated on identifying the slightest hitch. Two full revolutions later, he stopped the dial. "What number?"

"Thirty-seven."

He turned the dial back the other way, but he couldn't tell if any of the tumblers opened. After resetting the dial and starting over a dozen times, he dropped the lock and shut his eyes. This would be easier if he could see what he was doing.

"What do the bindings look like?" he asked.

"Old rusted chains, double looped around your wrists and then around the pillar, secured by the lock." Sarina licked her dry lips and repositioned herself so they were facing one another. She opened her mouth to say something but changed her mind.

He searched her face for a second, noting the grime that covered her skin. At least it wasn't blood. "Any idea where we are?" he asked.

"No. They knocked me out, and I woke up here."

"How many men?"

"Three. They always wear masks, but they go by different names. Alpha, Omega, and Zed." She sat closer to him, her voice practically a whisper. "These men took me because they want a computer program?"

"Yes."

"This is because of Logan?"

"Indirectly." Mercer turned to gauge her expression, but she was staring across the room at the broken phone. "He loves you. He'll do anything to get you back safely." It was possible Alpha had them under surveillance, so Mercer weighed his words carefully.

"Then why are we trapped in this godforsaken cellar? Why didn't he call the police?"

"Because the authorities do not understand the intricacies of ransom negotiations. Their job is to arrest criminals. That's why I was called instead."

"And what do you do besides make things worse?"

"Madam, my priority is your well-being."

"Sorry, if I have trouble believing that." She scooted farther away, settling onto a threadbare blanket that covered a few of the cold tiles. "They took my finger because of you."

"I'm sorry."

"Why won't you just give them what they want so I

can go home?"

"Once I do, they'll kill us. However, if Alpha agrees to release you, I'll give him the information as soon as you're safe." It was the lie Mercer chose. The more he repeated it, the more likely it would be believed.

"So why won't he let me leave?"

"He doesn't want to lose leverage over me."

"I'm his bargaining chip." The realization hit her, and she stifled a sob, wiping her eyes. "Damned if you do and damned if you don't."

"Precisely." Mercer reached blindly for the lock, endlessly spinning it in the hopes it would release.

"Logan's in danger," she said after the silence dragged on for too long. "He must have what they want. What if they decide to go after him and take it? Who's going to protect him?"

"He doesn't have it." Distracted by the conversation, Mercer lost his place on the combination lock. "Don't worry. Your husband's safe."

"How can you be sure?"

"I am." Mercer leaned his head back and relaxed his arms, giving his shoulder a reprieve. Donovan should be working on an exit strategy. What was taking so long? "Is there anything useful in this room?"

"I don't know. I haven't found anything." She shook her head. "The stairs are off-limits. As long as I agree to stay away from them, they don't tie me up."

"What about the cell phone?" Mercer nodded toward the destroyed item. "Is there anything salvageable?"

Obediently, Sarina retrieved the pieces and brought them to Mercer. The glass was cracked. The battery was of little use, and the plastic casing was destroyed. The circuitry inside might work, but without housing and the proper wiring to connect the battery, it lacked a power source and ability to transmit any data.

"Put the glass down," Mercer instructed, stomping hard on it until it broke into a few pieces.

"Do you have a plan?"

"No."

Before she could say anything else, the door opened, and she scurried back to the blanket, tucking herself into a ball in the corner of the room. That display sickened him, and he got to his feet, concealing the broken glass beneath his shoe. Alpha descended the staircase, scanning the room for Sarina. She cowered in the corner, so Alpha shifted his focus to Mercer.

After making sure the voice modulator was on, Alpha asked, "Where are the protocols?"

"Up your arse."

Alpha didn't say a word. He had grown tired of the game. They had reached a stalemate. He shifted his gaze to Sarina and removed a pair of handcuffs. He grabbed her by the wrists and clicked one of the cuffs in place.

"Please. Don't. Please," she begged, but Mercer silently watched as the woman was bound to a water pipe that ran along the wall. Alpha backhanded her, and she quieted, pulling her legs to her chest and hiding her face in her knees.

Alpha looked at Mercer, or at least in his direction since he still wore large, darkly tinted glasses that obscured most of his face. But he didn't speak. Whatever was about to happen wouldn't be pleasant. These were intimidation tactics meant to instill fear and aid in breaking a man.

A few minutes later, the Dane came down the stairs with a large bucket. He took off his jacket and rolled his sleeves up to his elbows. He put the bucket down and circled Mercer.

"A chair would make this easier," the Dane said. "You are familiar with interrogation techniques. Don't you agree it's easier when your captive is bound to a chair?"

"Looking for pointers?" Mercer asked.

"The SAS are all the same. You think you're the best, that you invented torture. Ha."

Without warning, the Dane lifted the bucket, showering Mercer in ice and water. Immediately, the frigid water soaked through Mercer's clothes, causing him to shiver uncontrollably. Before he could even blink, the man hit him across the face. The ice sent Mercer's nerve endings into hyperdrive, exaggerating the pain. First, it was white-hot from the shock, followed by a sharp stinging. Mercer involuntarily gasped, and the Dane smirked. He ripped Mercer's shirt open and picked up a blackjack, slapping him hard against his already bruised ribs. Mercer sunk to the floor. He shivered but ground his teeth to keep them from chattering.

"You can end this," the Dane said.

Mercer swallowed. "Afghanistan."

"What?"

"Danish special forces, maybe Jægerkorpset." Mercer lifted himself off the ground. "Pathetic," he spat. "You should know how to conduct a proper rendition, soldier."

Briefly, Omega's eyes widened in surprise. Then he snarled and delivered a right hook that knocked Mercer back to the ground. The restraints clanged against the pillar, and Julian knew he couldn't take much more before blacking out. Unfortunately, that was the best way to stop an interrogation and buy some time.

"Stop," Alpha commanded, but Omega was on a rampage. "I said stop."

Alpha strode across the room, but before he could pull the other man away, the Dane delivered a kick that sent Mercer spiraling back into the darkness. After an indeterminate amount of time, more ice water was poured over him, and Mercer sputtered awake, coughing as the frigid water burned his throat and lungs. On the bright side, Alpha hadn't resorted to waterboarding, yet.

"You will die if you don't tell me where the protocols are. Do you understand that?" Alpha asked.

Mercer stared up at him. He wasn't sure if he could even speak. His jaw was swollen and sore. He fixed Alpha with a death stare, wanting to rip those stupid glasses off his face and strangle him until the light left his eyes.

"Fine," Alpha turned to the Dane, "bring me the girl."

THIRTY-TWO

The shivering continued to worsen, so Mercer stopped fighting against it. It was the cold. There was nothing he could do about it, so he had to accept it. Instead, he concentrated his efforts on getting off the ground. With his arms still bound behind him, it was a struggle to get upright on shaky limbs, but he was determined.

Meanwhile, the Dane unhooked Sarina's handcuffs and dragged her toward Alpha. She fought against him, but he had a tight hold on her wrists. She let out a bloodcurdling scream, giving Julian the incentive he needed to get his feet underneath him.

"Alpha," Mercer's breath came in shallow gasps, "don't do this."

"Too late." Alpha didn't even bother to turn around. He nodded to the Dane, who threw Sarina to the ground. "On your knees."

Julian tugged against the restraints, but he couldn't break free of the metal. They scraped and clanged against the pillar. He lifted his arms higher behind his back, leaning forward and pressing his heels into the pillar, but the chains wouldn't give.

"On your knees, bitch," Alpha repeated, grabbing Sarina by the hair and forcing her to comply. "Face the wall."

"Sir?" The Dane sounded worried, but Alpha waved him off. The Dane stepped backward, focused on what was about to happen.

Mercer pushed harder, lifting his arms higher and using both heels against the pillar. Suspending himself in the air with his weight held by the chains and the angle of his body, Julian walked backward up the pillar, alternating bracing his feet against the pillar and moving his arms higher. Alpha cocked the gun and pressed the barrel against the back of Sarina's head. She cried and begged for her life, and Mercer knew he had to act. He had one chance to make this work, and he had to do it now.

Pulling his arms forward, he shifted his weight and kicked his legs out, managing to get his calves around the Dane's neck before he slid down the pillar. The momentum and surprise knocked the Dane off balance, and Mercer maneuvered into a better position to break the Dane's neck. The man choked, and his arms flailed. The Dane threw himself against the pillar beneath Mercer, and the metal made a loud clang. Alpha turned at the commotion.

"Drop the gun, or I'll snap your man's neck," Mercer's said, his voice strained, but he continued to hold tight. "Drop it."

"Or you'll kill him?" Alpha smiled. "You're chained up. How do you think this is going to end?" He made a tsk sound. "You arrogant little prick. You actually think I give a shit about him?" Without warning, Alpha fired on the Dane, shooting him in the chest. The man immediately went still. Blood blossomed on his white dress shirt, and he and Julian crashed to the floor in a heap. "Now what are you going to do?" Alpha asked.

Mercer fell to the side, a tangle of limbs and chains surrounded him on the icy wet floor. He glanced at the Dane, who had died instantly. Mercer didn't speak. Since Alpha was willing to kill his own man, he'd have no qualms about killing Sarina and Julian.

Sarina froze at the sound of the gunshot, but now she turned around, a silent scream etched on her face. Mercer prayed she wouldn't make a peep, but all too soon the shock wore off and her scream was no longer silent. Alpha hit her with the butt of his gun, knocking her unconscious.

"This is a fine mess you've caused." Alpha looked at the Dane's body and then Sarina. He aimed at Mercer and pulled the trigger. The gun clicked, but no bullet fired. He continued to pull the trigger until what would have been a full magazine was expended. Then he holstered his weapon. "Looks like I just had the one bullet." He smiled, a wicked dark look, and lifted the unconscious Sarina off the floor and took her up the stairs. The door slammed shut, rattling the walls and Mercer's already shivering body.

Julian took a moment to regroup. The scene that just played out was a nightmare. Negotiations weren't supposed to devolve into this. Swallowing, he kicked the Dane's body away, gaining a few centimeters of space between him and the deceased. Frankly, mourning another human being would have been the normal thing to do, but Mercer intended to kill the man the first chance he got. So he lacked remorse.

"Bastard," Mercer cursed. Every muscle in his body had tightened due to the cold, and from the strain of holding himself on the pillar, he could barely lift himself off the ground. Breathing was difficult, and he was positive the pain in his side must be excruciating by now. However, he couldn't feel it. That was the plus side of shock.

Lying on his side, he leaned his back against the pillar, feeling an odd shift in the restraints. At first, he thought it was the water playing a trick on him, but he shifted his left arm forward and noticed substantially more give. Sliding face first onto the ground, Mercer became aware something had happened to the chain. He turned his head to the side, hoping to find a way to free himself.

One of the rusted links had snapped under the pressure of his weight and the force of the fall. It weakened the double loop, turning it into a single loop. Carefully, Mercer sat up, reaching behind to feel the broken link and follow it through. While his practically numb fingers worked their magic to find the end of the chain and undo the bindings, he focused on the staircase. His eyes stayed trained on the door, and his ears listened for footfalls and the clanging of locks.

Alpha had taken Sarina, and Mercer could only imagine what sadistic things the cold-blooded killer had in store for her. Mercer had to free himself and get out of this basement before it was too late. Coming to the end of the long chain, Mercer pulled it forward to examine it. The broken link was in the center, making it difficult to wind through the rest. Luckily, he now had enough give to turn and face his bindings.

It took less than two minutes to free one wrist, and as soon as that feat was accomplished, the rest of the chain fell away. Mercer cautioned a look at the door then searched the Dane for anything of use. Inside the man's pocket, Mercer found a cell phone. Tucking the item away, Mercer continued the search but couldn't find any weapons. He peeled the mask off the dead man and studied his facial features. In the event he made it out of this mess, an identification might be useful.

The blackjack remained on the floor, along with one long sharp piece of glass from Mercer's destroyed cell phone. Ripping the bottom of the Dane's shirt, Mercer wound the cloth around the wider end of the glass, making a shiv. Then he crept toward the stairs. Sarina was just beyond that door, and Mercer had to find some way to get to her.

He went up the stairs with catlike stealth, counting each step in his head. Eight stairs. At the top of the steps was a door, and Mercer reached for the knob with his left hand. He held the shiv in his right and tried to turn the knob. It gave a centimeter in either direction, but the lock held tight. There were no keyholes or obvious means of getting the door to open from the inside.

Bollocks, he thought. Forcing the door open with brute strength wasn't feasible since it appeared to be reinforced steel, not to mention, loud. There had to be another way out. Mercer crept down the steps and searched the entire room. When he found nothing of use, he removed the cell phone he'd confiscated and maneuvered around the room in the hopes of securing a signal.

In the far corner, beneath the staircase, he had spotty service. A single bar kept blinking in and out, unable to support a phone call. Quickly, Mercer sent a coded text to Donovan's number, watching the "sending" message continue to spin on the screen.

"Come on," he said.

Before the message sent, he heard the sound of the latch from above. Leaving the phone beneath the stairs, Mercer dashed across the room, returning to his prior position on the floor. He put his hands behind his back, hoping whoever was about to enter wouldn't notice anything amiss. He held the shiv firmly. If Alpha came close enough, Mercer would cut his throat. It was time he ended this mission.

THIRTY-THREE

"What have you done with her?" Mercer asked.

"Didn't you mention something about not caring about her life any more than you care about the protocols?" Alpha rubbed his thumb across his lower lip and smirked. "Isn't this just a job?"

"It was." Mercer's eyes followed every movement and mannerism.

"Then how come your job performance continues to be disappointing?" Alpha asked. "You knew the rules. You were to bring the item to the exchange. Instead, you gave me shit and broke our agreement. I've been more than fair in our dealings. It is you who has lied repeatedly and botched the negotiation. I expected more from a professional with your reputation." Alpha looked down at his dead associate. "Needless to say, I've grown tired of this. Tell me where you hid the stolen protocols and I'll consider letting you live."

"No."

"Fine, I'll start over. Plenty of people work at Trila.

Someone will comply with my demands." Alpha cocked his head to the side. "After we're done, perhaps I'll pay a visit to Logan Porter or send him a special delivery. Since he wants his wife back, I'll let him piece her back together."

Mercer stood, keeping his arms behind his back. It was an arrogant act of defiance Alpha wouldn't tolerate. The kidnapper scoffed, practically sighing in exasperation over Mercer's continued insolence.

"Give up like the weak, pathetic pisser you are." Alpha stepped over the Dane's body. He grabbed Mercer's shoulders and moved to knee him, but Mercer sidestepped and punched him in the gut. Gripping the shiv, Mercer slashed at Alpha's throat. But the kidnapper deflected, and the blade sliced through Alpha's bicep instead.

Mercer shifted into a fighting stance, using the shiv as a dagger to stab in Alpha's direction, but the kidnapper was fast on his feet. He moved out of striking range and glanced at his bleeding arm.

"You'll pay for that," Alpha said.

Mercer stepped closer, keeping his fists up in a defensive position. Changing his grip on the shiv, Mercer lunged forward with a slashing motion aimed at Alpha's throat. With amazing reflexes, Alpha narrowly avoided the blade as it skimmed across the surface of his neck, destroying the voice modulator and drawing the slightest bit of blood. Enraged, Alpha followed up with a high kick to Mercer's sternum that sent him stumbling backward.

Without hesitating, Alpha removed the gun from his hip and fired. Julian went down, no longer having the strength to fight. His vision fogged, and he blinked. Blood. One shot, left side, near the ribs. His mind ran through the information even though he couldn't comprehend it. How could he let this piece of shit win? Mercer looked up to see Alpha standing over him, gloating.

"The protocols," Alpha said, "where are they?"

"Fuck. You."

*   *   *

Julian wasn't sure if he was dead or dreaming. It didn't matter. He was with her. Michelle, his wife, was lying against his chest. He had told her time and time again not to cuddle against him for fear he'd have a nightmare and accidentally hurt her in his sleep, but tonight, like most nights, she did what she wanted. He sighed, feeling a sharp pinch, but it was of little consequence. Having her in his arms was a comfort, and he relished the warmth of her body against his freezing cold skin. He'd missed this. He missed her.

"Wake up," a woman's voice insisted. "Please."

The voice didn't belong to Michelle, and Mercer looked down, realizing the woman pressed against his side wasn't his wife. He startled awake, pushing her away. He'd slept with other women since his wife's passing, but none of them had ever spent the night and he'd never fallen asleep with any of them. Nothing made any sense. Then the pain in his side grew worse, and he suddenly remembered everything that happened.

"Sarina?" he asked, unsure of this bizarre reality.

"Shit, I thought you had stopped bleeding." She pressed harder against his side, and he bit back a scream, swearing instead.

"Stop." He pried her hands off of him and looked down at his torso. "Is there an exit wound?" he asked.

"You're bleeding from the side too," she said. "I don't know if..."

"Yes," Mercer said, "that's what I needed to know."

He undid his belt, tugging it free from the loops. Removing his soaking wet shirt, he tried to wring out as much moisture as he could before pressing it firmly into the bullet wound. Hissing, he tried to secure the belt around it, but after his second failed attempt, Sarina took over, fastening it around his makeshift bandages.

"You need help." She gave him a tight smile. "We need help."

"Where's Alpha?" Mercer asked.

"I don't know." She looked away. "I woke up next to you. I don't know when they'll be back." She shifted her gaze to the puddle of blood and water near the center pillar. "I can't believe he shot his own guy."

"Fancy that." Mercer lifted his head and leaned against the wall. "One less target to eliminate."

"How can you seriously act so...indifferent, especially at a time like this?"

"What would you prefer?"

"Someone with human emotions." She was scared, but wasting time to coddle her wouldn't be a productive use of Alpha's absence.

"Underneath the stairs is a cell phone. Tell me if the message sent."

Her face brightened in actual hope, and she bolted across the room. "Message sent," she read from the screen. "Who did you text? Are the cops coming? When will they get here?"

Mercer held up his palm to silence the barrage of questions. He feared even if the message sent, it hadn't been received. Either that or wherever they were being held wasn't accessible. Donovan would come for them if he could.

"My team will do their best," Mercer said when she continued to stare at him. He assessed her appearance. The swollen cheek and bloody lip were nothing compared to the large welt and bruise at her temple. "Are you okay?"

Sarina practically laughed at the same time tears welled in her eyes. "You really want to ask that question now?"

Mercer started to shrug, wincing at the pain the movement caused. However, it reminded him of Brie Dawson. He still wasn't positive how Alpha had happened across Sarina's private e-mail account. "Distract me," Mercer said.

"What?"

"Had you not been taken, what were you doing that afternoon?" Mercer asked.

"I don't know." She blinked a few times. "Working, I guess." She exhaled. "It seems like a lifetime ago, or it was someone else's life. Do you think," she looked at the phone and Mercer's pale visage, "we'll actually live through this?"

"I made a promise." He was growing tired from the blood loss. "And I intend to keep it."

"How?"

He tried to think, but he kept losing his train of thought. She shook his shoulder, and he opened his eyes, realizing he had slipped out of consciousness. He blinked and sat up a little straighter, but it was a losing battle. He shivered, and she insisted on sharing her body heat with him. Eventually, he gave up the fight to keep her away when she nestled next to him.

"Don't leave me here alone," Sarina begged. "I don't know what will happen when Alpha comes back."

"He won't kill you," Mercer said. "He hasn't yet."

She looked up at him. "I guess he won't until he gets that stupid computer thing." She paused, watching Mercer drift in and out of wakefulness. "Are you sure he won't find it on his own? Where did you hide the protocols? Did you give them to your team for safe keeping?"

"No. He can't get them. No one can."

THIRTY-FOUR

The bang of the door startled Mercer and Sarina awake. Julian blinked, pushing himself up in order to use his body as a shield. He placed himself between Sarina and the three men who came down the stairs in full tactical gear. His mind screamed raid, but that made no sense. He narrowed his eyes, suspecting this was another ploy Alpha was using to terrorize and break them.

"Jules," one of the men said, lifting the mask from his face, "it's me."

"What the bloody hell took you so long?" Mercer had never been happier to see Donovan.

"You have no idea." Donovan looked at the woman behind him. "Sarina?" he asked. She nodded, and Donovan gave the two men waiting on the stairs a thumbs up. "Let's bring them home, boys."

The other two men never spoke, but they each took one of Mercer's arms around their shoulders and supported his weight. Practically carrying him, they went up the stairs, slowing at the door. One of them released Mercer and checked the hallway. He made a few hand signals, and they headed into the corridor. Sarina followed close behind, and Donovan took up the rear.

Fluorescent lights hung from the ceiling, but the grey walls and floor were indicative of a garage or basement. Mercer squinted, wrapping his mind around their location. Clearly, Alpha had been keeping his hostages in a subbasement. They rounded a corner and made a beeline for another set of stairs. This staircase was much wider and had ten steps instead of eight. At the top of the steps, they stopped.

"Put this on." Donovan handed Mercer a jacket. "If anyone gets a look at you, we may never get out of here."

"I need a gun," Mercer said, expecting to encounter armed combat.

"No, you don't." Donovan glanced at Sarina, but he didn't have anything to offer her. "Stay close. We'll go quietly."

"Agreed," Julian replied.

He struggled to put the jacket on while the two men removed most of their tactical gear. Then the men resumed their positions on either side of Mercer and walked into a brightly lit hallway. At first glance, it looked like an office building, perhaps for a prestigious law firm, but security was tight. The men wore dark suits, carried assault rifles, and had curlicue earpieces running down the backs of their collars. The signs in the hallway weren't in English.

The two men led the way down a side hallway and into a closed office. They shut the door and released Mercer. One took a position near the door, and the other went to the wall, entering a code into the security system. Mercer made his way across the room to the windows at the side. He looked out into the darkness. It was night or early morning.

"Three minutes," the man said.

"Thank you," Donovan replied. "Now we are even, comrade." The man nodded, crossing the room and opening the window next to Mercer. "Ladies first." Donovan offered a hand to help Sarina through the window.

She looked utterly bewildered, but Mercer nodded. She slid one leg out then ducked beneath the pane of glass and brought her other leg out. Donovan stepped through and waited for Mercer to join them. Once outside, he shouldered most of Mercer's weight, and they headed to the left.

"Patrols come through every five minutes. We have less than two until we're spotted," Donovan explained, bringing them to the rear edge of the property. "Johann reset the system. It'll be live in three minutes." Donovan gave the metal fence a wary look and placed his hand against it. "It's off." He glanced at the numerous security cameras posted around the property which were also temporarily disabled. "Up and over, madam."

Mercer leaned against the fence, and Donovan lifted Sarina up until she gripped the top of the iron girders. He gave her a boost, and she swung her leg over, falling to the ground on the other side.

"Ouch," she hissed.

"Quiet," Mercer whispered. He looked at the fence and the brick wall next to it.

"Your turn, commander," Donovan said, grinning slightly.

"Go."

"Sir, with all due respect, this is my rescue mission. Now move your arse." Donovan knelt down, making a makeshift step with his palms.

Knowing they didn't have time to argue, Mercer

stepped off Donovan and scaled the fence in a single motion that sent white-hot pain through his body. He landed on his back on the other side, biting his lip to keep from howling in agony. Donovan dropped down next to him, knowing they had less than a minute to get as far from the property as possible. The car was parked a block away, and he ducked underneath Mercer's arm, pulling him off the ground and dragging him down the street.

"You need medical attention," Donovan said, keeping an eye trained on Sarina. "You both do."

"No. Too many unknowns," Mercer said. "Is Porter secure?"

"Affirmative. I moved him to another location."

"Bastian and Hans?"

"In custody."

"What day is it?" Mercer asked, attempting to remain alert and regain control of the situation.

"Friday. You've been gone eighteen hours," Donovan said. "And from the looks of you, that was eighteen hours too many." He opened the car door, putting Julian in the back. Then he opened the passenger's side for Sarina. "I'm sorry it took us so long." He offered a polite smile. "Let's get you checked out and then we'll have you back with your husband in no time."

Mercer fought to stay awake, but he couldn't muster the will now that they were relatively safe. He blinked in and out, aware that they were in a back room of what smelled like an animal hospital. Sarina was seated in a chair near him, and a man in a lab coat was examining her hand. She protested, loudly arguing and pulling away from the man.

"Birds," Donovan muttered, "they are a fickle lot." He shook his head. "She's been through much worse, and she's acting like *this* is torture." He helped Mercer onto the operating table and assessed the damage. As a soldier, he had field medicine training, but unless it was absolutely necessary, it was better to leave surgery to the professionals.

"We need to go to ground and figure out our next move. Alpha's out there. He's determined to get the ransom," Mercer said.

Donovan unlatched the belt and removed the bloodied cloth from Mercer's torso. He poured a disinfectant over the wounds, and Mercer groaned. Reaching for the bottle of bourbon next to the surgical implements, Mercer took a swig.

"How soon until I'm mobile?" Mercer asked.

"We'll let the doctor answer that question." Donovan took the bottle from Mercer and swallowed a shot. "If I patch you up, it won't be pretty."

"I don't care. We don't have time for this."

"It's fine. We'll handle it," Donovan insisted. "Let's just get you stitched up."

After determining Sarina would survive, the vet turned his focus on Mercer. It was a clean shot that missed his vital organs. The projectile had glanced off his already broken ribs and exited to the side. His lung partially collapsed from the trauma, but after a brief and painful procedure, he was breathing normally again. The doctor hooked a few bags of antibiotics, painkillers, and fluids to the intravenous and went to work cleaning and cauterizing the wound.

Four hours later, Mercer was bandaged and able to leave. Donovan paid the man with a wad of cash, taking the prescription bottles and putting them in his pocket.

"We were never here," Donovan said, and the man nodded.

They climbed back inside the car, and Donovan cautiously checked their surroundings before shifting into drive.

"Who are you people?" Sarina asked. It was one of the first times she had spoken to Donovan, and from the look on her face, she might have been more frightened of Mercer's teammate than she was of Alpha. "What the hell is this?"

"We're security specialists, and until further notice, we're staying under the radar," Donovan said. "It's for your protection."

"You think Alpha will be back?" The realization caused her to panic, and she began to hyperventilate. "Julian," she turned around to look at Mercer, "what do we do?"

"Yes, Julian," Donovan said, eyeing the commander through the rearview mirror, "do tell."

Mercer closed his eyes, trusting Donovan to handle things. Right now, he wanted nothing more than to fall into the drug-induced haze and give his body and mind a chance to recover. The last eighteen hours had been hell, and it needed to be properly compartmentalized, or else it'd fester. He needed a brief reprieve to see things clearly. Something was bubbling beneath the surface concerning Alpha and the ransom demand, but at the moment, Julian couldn't think straight. All he knew was something didn't feel right.

THIRTY-FIVE

"Mr. Mercer?" Logan took two steps toward Mercer before he realized Sarina was behind him. "Oh my god. Sarina. Baby."

"No thanks necessary." Donovan gave the hallway a final look before closing the hotel door. It was the second hotel they'd checked into since taking this job. "Has anyone been here?"

When no answer was forthcoming, Mercer turned to see Logan with Sarina in his arms. Tears, hugs, and kisses abounded. Whispered "I love you"s and "are you okay"s were uttered throughout the affectionate display.

Julian cleared his throat, but the reunited couple paid him no heed. "Are you sure we're secure?"

"We're shorthanded. Being in public with already established security measures is our safest bet," Donovan said. "I've tapped into the hotel's camera feed."

Mercer spotted the hole in the wall and the wires that had been spliced and reattached. "Bastian would have hacked their system."

"This works just as well."

Mercer sighed. "We need the rest of our team. With Alpha on the loose, we can't leave them exposed."

"I agree." Donovan handed Mercer a business card. "I found a solicitor. She's supposedly one of the best, but I haven't contacted her yet."

"That will take too long."

"I spent the night calling in favors in order to free your arse from an embassy bomb shelter. We don't have the manpower or resources to break them out of the local prison," Donovan said.

"Trila has the resources. We need to convince them to drop the charges and call off their dogs." Mercer looked at Logan Porter who hadn't moved from the spot near the doorway. "We have to present Trila International with something substantial."

"What do you have in mind?"

"Let's give them Alpha." Mercer inhaled, testing his pain threshold. A shooting pain joined the constant dull ache, but it was manageable at the moment. He checked the time. "I need a few hours."

"Of course." Donovan took a seat at the desk. "The bedroom to the left is yours."

"Sarina will need supplies," Mercer added as an afterthought.

"I'll take care of it," Donovan assured. Normally, they would do an immediate debrief and exchange the pertinent information, but since Mercer wanted to rest before getting to work, that was a sign the commander was in rough shape. But Donovan knew better than to inquire about his condition.

"I want an updated dossier on Alpha. Everything we have. And I want specifics about where we were held. Who were those men who assisted in our escape?"

"Former military intelligence that I helped in Bosnia. They're now diplomatic attachés."

"Spies?" Mercer shook his head. "Add it to the file."

"What about your intel?" Donovan asked.

"Sarina can answer your questions." Mercer went past the couple, finally gaining their attention. "You're safe, but this isn't over. Help us."

"Anything," Logan said. "I can't thank you enough." He held out his hand, and they shook.

"You kept your word," Sarina whispered. She pressed her lips together to keep from crying.

"Always." Mercer went into the bedroom and shut the door.

Opening the drawers, he found the lockbox, entered the code, and removed a handgun. Alpha had taken his Sig and backup, but the team never traveled light on weaponry. After checking the clip, he placed it on the bedside table and eased onto the mattress. Taking a few more painkillers, he shut his eyes. Eventually, everything became a quiet hum until his thoughts turned to Alpha and the mission.

Balling the covers in his fists while he let the last twenty-four hours wash over him, Mercer realized one thing. Alpha let him live. No one could make a perfect shot and then hit a glancing blow. It wasn't a fluke. It had been intentional. Whatever Alpha planned wasn't over yet.

* * *

"Where are they?" Mercer asked, returning to the main room.

Donovan had opened the pullout and blinked a few times. Sitting up, he rubbed his eyes and pointed to the other bedroom. "Getting reacquainted, I would imagine. I updated the dossier. I don't like how this reads. However, you rescued the damsel in distress. I believe that makes this a job well done."

"We aren't done. Alpha hasn't given up on getting the protocols." Mercer picked up a duffel bag and rummaged through the contents for the RF reader. After performing another quick scan, he was reassured Alpha didn't leave them with any unwanted trackers. "That's why he didn't kill me."

"Maybe you're just lucky."

"Rubbish." Flipping through the dossier, Mercer read the newly updated information.

"I'd wager Alpha's a diplomat or someone with diplomatic immunity. It would explain the lack of information and the targets of his previous kidnappings. Normal people don't have access to royalty, even an unknown duke and duchess. He must travel in those circles."

"Call a duck a duck," Mercer said, getting agitated by the conjecture and uncertainty. "Alpha held us inside the Austrian embassy."

"He must be part of the inner workings. It'd be necessary for him to have access to the basement and the antiquated bomb shelter." Donovan folded the mattress into the sofa and straightened the cushions. "Johann said no one has used the bomb shelter in decades. Initially, it was a secure bunker in case of attack, but they've installed panic rooms and other modern security protections. Until last night, he thought the door to the subbasement had been sealed."

"Why would Johann let you break into his embassy?" Mercer asked.

"It isn't exactly his mother country. Just be thankful I called in a chit on your behalf." Donovan flipped on the television, but there was no mention of Trila, the embassy, or anything related to the kidnapping. "Alpha must know you've escaped. He'll probably realize you had help."

"I'm aware." Mercer sifted through the pile of documents again, but it was old news. Sarina should know more than what Donovan noted. However, she had mostly recounted what had happened after Mercer's arrival. "We've burned most of our disposables. Are we able to receive incoming communications?"

Donovan went into the kitchenette and poured a cup of cold coffee. Picking up a cell phone, he brought it back into the living room. "It'd be bloody ballsy of him to phone after everything that's happened."

"He's desperate, and he believes we're in possession of the object of his desire. He doesn't have a choice."

"Not to state the obvious, but what the bloody hell can be so important? And if this thing is that important, someone needs to do something to keep this psychotic wanker from getting his grubby paws on it."

"Contact the police. Make sure no one with diplomatic ties has been vying for the release of Bastian and Hans. We rescued Sarina. Alpha needs new leverage, and he'll want to make it personal." Julian went to the closed door and banged against it. "Mr. Porter, we leave in fifteen minutes. Don't dawdle."

"Alpha would have to be bloody mad to march into a police station, intent on finding new captives, and he'd have to be out of his mind to think Bastian and Hans couldn't put him down, even unarmed." Donovan studied Mercer's expression for a time. "You're worried."

"He's been trained. So have his associates. I need a list of former Trila employees. We're looking for a

Dane, six foot two, roughly one hundred and eighty pounds, probably a Jaeger, served in Afghanistan, blond, blue eyes, what you'd expect."

"Deceased?" Donovan asked.

"As of yesterday."

"But if he worked for Trila, why wouldn't he have stolen the protocols for Alpha?" Donovan asked.

Logan and Sarina emerged from the room. She smiled at Julian and ducked into the kitchenette while Logan listened to the tail end of the conversation.

"Where are we going?" Logan asked.

"To make amends," Mercer replied.

THIRTY-SIX

"You have two minutes to explain why I shouldn't have you arrested right now," George Browne said.

Instead of meeting inside the Trila building, Mercer phoned ahead, offering to turn himself in if Browne was willing to meet him outside. At first, the head of Trila's security wasn't interested, but after listening to Logan express his heartfelt appreciation that the company hired Mercer on his behalf, the head of security had a change of heart. Either the implied threat of blackmail worked, or Browne was relieved Mercer wasn't attempting to storm the offices again.

"I don't know what business you're in, and I don't care. I do know your latest computer system and the related data are highly valued," Mercer said. "You're not a fool. You are aware my team did not take your property."

"You tried," Browne said. "You entered the building under false pretenses, assaulted members of my staff, destroyed property, and attempted a burglary. The success of which is not relevant in the least."

"It's highly relevant." Mercer hid his scowl. "The man responsible for kidnapping Mrs. Porter remains at large. He is desperate to obtain this information."

"That's true," Logan said. "Sarina's afraid for her life. Mine too. We can't go on like this. You have to do something."

"We offered you help. We provided you security. We hired this pain in the ass," Browne looked pointedly at Mercer, "and you betrayed us."

"This isn't about betrayal," Mercer said. "Trila's security is your problem. The safety of your employees and their families is your problem. You ought to take this threat seriously."

"You're the biggest threat I see," Browne yelled.

"So call the police." Mercer sat back. "Just know, I will talk to every reporter, solicitor, and officer I can find and tell them precisely how Trila *protects* its employees."

"No one will believe you. You'll be discredited. A madman caught red-handed who wants nothing more than to save his own skin," Browne argued.

"What about me?" Logan asked. It was the bravest thing he'd said to date, and Mercer was glad his client was willing to follow through with their plan. "And my wife? Will we be as easily discredited?"

"You helped him. It's coercion. A conspiracy. You're all nuts," Browne insisted.

"Wake up. Blaming my team won't get you any closer to tracking the real threat. You know this. Your people should be aware of this." Mercer watched the truth register in Browne's eyes. The man wanted to pretend the threat was removed, but he knew that wasn't the case. "As a show of good faith, I'm going to share information with you. It is my belief a former employee provided the kidnapper with information about Trila's property and assisted in designing the scheme to obtain it."

"Who?" Browne asked.

Mercer checked his phone. Donovan was working on the profiles, but he wasn't Bastian. Thankfully, Bastian had accessed the Trila employee database prior to his incarceration, so it was a matter of finding the pertinent records for former employees. Right now, Julian needed a name, but he didn't have it yet. Luckily, he had become an expert at stalling.

"Will you agree to drop the charges against my team and reinstate Logan Porter's position at the company?" Mercer asked.

Even though Browne wasn't able to directly hire or fire someone, his position afforded him the ear of those in charge. Porter had been deemed a threat and was facing termination in addition to criminal charges dependent on Browne's assessment.

"Let me think about it," Browne said. He checked his watch. "Stay close. I'll give you an answer in an hour."

Once Browne returned to the Trila building, Mercer sent a text to Donovan, urging him to hurry. This new theory was nothing more than a hunch, but Mercer was counting on it. Unfortunately, they had another ticking clock to worry about.

"So we just wait?" Porter asked. He fidgeted uncomfortably. "Do we have to stay here?"

"Yes."

Porter let out an audible sigh. "Okay."

"She's safe. Donovan won't let anything else happen to her," Mercer said, reading his client's mind.

"Are you sure? I barely had any time with her. What happens if Browne calls the cops on us?"

"He won't."

"How do you know?"

"I do."

"But how?"

"Because he knows we're right."

"He said we were to blame. That we're nuts. That..."

"Quiet." Julian shifted and winced at the sudden stabbing pain in his side. He unbuttoned his shirt to make sure he hadn't bled through the bandage.

"Sorry." Logan turned to face Julian. "I'm sorry for what they did to you." His eyes shifted to the damage to Mercer's face which was nothing compared to what Logan couldn't see. "Sarina told me how you saved her. She said you were nearly killed."

"Silence," Mercer ordered. He didn't need to rehash these things with a civilian. He'd already discussed them with Donovan at length and reached his own internal peace. Softening, he added, "I know the risks. This is not uncommon. It need not concern you."

"Assuming Browne agrees to your terms, my life will be back on track," Porter said, changing the subject. "You brought Sarina home, and you're still willing to put your life on the line for us. How can I repay you?"

"Our fee has been paid by your insurance."

"That's not what I meant. I want to do something for you or Bastian or whoever."

Mercer cocked his head to the side. Logan Porter had been a hindrance, a threat, and an otherwise difficult client. It wasn't uncommon to receive gratitude after a positive recovery was made, but he never pegged Logan as the type to show it.

"If you mean it, tell me about your business associate."

"What associate? You mean Browne?" Logan asked, but Mercer saw the recognition and guilt on Logan's face. "He's the head of security."

"Fine." Mercer leaned back, feeling the weight of the handgun on his hip. "Did Donovan inform you where Sarina was being kept?"

"No." Logan continued to look uneasy.

"In the subbasement of an embassy." Mercer narrowed his eyes. "Would you like to reconsider your previous answer?"

A shiver traveled down Porter's spine, and for a moment, he looked like he might pass out. "I was afraid. He led me to believe he'd kill her." Mercer waited for Porter's mumbling and denial to wear itself out. Eventually, he shook his head. "I don't know his name. He met me at work Thursday, right after Sarina was taken. My head was in a fog. I don't remember much from that day other than the fear." Porter shook off the memory. "The head of sales introduced us, but I didn't catch a name. They acted so chummy, like they knew each other for years. It wasn't until a few days later that I found out they just met. This guy wanted us to engineer a secure system for their mobile devices. With all the hacking of government e-mails and celebrity nudie photos, it sounded reasonable."

"You aren't a programmer," Mercer pointed out.

"No, but I am the numbers guy. I gave him a ballpark figure for what it would cost, the types of security our programmers could design, and estimated how long it would take. He said he'd get back to me. Saturday afternoon, he phones my boss, insisting we had a meeting scheduled. I got chewed out, and somehow, this guy shows up at my house."

"How did he find out where you lived?"

"At first, I thought someone at Trila told him, but he walked into my home like he'd been there before. Something felt wrong. He was obsessed with our wedding photo. He asked where Sarina was. I said she was out, and he said it'd be a shame if she never came back."

"Why didn't you tell me this sooner?"

"He knew things. He came into my home. He...he made it sound like he would kill her if I said anything."

"Precisely what did he say?"

Porter shrugged. "I don't know. The thing about her never coming back and how he hoped we could do business in the future. Nothing direct. That night, you showed up in the middle of the meeting, and I was so twisted around at that point, I thought maybe I was projecting my fears onto this guy. A stranger in my home, asking about my wife. Maybe he was just being polite or something."

Fighting the urge to point out Alpha might have been stopped days sooner, Mercer swallowed his words, instead asking, "What did he look like?"

"He was tall and in shape with glasses and brown hair, I think. He should be on the footage from my security system. Didn't you review that data?"

"Unfortunately not. We downloaded the data from your system that morning. Will Trila security be able to provide an image of this ambassador?" Mercer asked, feeling as if his team were just as blameworthy for not taking the initiative sooner.

"He wasn't an ambassador. He was an attaché or consultant or something. He didn't have a discernible accent or anything. I asked about him when I returned to work on Monday, but no one seemed particularly sure of this guy's credentials or background. Someone thought his name was Geoff. Another guy thought Adam. It's like we weren't even talking about the same man."

"It was intentional to confuse details. Witnesses are often unreliable," Mercer said. "Let's see what Browne has to say. Maybe he'll be amenable to doing us another favor."

THIRTY-SEVEN

"You look like dog shit someone stepped in," Bastian said.

"Have you looked in the mirror recently?" Mercer retorted. He shifted his focus from Bastian to Hans. "Are the two of you done mucking about?"

"Absolutely." Bastian rubbed his wrists and gave the officer an uncertain look.

"You're free to go," the officer said, impatiently waiting for them to leave the holding cell. "Run before someone changes his mind."

"Tosser," Hans muttered under his breath, but he didn't need to be told twice. At the entrance to the police station, he spotted George Browne standing near Logan Porter. "Give me two minutes alone with him."

"Stand down," Mercer ordered. "Things have changed."

Bastian analyzed Julian and the scene before him. He always had a gift for reading people, a talent he'd put to use as an analyst. A lot had changed, so Bastian remained silent, blending into the background while Mercer spoke briefly with Browne.

The photo of the alleged diplomat would be e-mailed in exchange for the sharing of additional intel. So far, Donovan had found a name that matched Julian's description of Omega, Jorgen Black. Probably an alias, but Browne didn't say much on the subject. Instead, he insisted he needed to check his records and conduct an internal investigation. Not having a dog in the fight, Mercer agreed, and Browne departed. Logan watched him leave and turned to the group of security specialists. He tapped the face of his watch as if to say 'hurry', and Mercer nodded.

"Why didn't you let me knock his bloody block off?" Hans asked. "Do you have any idea what we've been through? Those Trila twats think they invented intimidation. I'd like to show them the proper way of intimidating someone."

"The recovery has been made," Mercer said, ignoring his friend. "We're reevaluating the situation. New facts have come to light, and until the threat has been removed, we can't leave the Porters vulnerable." Mercer eyed the area, feeling as though they were being watched. "Alpha believes we have the item in our possession. His focus may no longer be on our clients. However, it's hard to say for certain. Precautions must be taken."

After hailing a cab, Mercer gave the driver the address. Luckily, the four of them fit inside. Once they arrived at the hotel, Mercer led the way to their suite. But Bastian pulled him aside before they entered the room.

"Since when do we move from point A to point B without performing at least one switchback?" Bastian asked.

"It seemed unnecessary."

"You want to lead him here." Bas blew out a breath. "We're his new targets."

Mercer didn't answer. Instead, he strode inside. Donovan was stretched out on the pullout mattress again, but this time, he didn't make a move to return to the analysis. Hans was devouring everything he could find in the mini-bar, and Sarina and Logan were huddled together at the table.

"Jules, what happened?" Bastian asked.

Mercer took a moment to assess the room and his team. They were tired, beaten, and frustrated. At every turn, they had uncovered some new piece of information they should have possessed long before. The recovery had been their primary objective, but with that completed, the secondary objective was to identify Alpha and his remaining associates in order to ensure the Porters' safety.

"Alpha and his associates got the drop on me," Mercer said, unhappy about that particular detail. "It shouldn't have happened, but so be it." He looked around the room. "Sarina can provide additional details about Alpha's associates. But suffice it to say, there were three men, Alpha, Omega, and Zed. Those are the handles they are using. Omega is dead. Alpha has gone silent, and I never encountered Zed."

"As of an hour ago, we've identified Omega as Jorgen Black, the current alias of a former Jaeger turned private contractor," Donovan said, giving up on the idea of sleep. "He was briefly employed at Trila International until three months ago when he was fired."

"We're working under the assumption Omega provided Alpha with the information necessary to plan the kidnapping," Mercer said.

Bastian eyed the Porters who were staring at the exchange as if they were watching a horror film. "Does that name mean anything to you, love?" Sarina shrugged. "Mr. Porter?"

"Can I see a picture?" Logan asked, and Donovan gestured to the wall.

Crossing the room, Logan studied the blown-up employee ID, but he shook his head.

"Regardless, we know Alpha wants access to the backdoor to this operating system, and he's prepared to do anything necessary to obtain that access." Mercer shifted his gaze back to the Porters. Normally, they didn't conduct debriefs in front of civilians. "Alpha has political clout. We don't know how much, but he used an abandoned bomb shelter to hold us captive."

"Inside an embassy," Logan blurted out.

Hans's gaze shot to Mercer. "Seriously?"

Mercer nodded. "Alpha believes I'm in possession of the protocols, and he's made it clear he intends to make this personal unless I give him what he wants. The only reason I'm alive is because he believes I am of use to him. It's the same reason he didn't kill Sarina."

"Jules," Bastian cast a warning look in Mercer's direction, "there's no need to frighten the woman."

"It's true," Sarina said. Although she had never been properly introduced to Hans or Bastian, she didn't shy away from the confrontation. "But Julian said we're safe now and the four of you will protect us."

"Of course, he did," Bastian mumbled so only Mercer could hear. "Pardon us," he gave Mercer an insistent look, "but there are private matters we need to discuss alone." Giving Sarina the most charming smile he could muster, he added, "I'm sorry for your ordeal and our shoddy manners. I'm Bastian. That's Hans. If there's anything you need, please let us know.

You must be tired and hungry and in need of some peace. We will not burden you further."

"Thank you," Logan said before Sarina could respond. "We'll get out of your way."

"Julian," she said, ignoring her husband's attempt to retreat, "how could Alpha keep us inside an embassy without anyone noticing?" She swallowed. "If he has that much power, how are you going to stop him? Shouldn't you just give him whatever he wants and hope he goes away?"

"That's not an option, but we will stop him. You should rest now in case we need your help later. You've been up most of the night under extraordinary circumstances."

"Okay." She took her husband's outstretched hand, and they shut themselves inside the master bedroom.

"Birds." Hans took a seat on the vacant sofa bed. "So what really happened after we took the rap at Trila and let you escape?"

Mercer gave them the proper, uncensored debrief. After everyone was up to speed, Bastian took his usual spot behind the computer. Without being asked, he pulled up Omega's history which contained many gaps. Someone with a bit of know-how created Jorgen Black so he would look good on paper, but there wasn't enough information to create a proper profile or identify known associates.

"Is it a requirement that the security guards be named by Crayola?" Hans asked.

Donovan snorted in amusement. "You got your arses handed to you by a box of crayons."

"Enough," Mercer said. "Any idea how to lure Alpha out of hiding?"

"He isn't hiding," Bastian said. "He knows you're gone. Hell, he probably knows someone helped you escape. Frankly, it's a miracle you didn't risk an international incident." He studied Donovan for a moment. "We need to make sure Johann's cover remains intact. We aren't in the business of burning spies unless they've infiltrated our government. However, we need his help. Alpha must be on the embassy's CCTV footage. Jules said Alpha carried Sarina out of the bomb shelter and took her elsewhere, it must have been caught on camera."

"According to Johann, the security system doesn't cover the basement or subbasement. It was a blessing and a curse. It enabled us to bring Sarina and Mercer out without drawing too much attention on the approach. However, on the way out of the basement, the feeds were deactivated. Cameras were off," Donovan assured, putting the next question to rest. "No worries on blowing his cover."

"Couldn't he identify Alpha?" Mercer asked.

"He's keeping watch, but no one's gone back to the basement since your escape," Donovan said. "If that changes, we'll know."

"We can't assume that'll happen," Hans said. "It sounds like Alpha gave you the perfect opportunity to leave. He left you free to wander about."

"With a bullet in my side? Doubtful." Mercer ran a hand through his hair. "Sarina said they didn't typically bind her either. It could be purely circumstantial."

"Is there another way in or out of the basement?" Bastian asked. "It sounds like Alpha might have his own entryway or some other room down there away from official embassy business. He couldn't just traipse through the embassy with an unconscious woman in his arms. Someone would have noticed."

"If there is an alternate entrance or some hidden room, Johann doesn't know about it," Donovan said.

"I'll do some checking on blueprints and

renovations," Bastian sighed, "but we're talking a foreign country's sovereign property. Finding that information will be next to impossible. Hell, it's probably considered espionage in and of itself."

"Do what you can," Mercer said. He scratched his chin and considered the possibilities. Until now, he'd been focused on escaping that room, not on where the doorway at the top of the stairs could lead. "Sarina might be able to tell you more. I don't know what happened after he took her or how long she was gone." Mercer swallowed, uncomfortable with the possibilities. "I'll talk to her about it."

Bastian pressed his lips together, debating whether to speak his mind. Finally, he said, "Frankly, Jules, treating Sarina like she's a damsel in distress won't help the situation." He blew out a puff of air, drumming his fingers against the desk. "You have to stop doing this. We are ransom specialists. Once the asset has been recovered, our job is done. We do not offer protection. We are not bodyguards, so why did you volunteer to protect her and her husband from a threat we still know very little about? We are not equipped to handle this type of situation."

"I beg to differ, but we knock the shit out of this type of situation," Hans said. "We dealt with that killer bent on taking down that newspaper mogul. We can handle this too."

"You won't let us perform wet work. This is the opposite. You should be pleased." Mercer shook his head, dismissing whatever argument Bastian might make. It was of no matter. His team was exhausted. Except for Donovan, they'd each spent the night in shackles.

"Fine," Bastian leaned back in the chair, "what's our next move?"

"We wait for Alpha to make contact again. In the

meantime, we pool our resources and trust that Browne will flush out whatever moles might remain inside Trila and provide us with additional information on Alpha and his team."

"That's a lot of uncertainty," Donovan said. "Shouldn't we begin by questioning Sarina?"

"We'll let her rest first." Mercer went into the kitchenette to make some tea. "You should utilize this time to relax and prepare for whatever is to come. We'll take shifts. Donovan and I will go first."

"Fantastic," Donovan muttered.

THIRTY-EIGHT

"Anything?" Mercer leaned over Bastian's shoulder, staring at the e-mailed photograph of Alpha. An opaque white reflection blurred half of the man's face. "What is that?"

"Latest in technological advancements." Bastian rubbed the scruff on his chin. "I've set the facial recognition software to compensate, but it doesn't look promising. He must have sprayed his lenses with a reflective polymer that makes it impossible to accurately take a digital picture. Alpha knows precisely what he's doing. Some gamblers in Monte Carlo and Las Vegas have used similar devices and technology to thwart the cameras, but this is obviously very telltale. The real question is why didn't someone inside Trila stop him. They sure as hell stopped us."

"Someone on Trila's security team has been compromised," Mercer speculated.

"They haven't," Logan said from the doorway where he'd been eavesdropping. "No one monitors the security feed unless there's a reason. You know how many guards are stationed at the doors. They don't need to hire extra help to sit in a control room and watch monitors. That's not how it's done. If it was, you wouldn't have been able to break into the building."

"And we all know how successful that was." Bastian rose from his spot behind the computer. "It'll beep if there's a hit, but it'll be a few hours at the very least. I'm gonna get cleaned up and get something to eat."

"Dismissed," Mercer said. He turned his attention to Logan. "How's Sarina?"

"She's a trooper, but she wants to go home. She wants her life back. She wants things to go back to normal."

"Is she awake?"

"She's taking a shower." Logan let out a bitter laugh. "I'm probably worse off than she is. Every time she's out of my sight, I get this feeling in the pit of my stomach like she's going to disappear again. I didn't protect her before. I couldn't even get the damn computer protocols for the kidnapper. If her safety were solely up to me, she'd be dead. What do I do? How do I live with myself knowing that's the truth?"

"You do better," Mercer said.

"How?"

Taking a deep breath, Mercer turned his back on Porter and went into the adjacent room. He didn't have an answer. That was something he was struggling with himself. Crossing his arms over his chest, he leaned against the counter in the kitchenette. The room spun slightly, and he closed his eyes. *Damn blood loss*, he thought, forcing his mind to accept that as the truth.

When he opened his eyes, Sarina was standing in front of him. She wore the hotel robe, and her hair was wet. She opened the fridge and took out a bottle of water. When she couldn't find anything to eat, she closed the door.

"May we speak?" Mercer asked.

She nodded, leading the way to the couch in the main room. She pulled her leg underneath her and ran a towel absently through her wet hair.

"You want to know what happened that night." She gave him a sad smile. "To be honest, I don't know. I thought I was dead. And then there was nothingness." She used the towel to wipe at a wayward tear and looked away. "When I woke up, Omega was dead. You...," she swallowed, fighting to regain control of her trembling lip, "I thought I was alone. I thought..."

"I know." Mercer understood her fear. "You don't know where he took you?"

"I didn't know he took me anywhere," she said. "You told me that. I was facing the wall, and then I heard him fire, and then I woke up in almost the same spot." Wiping her eyes, she took an unsteady breath. "Are you sure you didn't imagine it? The only room I saw the entire time was that horrible dungeon."

"What about when you were first taken or when he took you to the rendezvous point?"

"I woke up in that room. There's nothing else but that room." She sniffled and began to cry.

"Baby, it's okay. You're safe. You're here. It's okay." Logan swooped in from where he'd been lingering a few meters away. "No one can hurt you. You're free."

"I don't feel free. I want to go home. I want things to go back to normal." She pushed away from her husband's shoulder and stared fiercely at Julian. "When will this be over?"

"Soon."

Considering her plea to return home, Mercer reached for the phone and dialed Browne. Trila had a lot of power, so Browne might be able to get the information they needed on Alpha faster and without the red tape that came from dealing with international bureaucracies. However, it was unclear whether Trila's head of security could be trusted. Either way, it would lead them to Alpha, Mercer reasoned.

*   *   *

Waiting was never easy. There was a reason patience was considered a virtue. Mercer stared at the second hand on the clock. It was after midnight, and he'd been stonewalled. The facial recognition had proved useless in identifying Alpha, and so far, the blueprints to the embassy were beyond their grasp.

Tunnels, Mercer thought, getting up and scouring their data for a city map. Alpha was aware of Mercer and Donovan's expedition through that booby-trapped abandoned building, and according to the map, the embassy was less than two kilometers away. Entering new search parameters for the city's infrastructure, sewer, and transportation system, Mercer hoped to find something that would indicate he was on the right track. After all, a fallout shelter used as a bunker for diplomats ought to have at least one emergency exit.

"You're still awake?" Sarina asked. They hadn't spoken since her meltdown. She looked around the room, but the rest of Mercer's team was absent.

"Yes."

"Can I ask you something?"

"Speak."

She winced at his harsh response but soldiered on. "Why would you risk your life for me? You don't know me. This is just a job, isn't it?"

"It's more than that."

"I don't understand."

"No matter."

But she wouldn't let it go. "You staged a heist at my husband's work. You could have been killed or imprisoned. Why go through all that trouble if you didn't even steal the one item that would free me?"

"That was my intention," Mercer said.

"Then why didn't you give it to Alpha? He might have spared us." She gingerly rubbed her bruised temple.

"I'm sorry things didn't go as planned."

"Julian, he nearly killed you. I saw what he did to you. I was so scared he'd do the same to me or worse. Much worse." She blinked, glancing at the closed bedroom door that contained her sleeping husband. "He's going to try again until you give him what he wants. Next time, he might hurt Logan too. Please, just give him what he wants so this will go away. I don't want to live in fear. I don't want him to hunt us. To hurt us. Please. Do something."

"I can't."

"Why not?"

"It's not that simple."

"Then make it that simple," she said.

"I don't have the protocols."

She looked as if she didn't believe him. "Yeah, whatever." Leafing through the stack of papers on the desk, she admitted, "I couldn't sleep. I keep thinking Logan and I should leave. We could go back to the States and live our lives free from this, but you said Alpha's a diplomat. He can travel. He can find us. We'll never be safe, will we?"

"This is what I do," Mercer said. "My team will find him if he doesn't find us first."

Sarina shivered at the implication, cinching the robe tighter around her body. She was sorely in need of clothing and other necessities. It was no wonder the woman wanted to return home, even if her house was the site of the abduction.

"Tell me about when you were taken," Mercer said, returning to the desk chair.

"Two men came into the house." Her eyes lost focus at the memory. "They had masks. Based on their eyes, I'd say one of them was Omega. I don't know if Alpha or Zed helped, but they were on me before I even knew what was happening. Then everything gets fuzzy, and I remember being carried past the bushes in the backyard." She shivered again. "On second thought, maybe I'm not too keen on returning home after all. I just want my things. I want to be around something familiar. I...I want everything to go back to the way it was before."

"It won't." He studied her shocked expression, realizing he should say or do something to demonstrate some level of sympathy, but no words came to mind.

"That's it?" she asked. "The life I knew is over?"

"You'll sort it out in time."

Suddenly, an involuntary snort escaped, and she reddened with embarrassment. "Sorry, I must sound like an ungrateful wretch. You rescued me. I just," she exhaled, "I don't even know what I want anymore. Yesterday, I wanted nothing more than to get out of that dungeon and see my husband again. Now, that I'm safe, I feel like I've traded one prison for another." She stood. "I'll put myself out of my own misery and go to bed. Good night, Julian." She turned at the doorway. "In case I haven't said it, thank you."

"Women," Mercer muttered. He had barely said anything, and she'd rambled on about her feelings. Obviously, she understood the situation was complicated, but handing over the protocols wouldn't solve anything.

While Mercer sat alone in the dark room, contemplating his thoughts, Bastian returned from a quick outing to a twenty-four hour market. He put the bags of groceries on the couch and brought the already opened bag of crisps to the computer, shooing Mercer away. After clicking a few keys, Bastian reached into the bag and withdrew a handful of crisps. He examined the searches Mercer had been conducting and the lack of progress the facial recognition software had made.

"Something's bugging me," Bastian said, "but I'm not entirely sure what it is." He opened the file containing copies of Sarina's private e-mails. "There's something here. I can feel it."

"Figure it out." Mercer removed a premade sandwich from the bag and put the rest of the cold items in the fridge. "I want to move on from this mission, and we can't do that until Alpha's neutralized."

"Donovan asked his contact to scout the embassy. He wants to make sure we didn't miss something. He figures it'd be faster than waiting for blueprints and renovation work orders. Frankly, it sounds like a fool's errand." Bastian smirked. "Then again, so was storming in to save your pathetic life."

"You aren't planning on letting me live this down?"

"Hell no. I sacrificed myself for the good of the mission, and you get captured," Bastian teased. It was the usual ribbing that often followed a harrowing experience. "Ridicule will abound, my friend." He watched as Mercer eased uncomfortably onto the couch. "Your only other option is to keel over."

"I could shoot you instead."

"Then who would work the bloody computers?"

THIRTY-NINE

"I find it odd," Hans said from the table. "This bastard had everything meticulously planned. The abduction went perfectly. He makes sure the panic and desperation set in before he issues his ransom demands. He cuts off the lady's finger and has it delivered by a florist to show what a tough nut he is, and then the wanker puts a bullet in you and lets you escape. What the fuck? Does this guy have multiple personalities?"

"What about Zed?" Bastian asked, shoveling a spoonful of cereal into his mouth. "Are you certain Alpha is the brains behind the operation?"

"You're thinking we're dealing with a puppet master," Mercer said. "What about Alpha's past offenses?"

Hans shrugged. "It's speculation made by law enforcement. They get a lot wrong, mate."

"Yes, they do." Mercer sighed. His body ached. His injuries were taking a toll on his concentration, and he noticed he was zoning out of the conversation.

"We should go to the Porters' estate," Bastian suggested. "Now that we don't have to worry about Trila shooting us on sight or having us arrested, we should make sure Alpha hasn't left us a message. Plus," he turned to glance at the opened bedroom where Sarina and Logan were eating their breakfast alone, "she could use a few of her belongings."

"Have them make a list. We'll drop by in a couple of hours." Mercer pushed away from the table. "I need a moment."

"Are you all right?" Bastian asked.

"Brilliant." Mercer's attempts to sleep last night didn't pan out, and he knew it was important to take advantage of the current lull. At any moment, things could change. He walked past the bathroom, hearing Donovan speaking on the phone. They were in tight quarters on account of the two civilians, but keeping the team close was the safest choice right now.

Shutting himself in the other bedroom, Mercer changed the bandage and examined the shoddy stitching. Normally, they would have taken Sarina to a hospital, but with Alpha at large and half the team incarcerated, Mercer didn't believe it was the best idea, particularly since they had been wanted criminals at the time. Pulling a clean shirt over his head, he took a deep breath, feeling a sharp stabbing in his side. One of these days, his luck would run out. Truthfully, it should have long ago.

"Commander," Donovan knocked on the door, "I have news."

"Enter," Mercer replied, shaking off any thought he might have had of getting some shuteye.

"You were right. There are tunnels beneath the embassy that connect to the sewer lines. Johann discovered a hidden passage in the basement. However, the tunnels themselves have a laser grid which was installed in the 1990s. If there's a breach, it would be noticed."

"There are ways around that," Mercer said. "Where do the tunnels lead?"

"Conceivably, anywhere. It would explain how Alpha was able to get in and out with Sarina without arousing suspicion."

"Is it possible to track where he went?"

"Probably."

"Okay." Mercer opened the drawer and put two additional magazines in his pocket. Then he slipped a jacket on to conceal his weapon. "Let's find out."

"Jules, I can handle this," Donovan said, following the commander out of the room and back to the kitchenette.

"I know, but Alpha's mine." Mercer gave orders to Bastian to send maps and information on the sewer lines to their phones and to keep guard at the hotel. Under no circumstances were the Porters to be left unprotected. "We need an access point."

"I found one," Bastian said. "The area should be familiar. It's where you were almost blown-up."

Without another word, Mercer selected a set of keys and went out the door. Donovan grabbed the large black duffel containing his gear and followed after the commander, catching up to him in the garage.

"I'll drive," Donovan said. "You shouldn't be operating heavy machinery in your condition."

"Fine." Mercer tossed him the keys. They had just exited the garage when Mercer's phone rang. He checked the display, surprised to see the caller. "Mr. Browne," Mercer said, waiting for the man to speak.

"Have you any additional information to share?" Browne asked.

"Not at the present."

Browne made a disgusted sound. "Against my better judgment, I'm being forced to divulge the progress we're making. As you may know, we have numerous contracts with various governments. That position allows us access to information that isn't readily available to others. I checked into the diplomat in question. We've reviewed the sign-in sheets and the security footage. As you know, the identity of the man you believe to be a kidnapper has proved difficult to ascertain. However, our surveillance footage from the garage has provided a clear license plate number. Our police pals have traced it back to one of many vehicles used by the embassy. I've contacted the embassy, and that's the vehicle the cultural attaché and his staff use."

"Does the attaché have a name?" Mercer asked.

"I've already compared his photograph to that of the man on our security footage. They don't match," Browne said.

"Then why did you phone?"

"Various embassy staff members and civilian personnel have access to the car in question. It is my belief the person who used that vehicle is responsible for the threat to Trila. After reviewing Mr. Black's file, I believe your assertion is correct that Mr. Black was placed inside Trila to provide information on our developmental software to someone else, and that unknown entity is to blame for the threat against Trila and Logan Porter."

"What do you want?"

Browne swallowed the lump in his throat. "I've been authorized to offer you a finder's fee if you can verify these details and identify the threat."

"We do not work blind." Mercer shifted the call to speakerphone. "What interest would members of the embassy have in your computer systems?"

"Those protocols allow total access to an operating system used in the housing of weapons systems. If a nation-state or individual could gain access to the system via the backdoor protocols, they would control a sovereignty's defenses. Handling this quietly would be particularly beneficial for us and lucrative for you."

"Bollocks," Donovan muttered.

"Avoiding an international crisis is no longer my focus," Mercer said. "However, ensuring the safety of my client is. Whatever the overlap might be, so be it." He disconnected the call.

"Guess we know what makes those protocols so valuable," Donovan said. "Alpha must believe they're in our possession. That means we're walking targets."

"Browne's wrong. Alpha's actions aren't sanctioned by a government that lost a bidding war. Alpha killed his associate. He wants the information to sell to the highest bidder. He's a bloody arms dealer on a massive scale."

"Which means he'll eliminate anyone who causes problems." Donovan parked the car. "Logan and Sarina are a problem."

"Overlap," Mercer replied, opening the door. He stared at the entrance to the maintenance tunnel. "Let's get on with it."

FORTY

"Shit," Donovan griped, cautioning a glance at Julian. The maintenance tunnel had split in multiple directions, and cell service underground was spotty. The GPS had blinked out after a few dozen meters, so they were relying on Donovan's natural sense of direction. They had stopped at a metal door that looked far too clean to be in the middle of the sewer system. It had a keypad next to it. "We should have taken Bastian with us."

"I can override it," Mercer offered.

"No," Donovan shook his head, "if I'm right, this ought to lead to the embassy's underground tunnels. The door could have an alarm." Unzipping the duffel bag, Donovan removed a container with fingerprint powder. He brushed the keys, seeing obvious marks on four of the numbers.

"Take a guess," Mercer said. He turned to look behind them. Since entering the tunnel, he'd heard echoes and pings, making him believe an attack was imminent.

"Light to dark." Donovan pressed the keys, hearing an angry beep. "We'll try again." He entered another combination and another, each time, hearing the same negative beep.

"Any progress?"

"Do you want to give it a go?" Donovan asked.

Mercer glanced at the permutations Donovan already tried. "Have you tried all the combinations?"

"Not yet." Donovan entered another set of numbers. This time, the lock unhinged. "Jolly good." Slowly, he cracked the door, slipping a fiber optic cable into the gap. His embassy contact warned of lasers, but the grid was undetectable. "Wait."

Pulling out a spray can, Donovan lightly misted the area, catching the slightest hint of a laser grid against the sides of the wall. Confused, he carefully pushed the door open, seeing reflective material placed parallel to the walls in order to thwart the system.

"Someone's been here," Mercer said, raising his gun.

Instead of taking point, Mercer followed Donovan into the tunnel. Donovan kept his eyes on the grid, occasionally checking to make sure there were no lasers or other security measures to trip. The tunnel grew darker, and Julian turned on a torch, keeping it aimed at the ground in front of them. At a juncture, he took point, continuing on the path that would most likely lead to the embassy.

Donovan tapped him on the shoulder, halting their progress. "Twelve o'clock."

Mercer nodded, carefully stepping to the side so they could make the approach together. On the ground was a large indecipherable object. As they got closer, they realized they found a body.

"Is it Omega?" Donovan pushed the man over with the toe of his shoe.

"No." Julian stared at what was left of the man's face. A gunshot had gone through the back of his skull and exited below his eye socket, taking most of his cheek and upper jaw with it. However, the sunglasses inside the man's shirt pocket were the only evidence Mercer needed. "It's Alpha."

Kneeling down, Mercer checked the deceased's pockets for identification, finding an embassy access card but no identification. Beneath the body was Mercer's backup sidearm.

"It's him." Mercer pocketed the gun, wondering who shot Alpha. Before he could say another word, he heard a sound.

"Footsteps," Donovan whispered. They were trapped with no place to hide. This would not be pretty.

Mercer extinguished the light. The footfalls sounded like they were coming from behind. Then the sound grew louder from somewhere in front of them. They were surrounded. The former SAS took up positions back to back, waiting to see what was about to happen.

"We must have tripped the alarm," Donovan said, "unless Alpha has a team of mercenaries guarding his rotting corpse."

"Silence." Mercer's mind was analyzing the situation. Assuming the footfalls belonged to the embassy's security team, it'd be best to surrender.

"Police. Freeze."

"Hold your fire," Mercer said.

Donovan held his weapon by the handle, carefully placing it on the ground. Just as Mercer began to follow suit, additional voices shouted commands from the other end of the tunnel. He turned, seeing assault rifles aimed in his direction. He drew a bead on one of the men, watching Donovan scoop up his weapon and shift his focus while the police continued to bark orders at them to drop their weapons and surrender.

"This is sovereign property," one of the embassy guards yelled. "You have no jurisdiction here."

"What embassy? This is part of the city's tunnel system," the cop responded. He was too far away to make out the dead body, but Mercer knew things would turn ugly soon.

"Identify yourselves," someone yelled, focusing laser sights on Mercer and Donovan. Embassy security and the police unit closed the gap from both directions, noticing the man on the ground. "Don't move."

"Easy," Donovan said, "we're personal security consultants."

"Lower your weapons," the police ordered. "Now."

"Not until the men with the assault rifles do the same," Mercer said.

"Are you trying to start a turf war?" Donovan whispered. "We'll be shredded in the crossfire."

A booming voice broke through from the back of the police unit. "Those men are working for us."

"Browne," Mercer said, "you tracked my phone. It's why you called."

"I wanted to know what you were doing." He made his way toward Mercer, holding his hands up as he broke past the police officers and entered the kill box. He smiled at the embassy security guards. "I'm George Browne. I work for Trila International. I phoned earlier about a threat. Your superior should have the details to explain this away." He looked down at the body. "Well, most of it."

The embassy guards seemed uncertain. One radioed for advice, and during the confusion, Browne urged Mercer and Donovan to back away from the body. The police were the better option, so the former SAS retreated, letting the cops and embassy guards duke out who was to take possession of the crime scene.

"Get out of here," Browne said as soon as they safely exited into the maintenance tunnel.

"They can't leave. They're suspects in a murder," the detective on scene protested.

"I said they can go." Browne gave the detective a pointed look. "I need to know the dead man's identity and his affiliation with the embassy. Send a photo as soon as you take possession of the crime scene. Time is of the essence."

Mercer and Donovan watched the exchange. It was one thing to know the police force was in Trila's pocket. It was another to actually see a civilian order an officer of the law to act. Money was the controlling power, especially here.

"You're free to go," the detective said. "Mr. Browne will provide us with your contact information. Assume we'll have plenty of questions later."

"Let's go." Donovan dragged Mercer back the way they came before the commander could say or do anything that would get them arrested, killed, or turned over to a foreign power.

"Mercer," Browne called after them, "is that Alpha?"

"Yes."

"Good. You nailed that son of a bitch. We'll talk in my office later."

Mercer didn't respond. Alpha was dead. He should feel relief. It was good news to share with Sarina. However, this meant someone else had been pulling Alpha's strings — Zed.

FORTY-ONE

"We have a new player on the scene," Donovan said into the phone. As soon as they were out of the subterranean shithole, cell service was restored. "Alpha's been neutralized." He grunted a few affirmatives and disconnected.

"We have nothing to go on." Mercer's calm demeanor meant the wheels were turning.

"It could be over. With Alpha and Omega eliminated, Zed is out of puppets. He probably cut ties and has gone to ground."

"Alpha's need for the protocols bordered on mania," Mercer said. "Why would Zed walk away without the score?"

"Maybe Alpha's life was dependent on obtaining the computer data," Donovan suggested. He monitored the traffic in the rearview mirror. "Did Sarina actually encounter Zed?"

"Yes, but their interaction was limited." Mercer glanced at the younger man, knowing he had insight to offer.

"How can we safeguard the Porters against a threat we can't identify? We had enough trouble discerning if Sarina had even been abducted, and then we had plenty of trouble finding Alpha." Donovan shook his head. "For once, we need military intelligence to call the plays. A state's weapon systems could be anything from defensive measures to prevent an airstrike to nuclear capabilities. How can these Trila shitheads sell that kind of technology with such an extensive flaw in the design? We're all fucked."

"We fight," Mercer said. "It's all we can do."

"Bugger. Now you're turning into a freaking Pollyanna. That's never good." They continued the drive in silence for a time before Donovan asked, "Should we go straightaway to the hotel?"

"Yes. If Zed comes to us, it would make this less complicated."

"It depends on the amount of firepower he brings with him."

Despite their hopes that the mysterious Zed would make an appearance and put this entire situation to rest, no one followed them back to the hotel. The room remained secure. Bastian had torn down most of their work. He needed a clean slate to compile the new information. And Hans had the television on. To the untrained eye, it would appear he was deeply enthralled in the program, but Mercer knew better. Hans was evaluating their location from a tactical standpoint, imagining how he would conduct a breach.

"Where are our guests?" Donovan asked.

"Inside," Hans said, not bothering to turn his head. After he finished his mental assessment of the tactical weaknesses of their current position, he turned to Mercer. "Are we working for those sods at Trila now?"

"No."

"Except we are," Hans retorted, embittered by this fact. "We don't have a choice. It's tangled together. Serve the greater good. Straighten out the karmic scale." He gave Bastian a disgusted look. "Did I miss anything?"

"Nope," Bastian smirked, not letting his friend's annoyance deter him, "that covers it." Pushing away from the desk, Bastian picked up a sheet of hotel stationery. "Here's the list of things our guests want from their home. Shall we?"

* * *

The Porters' home remained undisturbed. Despite Mercer's assumption that Trila would have conducted a search to determine where their wayward employee had gone after the break-in, there were no signs of tampering. However, the guards at the post would have reported any activity on the premises had they returned after the failed heist. Mercer looked at them again, annoyed by their incompetence in allowing Sarina to be taken in the first place.

After collecting the items on the list and a few she was probably too modest to request, Mercer and Bastian gave the perimeter a final sweep, checked whatever parts of the security system Mercer hadn't dismantled in a paranoid fit, and left. As they made their way through the streets, Bastian noticed a tail behind them. He performed a few unplanned turns to make sure they were being followed.

"How do you want to handle this?" Bastian asked, hoping Mercer didn't want to risk a shootout in the middle of a crowded street.

"Let's pay Mr. Browne a visit," Mercer said. He remained outwardly impassive, but Bastian noticed the handgun now rested on Mercer's lap.

When they stopped in front of the Trila building, the car that had been following them double-parked. Mercer opened the door, prepared for the worst, but instead, he was met by a professional nod from the detective he encountered earlier that morning in the sewers.

"Nice driving," the detective said. "You saved me the trouble of having to track you down. I was on my way to speak to Mr. Browne. You might as well join us."

Bastian watched the exchange with a morbid fascination but followed Mercer's lead and remained silent.

Unlike their previous visits to the Trila building, this time, the kidnapping specialists weren't treated with outward hostility. The detective spoke to the receptionist, offering his credentials, and waited patiently for the guards to escort them to Browne's office. No one demanded Mercer's weapon or asked for any identification. Even Bastian, whom they had detained, was treated like a guest.

"Ah," Browne stood, "just the men I wanted to see." He waited for the three to enter, and then he shut the door to his office, returning to the spot behind his desk. "Detective Maxwell, do you have what I requested?"

Maxwell pulled a sealed envelope from his pocket. "We took fingerprints and determined the cause of death, but before we could conduct any other tests, the body was claimed by diplomats. Since it was located inside the sealed door, the state department ruled it was on embassy property, and since the deceased is a foreign national, we have no jurisdiction." The cop turned to Mercer. "What can you tell me about the body?"

Mercer snorted, amused by Browne's quick headshake. "Nothing."

"Why were you in that tunnel?" Detective Maxwell opened a manila folder. "In the past week, you've been arrested for grand theft auto and wanted in connection with numerous crimes that happened on this property." He shifted his focus to Bastian. "You've been inside our holding cells on two separate occasions. Are you trying for a third?"

"Do you have a punch card?" Bastian asked. "Is my next visit free?"

Browne cleared his throat. "These men are currently in Trila's employ. Those prior incidents were miscommunications and need not see the light of day." Browne lifted the envelope. "This is everything?"

"It's everything I could get. You have more pull and vaster resources. They'll serve you better in this situation than I can." Maxwell nodded at Mercer and Bastian. "I don't know what's going on here, but when this is over, I don't want to have another run-in with any of you." Giving the group a curt nod, he let himself out of the office.

"The detective followed us from the Porters' estate," Mercer said. "He knows more than he's letting on."

"Don't we all?" Browne tore open the envelope, pulling out the data the police department had on the body. Pointing to a photo, he asked, "Is this Alpha?"

Mercer nodded without looking. "Whoever executed him might pose a threat to the Porters."

"And Trila," Browne added. "Do you know who did this?"

"A third party," Bastian said. "According to Mrs. Porter, three men were responsible for her abduction. That's the only information we have."

"Is that true?" Browne asked, leering at Mercer.

"Yes."

"Okay," Browne clicked a few keys at his computer, "I'll deal with this matter."

"How?" Bastian asked. "If those protocols get into the wrong hands, the situation could be disastrous. Large-scale destruction." He placed his palms on Browne's desk, leaning forward and towering over him. "I don't believe a pencil-pushing pissant like yourself knows how to deal with this." He slammed his palms against the desk for emphasis. "What are you going to do?"

"I remember you," Browne said. "You were the friendly one until we roughed up your buddy. Admirable really. But stupid. You might be former SpecOps, but I've been handling security at Trila for a long time. This isn't the first time the stakes were this high. I doubt it'll be the last. Don't you think there's a reason we have the security personnel we do? We can handle it."

"So be it," Mercer said. "Until you deliver proof of Zed's demise, we'll guard the Porters. Do not interfere."

"Zed," Browne smiled, "interesting codename. It might prove useful." He looked up at Bastian. "You're dismissed, soldier."

Mercer grabbed Bastian's arm before he could take a swing at Browne. It was obvious whatever occurred the night of their botched heist had left a bad taste with Hans and Bastian. "Not here. Not now."

Neither man spoke until they were back at the hotel. Bastian went to the computer, immediately returning to the task of identifying Zed. It was personal now. It was a matter of dignity that Mercer's team find Zed before those blowhards at Trila. However, after a few hours of hitting nothing but dead ends, Bastian slammed the laptop shut.

"What's wrong?" Sarina had changed into her own clothes, and her spirits seemed higher than they had been. "Is the house okay? Are we safe?"

"The house is secure." Mercer took a seat next to her. "Trila is doing everything they can to find Zed. They want to put a stop to this."

"Then what's the problem?" Logan asked.

"We don't know if they can."

FORTY-TWO

"You're making yourself crazy," Mercer said. He reached over and ripped the cigarette out of Bastian's mouth. "This is rubbish." He broke it into pieces and tossed it into the trash receptacle.

"It wasn't even lit. This bloody hotel doesn't allow smoking in the rooms," Bastian replied, angrily clicking the mouse in the hopes of making it cooperate.

"Lighter." Mercer held out his hand. Reluctantly, Bastian handed him the Zippo. "Report."

Bastian muttered a slew of derogatory comments, letting out his frustration. Then he spun the computer around. "Zilch. Nada. Nothing," he huffed. "I've gone through the Porters' security feed again. I even had Logan and Sarina review it. We can't identify Zed. There are two men on the feed. Two. One is Omega. We don't even know if the other is Zed. He might have been the driver, but we can't access that feed. Or it's shit. Useless shit."

"What about the embassy information Donovan's contact leaked to us?" Mercer asked.

"More shit. I can run every person through facial recognition. The damn footage doesn't even show Jorgen Black. And since we don't know Alpha's real name or any of his other aliases, I don't know if we have any hits on him. I could be staring at him right now and not know it."

"Take a break."

"Jules," Bastian pushed away from the desk and picked up an empty bag of pretzels, searching for a missed crumb, "we're chasing a ghost. If it weren't for Alpha's body, I'd say Zed doesn't exist."

"Take a break, and when you have fresh eyes, conduct a threat assessment. If Zed's gone, we don't need to stick around." He clapped Bastian on the shoulder before returning to the kitchen to see if his other teammates had made any progress.

"The embassy has tightened its security," Donovan said. "Johann won't risk our communications being intercepted, so he's gone radio silent. It appears Alpha was an embassy employee, and he used the tunnels as his own personal entrance. It's how he smuggled you and Sarina inside."

"I made some calls. Diplomatic passport records are being checked for the time of the other two Alpha abductions. Assuming our intelligence friends get a few hits, we might know Alpha's identity soon. It could lead to Zed," Hans added.

"Good work." Mercer slumped into a chair. "It's no wonder Alpha was so pompous. He picked a completely secure location to hold his hostage."

"Clearly, he didn't count on Donovan's mate breaking you out," Hans offered. "From the sound of it, he didn't count on taking a bullet to the back of the head either."

"The shot wasn't precise," Donovan interjected. "Normally, at that range, it would be at the base of the skull or higher on the head. This was in between. It doesn't seem professional."

"Zed's a lousy shot," Hans said. "He probably orders others to conduct his hits for him." He narrowed his eyes. "But it's weird he left the body. It's a sewer. How difficult would it be to dump it in one of the outflow tunnels?"

"It was probably safer to leave him on embassy property. The locals would never be involved, and it was unlikely anyone else knew of the tunnels," Mercer said.

Bastian cursed loudly, slamming the chair against the desk before joining the group in the other room. "Jules, you thought you spotted a camera inside that booby-trapped building. I want to check it out." Mercer moved to stand, and a sharp pain spread through his torso. Grunting, he grasped the table. "Whoa, easy." Bastian's eyes homed in on the growing bloodstain on Mercer's shirt. "You're not going anywhere. You ripped a stitch."

"A few, from the looks of it," Hans added. "I spotted a sewing kit in the loo."

"I'm fine." Mercer pushed away from the table. "I'll deal with this when we return."

"Stay. I'll go," Donovan said. "The Porters need protection, remember?"

"Careful," Mercer called to their retreating backs. Taking the needle and thread from Hans, Mercer grabbed a few additional supplies, removed his shirt, and settled at the table. "Have you updated Logan and Sarina?"

"They're aware of the situation," Hans said, watching Mercer thread the sterilized needle and push it through his skin. "Do you want help with that?"

"I've got it."

"In that case, I'd prefer not to watch."

Biting his lip, Mercer continued to thread a few additional stitches in his side. It felt like hell, and he knew having to remove the thread after the wound healed would be just as painful. Sometimes, it would be nice to live a normal life, but that option had been taken away from him long ago.

The sounds of Sarina's laughter filled the suite, and Logan chortled. They were happy because of his team. Struggling not to allow his own foul mood to sour everyone else's, he finished the stitches, bit the end of the thread, and cleaned up the mess. He had just picked up his shirt when the Porters entered the room.

"My god," Logan said, "should we call a doctor?"

"I'm fine," Mercer said, stumbling slightly.

"Lie down," Logan insisted, ducking beneath Mercer's arm. "You've done enough for us today." Helping Mercer to the couch, he nodded at Hans. "We're not invalids. We can help. Tell us what we can do."

"Can you make the phone ring?" Hans asked. "Because we're waiting on intel. Until then, there's nothing any of us can do."

"I'll get you something to eat," Sarina offered. She looked at the two men. "Pizza?"

"Sounds lovely," Hans said.

"Irish whiskey," Mercer said.

"Neat?" Logan asked, searching what was left in the mini-bar.

"Yes."

Hans requested a Guinness from the stash Bastian had purchased, and the four of them sat down to share a meal. It was the first normal thing that had happened since Sarina's rescue, and soon, the Porters were sharing personal stories as if Julian and Hans were their lifelong friends.

"Wait," Hans said, "you met here?"

"After my transfer," Logan said, "I didn't know anyone. I worked all the time. So I never had a chance to meet anyone outside the office. One night, I went into this dive bar after work." A big, goofy grin erupted on his face, and he winked at his wife. "There you were in that neon pink sundress and the stupid hat."

"Hey, it was vacation. I just got my MBA and treated myself to a quiet trip. It's not my fault geography wasn't my strong suit." She returned his smile, downing another mouthful of some flavored vodka concoction that made Mercer grimace. "I met you and never left."

"C'est la vie," Logan said. They shared a quick kiss. He looked down, seeing her bandaged hand, and the nauseating sweetness plummeted into sadness and anger. "We can pack up and leave. You have family and a life elsewhere. We can escape this. Start over." He looked at Mercer. "Now that Sarina's safe, wouldn't it be best for us to leave?"

That question had been asked a dozen times in the last two days. "From what I gather, Zed wants to remain protected. If getting to the two of you is easy, he might try it." Mercer put his glass down, noticing the four empty miniature whiskey bottles. He didn't mean to drink so much, and he was relieved Hans had shown restraint. "But if you truly plan to walk away from the life you have here and can avoid Trila, your friends, co-workers, and everyone who connects to you, it would be a safe move."

"Like we'd be entering witness protection or something?" Logan asked, realizing the extent of their departure.

"Sure," Hans said. "Which won't be a small feat. However, if our intel pans out, we might identify Zed, and nothing has to change."

"What's the chance of that?" Sarina asked. The topic had sobered her, and she was anxious for an answer.

"We'll know soon," Hans reassured.

Sarina gripped her husband's arm. "We'll talk about it later." She looked at the time, wondering where the day had gone. "Let's go to bed. I'm tired. And I've missed you." She forced a tight smile onto her face. "Good night."

"Night," Hans said, and Mercer gave them a nod. Once the bedroom door closed, Hans leaned closer to Mercer. "Do you think they'll decide to leave?"

"It depends." Mercer shifted on the couch. "Logan would go. He'd do anything for her. It will be her decision."

"They'll go," Hans said. "She's made it extremely obvious she wants to leave this behind."

"They don't have many friends or close ties," Mercer said. "It wouldn't be much of a sacrifice. She could start her own business again elsewhere and without that ditzy assistant."

"Shall I have documents ready for their departure?" Hans asked. The team had connections to obtain fake passports and new identities when the situation warranted it.

"Go ahead and have them drawn up, but we'll wait on the photos. Bastian has something up his sleeve." Mercer noticed the late hour, wondering what was taking Bastian and Donovan so long.

"I'm on it." Hans took a seat at the desk. He hit a few keys, and Mercer shut his eyes to contemplate what Bastian could have possibly hoped to gain by visiting some drug dealer's den.

FORTY-THREE

When Julian opened his eyes, it was daylight. Bastian was at the table, enjoying an omelet from a foam container. Sarina and Logan were sharing a bagel, and the chatter seemed light and easy. Grunting, Mercer sat up.

"Nice to see you're back among the living," Bastian said. "I planned to poke you with a stick if you didn't wake up soon." Rubbing his eyes, Mercer looked at the clock. He'd been out for over twelve hours. "You shouldn't drink when you've lost that much blood, mate. It's not smart."

"How did last night go?" Mercer asked.

"It went," Donovan said. "We're working on it."

"Got it." Obviously, they didn't want to share their intel in front of the Porters. "Hans?"

"He's asleep, but unlike you, he waited until after we returned before knocking off." Bastian grinned. He was in a cheeky mood which might have been an improvement from yesterday if it wasn't irritating the shit out of Julian.

"We've come to a decision," Logan declared. "We want to leave. Staying here is foolish. I can't put her at risk." He shook his head, pressing his lips together and giving his wife's hand a squeeze. "Nothing is worth that kind of torment. So how do we do this? How soon can we leave?"

"It'll take a few days. Possibly a week," Bastian said. "The priority is making sure you disappear without a trace."

"What about our things?" Sarina asked.

"You can't take everything, love," Bastian said. "But the important items shouldn't be a problem. Most times, those are the sentimental trinkets. Just remember, the majority of your material possessions can be replaced."

She nodded. "Do we make a list?"

"It's about time you return home." Mercer rubbed his eyes, hoping to shake off the headache. "We'll make the move this evening." Bastian and Donovan agreed, and Mercer left the kitchenette to shower and prepare for another long day.

When he returned, their clients were planted in the middle of the suite, aimlessly flipping through channels while discussing what knickknacks warranted saving. They were currently arguing about a commemorative plate that had belonged to Logan's grandmother. The security specialists huddled together in the back bedroom, discussing the intel Hans had received and the progress Bastian had made.

Bastian put his finger to his lips before Julian could utter a word. Giving the doorway a quick glance to make sure they were alone, Bastian handed him a folder. Inside were photographs of Alpha, along with a list of known aliases. While the man traveled as a diplomatic attaché or a member of the support staff for the Austrian government, it was abundantly clear he was involved in clandestine operations.

"Our kidnapper was one of the good guys." Hans put the word good in air quotes. "He worked black ops for his government, obtained valuable intel, conducted illicit trades, and who knows what else. However, I'm guessing his loyalties ended when he realized he could make ten times what the Austrian government was paying him by pursuing his own ventures on the side."

"His superiors knew and did nothing?" Mercer asked, his voice low and gravelly.

"I don't know." Hans shrugged. "It doesn't matter anymore. He's pushing daisies."

"What about Zed? Is he another operative or a sleeper?" Mercer asked.

"From the looks of this, Alpha worked alone."

"Bollocks." Mercer handed the folder back to Hans and gave the doorway an odd look. They hadn't made any real progress other than to verify their assumptions. "Why the secrecy?"

Bastian produced a damaged button camera. It was tiny and would have been difficult to spot, but the green light Mercer saw following the explosion had been a reflection from the lens. The item had been disassembled, and the small internal chip that broadcast the feed was plugged into Bastian's computer.

"I've pulled the IP address and have conducted a reverse trace. Whoever's on that network is active."

"We should move," Mercer said.

"No," Bastian shook his head, "the trace links back to the Porters' estate. I'd guess they're piggybacking off the Porters' internal system. We suspected a breach with the missing seconds of footage prior to Sarina's abduction. Someone must still be connected."

"How do we find them?" Mercer asked.

"We need to be back on the property. They must be close. Once there, I might be able to triangulate where the usage drain is coming from directionally."

Mercer's brow furrowed. "English."

"He can use this as a divining rod to point us in the proper direction," Donovan said. "However, it won't do much more than that."

"You said whoever hacked their system had to be close," Mercer recalled. "Does that mean Zed's on the property?"

"It might, or it might mean one of them left a device behind." Bastian shrugged. "It's worth a look, but what about our clients?"

"Hans, Donovan, scout ahead. Use infrared or thermals if necessary to make sure the house is secure. Once it is, we'll join you."

"Yes, sir," Hans said. Shouldering bags with the necessary equipment, Hans and Donovan quietly exited the suite.

"I don't think he's there," Bastian said.

"It won't matter. We need the Porters to return to their normal routine until we can get them out of the country. It's time they go home."

* * *

"Park wherever the hell you want," Logan said when Mercer pulled to a stop at the front door. Donovan and Hans had left their SUV on the cobblestone path, and Mercer expected his client to throw a fit. "This house was a dream. A symbol of what I achieved. I wanted it to be pristine, untainted, picture perfect because we were living the idyllic life."

"That dream was shattered." Sarina peered out the window at her home. "Are you sure we're safe here?"

Bastian plastered a reassuring smile on his face. "Of course, love. Nothing to fret over."

"Julian?" she asked uncertainly.

"We're here. We're not leaving." Mercer got out of the car and opened the back door. "Come on." He jerked his chin at the house, and reluctantly, she stepped out of the vehicle.

As if on cue, Hans opened the front door, ushering them inside. "Place is clean."

"I should hope so," Logan replied, the haughty tone back in his voice.

"I'll take a looksy around," Bastian said, disappearing after Hans.

Donovan lingered near the back door. His rifle was propped against the wall, and his side arm was visible in his thigh holster. He nodded to Mercer but remained silent, allowing the Porters to get reacclimated to their home.

Eventually, Sarina dropped onto the couch in the living room, letting out a sigh. She leaned her head back and closed her eyes. For the first time since the rescue, she appeared truly relaxed. Even when they'd been slightly inebriated while sharing a pizza, she had remained tense, like a wound coil, but now, she let her guard down. Logan puttered around the kitchen, keeping one eye on his wife the entire time. After making a platter of sandwiches, he joined her on the couch.

"I can't get enough of you," Logan whispered. "I wish I could sleep with my eyes open just to make sure you were beside me."

Donovan glanced at Mercer. Keeping his voice low, he said, "If this keeps up, I'm likely to shoot myself in the head."

"Go see how Bastian is faring." As soon as the perimeter was secure, they wouldn't have to remain in such close proximity to the reunited couple.

Five minutes later, Donovan returned. "All clear." He smiled brightly at them. "Stay inside. Avoid the windows. And everything else will fall into place. You're safe here."

"Thank you." Sarina practically bounced off the couch. "I want to take a nice long soak in our tub."

"Help yourselves to the sandwiches," Logan said. He surveyed the room. "On a normal day, I'd be finalizing a report for work or going to some meeting. I'm not sure what to do now. It's strange. Everything looks the same, but it's all so different." He picked up a Lucite award he'd received from Trila. "I guess I can start sorting through this junk. We only have a week to figure it out. I don't even know where to begin."

"Use your best judgment," Donovan said.

"Like I did when I let that psycho into my house?" Logan asked, his tone angry.

"Stop." Mercer slammed his palm against the sofa. "It's done. You can only move forward." Making sure his earpiece was functioning, he nodded to Donovan. "I'm going to give Bastian a hand. Signal if there's trouble."

Upon entering the dining room, Mercer could hear Bastian's voice from two rooms away. Continuing through the house, he found Bastian and Hans inside Logan's home office.

"Dammit," Bastian cursed, "it's gone." He tapped a few keys, checked his connection strength, and picked up the device. "The signal's gone. It just blinked out. Literally, five minutes ago, it vanished."

"Whoever's using the system knows we're here," Hans said. "I'm gonna have a chat with the guards posted at the gate."

Mercer nodded, and Hans exited through the back door, hoping to use the element of surprise to his advantage. In the event the men Trila hired to guard the estate were cooperating with Zed, it'd be best to find out posthaste. In the meantime, Bastian hardwired his computer to the Porters' system in order to monitor usage activity.

"Someone must know we're here."

"Let them come," Mercer said. "We'll be ready."

FORTY-FOUR

Three days passed, and nothing occurred. No additional threats were made. The signal Bastian hoped to find would flicker on and off occasionally, but it never lasted long enough to allow for triangulation. Will Franco and Thomas Redding, the men stationed at the front gate, proved to be uninvolved, so Mercer assigned them the task of monitoring the exterior cameras. He didn't know if he could trust them completely, but it was an additional set of eyes. In the event the property was breached, the question of their involvement would finally be answered.

After briefing the Porters on how they should act while the necessary travel documentation was created, Sarina returned to her office to put things to rest. She informed Brie it'd be best if they took a few weeks off to recover. Brie agreed happily. Her tossed apartment and overprotective boyfriend were all the incentive she needed.

Logan Porter returned to Trila with Donovan in tow. Hans and Bastian couldn't stand the thought of being anywhere in the vicinity of that wretched building, and Sarina had insisted Mercer remain close to guard her. She had a fondness for the commander after what they endured together in the subbasement of the embassy.

Meeting upon meeting ensued. Logan was welcomed back and questioned as to his loyalty and involvement. He stuck to the script, making sure no one at Trila knew of his impending departure. The company continued its internal investigation, limiting his job duties and role until they were positive he and his cohorts hadn't absconded with any sensitive materials. However, his boss promised he wouldn't be demoted and assured him it was temporary.

After enduring another performance evaluation, Logan returned to his office, surprised to find Sarina and Mercer inside. Donovan was seated in the corner of the room, listening to a book on tape. Logan dropped into his chair, amused by the absurdity that had become his life.

"What are you doing here?" Logan asked.

"I just gave Brie two weeks off," Sarina said, repeating her cover for anyone who might be listening. "I can't focus on work right now. I wanted to see you."

"Here I am. I can't wait for this week to be over. I never realized just how intrusive this job can be and how much I miss you." He glanced out the opened door at his assistant who was obviously eavesdropping.

"Can you come home for lunch?" Sarina asked.

"Definitely. Maybe I'll make it a half day. It won't hurt, right?"

"Under the circumstances, I think it should be fine. Tell whoever that your wife insists."

"Yes, ma'am." Logan grinned, collecting his things.

Mercer led the way out of the office, nodding at the two Trila security guards waiting outside. Things had changed drastically since the head of security was bending over backward to keep Julian on his side. Mercer was painfully aware George Browne's vast power and resources had fallen short of identifying Alpha and his accomplices. Browne wanted the former SAS to do the heavy lifting for him, and at the moment, it was beneficial to let the man believe they were cooperating.

The ride home involved additional planning and debate on what the Porters needed for their departure. Their cover identities had been created, but the passports hadn't arrived yet. Along with their travel documentation, they had to get credit cards under their new names and a reasonable background established. In another two or three days, everything would be set.

Upon returning home, Logan went upstairs to change. Donovan went to see what Bastian and Hans were working on, so Mercer followed Sarina into the kitchen. She was rooting through the refrigerator, looking for something to eat. As she pulled containers out of the fridge, giving some of them a sniff and tossing the spoiled contents into the trash, Mercer noticed the full block of knives on the counter next to her cell phone.

"When did you and Logan meet?" Mercer asked.

"Almost five years ago. I never expected our life together to turn into this."

"Obviously."

Something didn't feel right. He continued to make small talk, urging her to continue speaking while he did a quick check of the area. In order to avoid causing her alarm, he sent a text to Bastian, asking for the status of the home. When he received an "all clear" in return, he examined the knife set.

"I see you found the knife," Mercer said.

"Yeah," she shrugged, "I came across it the other day when I was cleaning out the drawers."

"You came across it?"

"Yes." She gave him a confused look. "Logan can be so anal about things. I'm surprised he didn't say something."

"Odd." Mercer moved around the kitchen island. "We were under the impression the knife was used to subdue you."

"No." She shook her head, turning away.

"Sorry, we must have been mistaken." Mercer spotted her opened purse on the counter and another cell phone inside. "How did they get you to comply?"

"They broke in and grabbed me."

"That was it? You didn't fight?" Reaching into her bag, he picked up her phone and turned it on. It was an oddity for a civilian to possess an encrypted phone. Entering the override code for that model, he unlocked the phone and saw the text he had sent to Donovan. Continuing to examine the device, he opened the private e-mail account. Scanning the sent messages, he saw the encoded replies that had been written.

"Of course, I fought." She turned to see him with her phone. "That's mine."

"Are you sure?"

"It was in my bag. Put it back."

Placing the phone on the counter, Mercer gave her a look. "Brie told us about your private e-mails. Does your husband know about them?"

"You think I'm cheating on Logan?" She stared at him. "If I were, why would I be willing to give up everything and escape with him?"

Mercer contemplated the facts, but he had reached an unsettling conclusion. She lunged for her phone, and he pulled his Sig. "Don't move."

"Are you out of your mind?" she screamed. "You must be working for them."

"No," he pressed his lips together in a grim smile, "are you?"

"What? How can you ask me that?" She held up her hand. "He cut off my fucking finger."

"Was it your idea to steal the protocols? Or did Alpha approach you?"

"You're insane." She stepped to the side, but he blocked her path, keeping his gun trained on her.

"How did it happen?" Mercer asked.

"Jules," Bastian called from the next room, "the signal's back, but it's coming from inside the house." He walked into the kitchen to find Julian holding Sarina at gunpoint. He took a step back, automatically reaching for his holstered weapon. "What's going on?"

"He's crazy. He's spouting out crazy accusations. Help me," Sarina implored. She raised her hands and backed against the counter. "Please, Bastian."

"Are you daft?" Bastian asked. "We rescued Sarina, remember? She's the victim."

"Check her phone. I believe that's the signal you're tracking." Mercer nudged the phone toward Bastian, never taking his eyes off Sarina.

The commotion in the kitchen drew the attention of everyone else inside the house, and soon the kitchen was crowded.

"What do you think you're doing?" Logan exclaimed. Before he could step between Mercer's gun and Sarina, Donovan grabbed Logan from behind, pulling him away from his wife.

"Tell him," Mercer warned, "or I will."

"You're a psychopath." She looked beseechingly at the other members of Mercer's team. "You can't let him get away with this. Please, help me."

"What's this ruckus about?" Hans asked.

Bastian scrolled through the data on the screen and handed the phone to Hans. Hans read the information, looking up with hatred. He slammed the phone down.

"Jorgen Black," Hans said, "how did it happen?"

"Sarina, what's going on?" Logan asked. He continued to struggle against Donovan's grip, but his efforts had significantly decreased. "What are they talking about?"

"Tell him," Mercer repeated. "You owe him that much."

"I owe him nothing," she spat. "He wanted nothing more than a trophy wife. Give it five years, and he'll be cashing me in for a newer model. It's just like this house and everything else. It's all for show. None of it is real. Not even our marriage."

"What?" Logan blinked, processing her words.

"I should have had you pegged from the moment we met. You were just like the guys I'd spent the last three years with. You were driven by work and the prestige and glory that came with a lot of money. You were using me as a status symbol, and I used you for a paycheck." She glanced around for a way out but didn't find one.

"That's not true." Logan shook his head for emphasis.

"It is, and you know it." She shifted to the right, and Mercer moved to block her path again.

"I'd do anything for you. When you were taken, my world came crashing down," Logan said.

"How long did it take before you noticed I was gone?" Her words were cold. "Don't lie to me."

"Sarina," Mercer said, interrupting the lovers' spat, "the truth."

She swallowed. "I used to bring Logan lunch, but he was too wrapped up in work to even come down to the lobby to see me. I became friendly with one of the guards. He was nice. He enjoyed seeing me every day."

"I never neglected you," Logan insisted.

"Jorgen Black?" Bastian asked, continuing to read the coded e-mails.

Sarina closed her mouth and glared at them.

"Answer the question," Mercer ordered, his aim never wavering.

"Yes."

"Did you screw him?" Logan asked, more concerned with his marriage than what was unfolding.

"Why do you care? It's not like you ever bothered to touch me." Her expression was angry and hurt, but Logan looked like he'd just been punched in the gut.

"Black proposed you get revenge on your husband by helping him steal the protocols," Bastian said. He copied the relevant data off Jorgen's phone and placed it on the counter. Picking up Sarina's phone, he realized Black had cloned it so the kidnappers would have access to the home security system, surveillance feed, car service schedule, and other private information that only the Porters possessed.

"He said someone approached him, and they needed my help to pull it off. He said it was the project that Logan had been working on for the past year." She wiped at a wayward tear. "That was around the time you stopped paying attention to me. I guess I wasn't the new shiny toy in your life anymore."

"Baby," Logan said, but a sharp look from Mercer forced him to shut up.

"You weren't taken," Mercer said. "You went willingly."

"It was the worst decision of my life." She trembled. "At first, it was fine. Jorgen's friend had a hideout. We were safe. No one bothered us, but then," she glared at Julian, "you showed up. You wanted proof of life." She looked at her hand. "I didn't agree to this, but Jorgen didn't care. He had used me worse than this asshole," she gave her husband another dirty look, "but they insisted the payday would make it all worthwhile. I'd be able to afford whatever life I wanted. The misery would be worth it in the end. I chose to believe that." Taking a deep breath, she added, "They told me to get close to you, Julian. That you would tell me where the protocols were. You had no reason not to trust me." She gulped down some air. "Except Alpha killed Jorgen. And I knew that I was next. I told Alpha you'd given me the location of the protocols and that I'd lead him to them. We went out to the exit tunnel, and I grabbed your gun and shot him. Then I went back inside. I wanted to make sure you were okay."

"You wanted the payout," Mercer said. "You thought I possessed the data."

"Jules," Bastian watched Mercer's finger tense slightly on the trigger, "put the gun down."

"How could you do this?" Logan asked. "How could you be this unhappy and not tell me? How could you destroy us? Destroy yourself?" He shook his head. "Even now, you said you'd run away with me. That we could start over. Start fresh. Did you mean any of that?"

"Obviously not," Mercer muttered before Sarina could reply.

"Jules," Bastian said again, "killing her won't change things." He put his hand on top of Mercer's gun and forcibly lowered the weapon.

"There is no Zed," Mercer said. "She's Zed." He gave his team a look. "Do what you like. I'm done."

"What are you going to do to me?" Sarina asked.

Donovan released Logan, but the man didn't make a move toward his wife. He took a seat at the counter and picked up her phone, reading the correspondence. They were difficult to decipher, but once he broke the code, he saw the extent of their planning and conniving.

"You lying bitch," Logan said. "I loved you. I gave you everything. You could have come to me. We could have worked it out." His love had shifted to sheer hatred. "You're the psychopath. This is crazy." Picking up the phone, he dialed the police. "You put me through hell. I'm glad things weren't so easy for you." He sneered and stormed out of the room.

"Looks like you did this to yourself, love," Bastian said. "It's a shame. That man really did love you." He caught sight of Julian's clenched fists. "And that other man literally put his life on the line to save yours. It's a shame you weren't worth a damn."

FORTY-FIVE

"I'm sorry for the trouble," Logan said. "Had I known, I wouldn't have wasted your time or mine." He had been cold since his wife's arrest. He extended his hand to Julian. "I am in your debt. Take care of yourself."

Mercer nodded and climbed into the car, watching Logan slam the front door behind him. "He's lying."

"You showed him who his wife is," Bastian said. "He owes you for that. That bird was off her rocker."

"He would have preferred not knowing." Mercer turned the key in the ignition and pulled away. "He thought he had the perfect life. Because of us, he'll never have that again."

"I beg to differ, but that's on him." Bastian cocked his head to the side and studied Mercer. "You did save her, Jules. Alpha would have killed her."

Mercer let out a mirthless laugh. "She put herself in danger. She shot Alpha. I didn't do anything."

"You gave her the tools necessary to escape."

"And I got a bullet through my side for the trouble.

It wasn't worth it." He glanced in the rearview mirror, but the police cars had left hours earlier. "She got off easy."

"Would you have shot her?" Bastian asked.

Mercer didn't answer. He was lost in his thoughts. Had he not confronted Sarina or turned on her cell phone, she and Logan would have taken their fake identities and disappeared. They might have reconciled. They might have rediscovered what initially drew them together, but Mercer interfered. His actions took away that possibility.

"No, she wasn't armed. It wouldn't have been sporting," Mercer finally said.

"So what's the problem?" Bastian asked. "I can tell something is bothering you."

"Do you think Michelle felt neglected?" Mercer asked. His wife would go months on end without seeing or hearing from him. Their time together never seemed long enough, and before he'd leave, she always seemed so miserable.

"She loved you. You made her happy."

"I made her miserable." Mercer inhaled. "If I had been there..." He clenched his jaw. They'd gone over this many times, mostly late at night when he was hammered. "Forget it."

"We will get justice for her," Bastian said. "One of these days, we'll find that lead." He clapped Mercer on the shoulder. "It's a shame the Logans and Sarinas in this world don't know how good they have it."

"Aye," Mercer replied.

* * *

"Zed's in custody," Browne said, extending his hand to Mercer who made no move to reciprocate the gesture. "Without your help, we wouldn't have realized Mr.

Black had breached our system, but rest assured the protocols are being reworked in order to ensure the operating system will not be compromised again."

"Lovely," Bastian retorted.

"Can I ask if she told you why she did it?" Browne inquired.

"Does it matter?" Mercer was tired of reliving these facts. They had turned over the information to the police, answered additional questions about the staged kidnapping and murder, and had provided statements to the embassy officials as well. Trila's questions were of no consequence. "It's over."

"But you swore you'd protect her. That must take a toll," Browne said, continuing to wheedle. "Why do it? Why not settle down with a steadier gig and call it quits?"

"You're kidding me," Bastian said. He looked to the commander for approval, glancing around to make sure no police officers were lingering outside the station.

"I have my reasons." Mercer shut his eyes and inhaled. "I'll meet you at the car." Turning around, he walked away, knowing Bastian intended to even the score before their departure.

Five minutes later, Bastian joined him inside the vehicle. He didn't share what happened, but Mercer already knew. Instead, Bastian said, "At least we know their computer systems are secure, so we don't have to worry about World War III just yet."

"Brilliant."

"Hans and Donovan are meeting us at the airport." Bastian checked the time. Confused by the direction they were currently traveling, he asked, "Where are we going?"

"To drop off documents for Mr. Porter."

"He doesn't need them anymore. Isn't he planning

to stay?"

"He can change his mind. He might need a fresh start."

"It's not that simple. His life is here. She was his reason to go."

"She might still be." Mercer snorted. "Did you hear her begging him for forgiveness? The cold steel walls of a prison cell really changed her tune."

"Maybe she was sincere." Bastian studied his bruised knuckles. "You're afraid if he stays, he'll forgive her in order to get back a piece of what he lost."

"It's what she destroyed." Mercer swallowed. "It's what we destroyed when I made her confess. It's the appearance of the perfect life that he wants." He parked in front of the house and stepped out of the car. "This could be just as perfect." He held up the envelope. "It's an option I won't take from him."

Dropping the envelope on the front step, Mercer rang the bell and returned to the car, not waiting for Logan to open the front door. It was about time their client received a delivery that wouldn't flip his world upside down. This time, it might just flip it right side up.

"Bloody hell, you've lost your edge, mate," Bastian said. "How many painkillers did you take this morning?"

"Not enough." Mercer pulled down the drive, nodding to the men at the guard post before turning toward the airport. "Maybe we could use a short holiday to regroup."

"Now I know for certain you aren't sober enough to drive. Stop the car."

"Shut it," Mercer said.

"And you're back." Bastian smiled. "So where do you plan on taking holiday?"

Mercer thought for a moment, wanting to use their recent discovery concerning the Austrian diplomat as leverage to make his own gains on his wife's murder. He shrugged, trying to play it cool. "Austria, perhaps."

"Hans already leveraged the information on Alpha with Interpol to have investigators reopen Michelle's file. They have reviewed it before, but it doesn't hurt to encourage them to give it another go," Bastian said. "We could take some time to work through the new information while you mend."

"Like I said, holiday." Since his wife's murder, Mercer had been incapable of resting or relaxing, but going over the information again and searching for something the investigators missed was as close as he could get.

"Here we go again," Bastian muttered. He cleared his throat, hoping to get off the morbid topic before Mercer returned to his normal, tormented self. "What gave Sarina away?"

"First, it was the knife. It was back. She said it was in a drawer, like it had been hidden. Then I noticed her purse. It was the single item Logan couldn't recall seeing. At first, I thought she had taken it with her, but she didn't have it at the embassy. So where did it come from?"

"Where did it come from?" Bastian asked, confused by Julian's line of thought.

"I'm not sure. It had to be in the house."

"But we searched the house."

"It was intentionally stashed somewhere, so Logan wouldn't find it," Mercer said. "It just took a moment of clarity for me to realize her involvement. It's probably on account of the damn painkillers."

"Sure," Bastian said sarcastically, "that must be it."

Mercer glared at him, and they remained silent for the rest of the ride. Upon arrival at the airport, Mercer wiped the inside of the car for fingerprints, a habit he'd picked up a while ago. Then they grabbed their bags from the trunk and met Hans and Donovan at the gate.

"We're taking a holiday," Bastian said.

"Glad to know you realized we deserve one," Hans said. "Any particular destination in mind?"

"Somewhere far away from here." Mercer felt the familiar pang of loneliness that accompanied a completed mission because he didn't have a home to return to. "I might need your help."

"Always," Donovan said. "Can it be somewhere tropical that has topless beaches?"

"Here, here," Hans said, and Bastian grinned.

"Fine," Mercer agreed, "we could use a break."

SUBVERSION, JULIAN MERCER #3, IS NOW AVAILABLE IN PAPERBACK AND AS AN E-BOOK

ABOUT THE AUTHOR

G.K. Parks is the author of the Alexis Parker series. The first novel, *Likely Suspects*, tells the story of Alexis' first foray into the private sector.

G.K. Parks received a Bachelor of Arts in Political Science and History. After spending some time in law school, G.K. changed paths and earned a Master of Arts in Criminology/Criminal Justice. Now all that education is being put to use creating a fictional world based upon years of study and research.

You can find additional information on G.K. Parks and the Alexis Parker series by visiting our website at
www.alexisparkerseries.com

Made in the USA
Las Vegas, NV
09 December 2022

61658819R00173